THE
TAKING

THE
TAKING

DEAN KOONTZ

HarperCollins*Publishers*

HarperCollins*Publishers*
77–85 Fulham Palace Road,
Hammersmith, London W6 8JB

www.harpercollins.co.uk

Published by HarperCollins*Publishers* 2004
1 3 5 7 9 8 6 4 2

A catalogue record for this book
is available from the British Library

ISBN 0 00 713075 9

Set in Trump Mediaeval

Printed and bound in Great Britain by
Clays Ltd, St Ives plc

This book is dedicated to Joe Stefko:
great drummer, publisher of exquisite special editions,
dog-lover . . . three virtues that guarantee Heaven.
The bad feet can be overlooked.

"When you're alone in the middle of the night and you wake in a sweat and a hell of a fright . . ."

—T. S. Eliot, *Fragment of an Agon*

PART ONE

"In my beginning is my end."

T.S. Eliot, *East Coker*

I

A FEW MINUTES PAST ONE O'CLOCK IN THE MORNING, a hard rain fell without warning. No thunder preceded the deluge, no wind.

The abruptness and the ferocity of the downpour had the urgent quality of a perilous storm in a dream.

Lying in bed beside her husband, Molly Sloan had been restless before the sudden cloudburst. She grew increasingly fidgety as she listened to the rush of rain.

The voices of the tempest were legion, like an angry crowd chanting in a lost language. Torrents pounded and pried at the cedar siding, at the shingles, as if seeking entrance.

September in southern California had always before been a dry month in a long season of predictable drought. Rain rarely fell after March, seldom before December.

In wet months, the rataplan of raindrops on the roof had sometimes served as a reliable remedy for insomnia. This night, however, the liquid rhythms failed to lull her into slumber, and not just because they were out of season.

For Molly, sleeplessness had too often in recent years been the price of thwarted ambition. Scorned by the sandman, she stared at the dark bedroom ceiling, brooding about what might have been, yearning for what might never be.

By the age of twenty-eight, she had published four novels. All were well received by reviewers, but none sold in sufficient numbers to make her famous or even to guarantee that she would find an eager publisher for the next.

Her mother, Thalia, a writer of luminous prose, had been in the early years of an acclaimed career when she died of cancer at thirty. Now, sixteen years later, Thalia's books were out of print, her mark upon the world all but erased.

Molly lived with a quiet dread of following her mother into obscurity. She didn't suffer from an inordinate fear of death; rather, she was troubled by the thought of dying before achieving any lasting accomplishment.

Beside her, Neil snored softly, oblivious of the storm.

Sleep always found him within a minute of the moment when he put his head on the pillow and closed his eyes. He seldom stirred during the night; after eight hours, he woke in the same position in which he had gone to sleep—rested, invigorated.

Neil claimed that only the innocent enjoyed such perfect sleep.

Molly called it the sleep of the slacker.

Throughout their seven years of marriage, they had conducted their lives by different clocks.

She dwelled as much in the future as in the present, envisioning where she wished to go, relentlessly mapping the path that ought to lead to her high goals. Her strong mainspring was wound tight.

Neil lived in the moment. To him, the far future was next week, and he trusted time to take him there whether or not he planned the journey.

They were as different as mice and moonbeams.

Considering their contrasting natures, they shared a love that seemed unlikely. Yet love was the cord that bound them together, the sinewy fiber that gave them strength to weather disappointment, even tragedy.

During Molly's spells of insomnia, Neil's rhythmic snoring, although not loud, sometimes tested love almost as much as infidelity might have done. Now the sudden crash of pummeling rain masked the noise that he made, giving Molly a new target upon which to focus her frustration.

The roar of the storm escalated until they seemed to be inside the rumbling machinery that powered the universe.

Shortly after two o'clock, without switching on a light, Molly got out of bed. At a window that was protected from the rain by the overhanging roof, she looked through her ghostly reflection, into a windless monsoon.

Their house stood high in the San Bernardino Mountains, embraced by sugar pines, knobcone pines, and towering ponderosas with dramatic fissured bark.

Most of their neighbors were in bed at this hour. Through the shrouding trees and the incessant downpour, only a single cluster of lights could be seen on these slopes above Black Lake.

The Corrigan place. Harry Corrigan had lost Calista, his wife of thirty-five years, back in June.

During a weekend visit to her sister, Nancy, in Redondo Beach, Calista parked her Honda near an ATM to withdraw two hundred dollars. She'd been robbed, then shot in the face.

Subsequently, Nancy had been pulled from the car and shot twice. She had also been run over when the two gunmen escaped in the Honda. Now, three months after Calista's funeral, Nancy remained in a coma.

While Molly yearned for sleep, Harry Corrigan strove every night to avoid it. He said his dreams were killing him.

In the tides of the storm, the luminous windows of Harry's house seemed like the running lights of a distant vessel on a rolling sea: one of those fabled ghost ships, abandoned by passengers and crew, yet with lifeboats still secured. Untouched dinners would be found on plates in the crew's mess. In the wheelhouse, the captain's favorite pipe, warm with smoldering tobacco, would await discovery on the chart table.

Molly's imagination had been engaged; she couldn't easily shift into neutral again. Sometimes, in the throes of insomnia, she tossed and turned into the arms of literary inspiration.

Downstairs, in her study, were five chapters of her new novel, which needed to be polished. A few hours of work on the manuscript might soothe her nerves enough to allow sleep.

Her robe draped the back of a nearby chair. She shrugged into it and knotted the belt.

Crossing to the door, she realized that she was navigating with surprising ease, considering the absence of lamplight. Her sureness in the gloom couldn't be explained entirely by the fact that she had been awake for hours, staring at the ceiling with dark-adapted eyes.

The faint light at the windows, sufficient to dilute the bedroom darkness, could not have traveled all the way from Harry Corrigan's house, three doors to the south. The true source at first eluded her.

Storm clouds hid the moon.

Outside, the landscape lights were off; the porch lights, too.

Returning to the window, she puzzled over the tinseled glimmer of the rain. A curious wet sheen made the bristling boughs of the nearest pines more visible than they should have been.

Ice? No. Stitching through the night, needles of sleet would have made a more brittle sound than the susurrant drumming of this autumn downpour.

She pressed fingertips to the windowpane. The glass was cool but not cold.

When reflecting ambient light, falling rain sometimes acquires a silvery cast. In this instance, however, no ambient light existed.

The rain itself appeared to be faintly luminescent, each drop a light-emitting crystal. The night was simultaneously veiled and revealed by skeins of vaguely fluorescent beads.

When Molly stepped out of the bedroom, into the upstairs hall, the soft glow from two domed skylights bleached the gloom from black to gray, revealing the way to the stairs. Overhead, the rainwater sheeting down the curved Plexiglas was enlivened by radiant whorls that resembled spiral nebulae wheeling across the vault of a planetarium.

She descended the stairs and proceeded to the kitchen by the guidance of the curiously storm-lit windows.

Some nights, embracing rather than resisting insomnia, she brewed a pot of coffee to take to her desk in the study. Thus stoked, she wrote jagged, caffeine-sharpened prose with the realistic tone of police-interrogation transcripts.

This night, however, she intended to return eventually to bed. After switching on the light in the vent hood above the cooktop, she flavored a mug of milk with vanilla extract and cinnamon, then heated it in the microwave.

In her study, volumes of her favorite poetry and prose—Louise Glück, Donald Justice, T. S. Eliot, Carson McCullers, Flannery O'Connor, Dickens—lined the walls. Occasionally, she took comfort and inspiration from a humble sense of kinship with these writers.

Most of the time, however, she felt like a pretender. Worse, a fraud.

Her mother had said that every good writer needed to be her own toughest critic. Molly edited her work with both a red pen and a metaphorical hatchet, leaving evidence of bloody suffering with the former, reducing scenes to kindling with the latter.

More than once, Neil suggested that Thalia had never said—and had not intended to imply—that worthwhile art could be carved from raw language only with self-doubt as sharp as a chisel. To Thalia, her work had also been her favorite form of play.

In a troubled culture where cream often settled on the bottom and the palest milk rose to the top, Molly knew that she was short on logic and long on superstition when she supposed that her hope for success rested upon the amount of passion, pain, and polish that she brought to her writing. Nevertheless, regarding her work, Molly remained a Puritan, finding virtue in self-flagellation.

Leaving the lamps untouched, she switched on the computer but didn't at once sit at her desk. Instead, as the screen brightened and the signature music of the operating system welcomed her to a late-night work session, she was once more drawn to a window by the insistent rhythm of the rain.

Beyond the window lay the deep front porch. The railing and the over-hanging roof framed a dark panorama of serried pines, a strangely luminous ghost forest out of a disturbing dream.

She could not look away. For reasons that she wasn't able to articulate, the scene made her uneasy.

Nature has many lessons to teach a writer of fiction. One of these is that nothing captures the imagination as quickly or as completely as does spectacle.

Blizzards, floods, volcanos, hurricanes, earthquakes: They fascinate because they nakedly reveal that Mother Nature, afflicted with bipolar disorder, is as likely to snuff us as she is to succor us. An alternately nurturing and destructive parent is the stuff of gripping drama.

Silvery cascades leafed the bronze woods, burnishing bark and bough with sterling highlights.

An unusual mineral content in the rain might have lent it this slight phosphorescence.

Or . . . having come in from the west, through the soiled air above Los Angeles and surrounding cities, perhaps the storm had washed from the atmosphere a witch's brew of pollutants that in combination gave rise to this pale, eerie radiance.

Sensing that neither explanation would prove correct, seeking a third, Molly was startled by movement on the porch. She shifted focus from the trees to the sheltered shadows immediately beyond the glass.

Low, sinuous shapes moved under the window. They were so silent, fluid, and mysterious that for a moment they seemed to be imagined: formless expressions of primal fears.

Then one, three, five of them lifted their heads and turned their yellow eyes to the window, regarding her inquisitively. They were as real as Molly herself, though sharper of tooth.

The porch swarmed with wolves. Slinking out of the storm, up the steps, onto the pegged-pine floor, they gathered under the shelter of the roof, as though this were not a house but an ark that would soon be set safely afloat by the rising waters of a cataclysmic flood.

2

IN THESE MOUNTAINS, BETWEEN THE TRUE DESERT to the east and the plains to the west, wolves were long extinct. The visitation on the porch had the otherworldly quality of an apparition.

When, on closer examination, Molly realized that these beasts were coyotes—sometimes called *prairie* wolves—their behavior seemed no less remarkable than when she had mistaken them for the larger creatures of folklore and fairy tales.

As much as anything, their silence defined their strangeness. In the thrill of the chase, running down their prey, coyotes often cry with high excitement: a chilling ululation as eerie as the music of a theremin. Now they neither cried nor barked, nor even growled.

Unlike most wolves, coyotes will frequently hunt alone. When they join in packs to stalk game, they do not run as close together as do wolves.

Yet on the front porch, the individualism characteristic of their species was not in evidence. They gathered flank-to-flank, shoulder-to-shoulder, eeling among one another, no less communal than domesticated hounds, nervous and seeking reassurance from one another.

Noticing Molly at the study window, they neither shied from her nor reacted aggressively. Their shining eyes, which in the past had always impressed her as being cruel and bright with blood hunger, now appeared to be as devoid of threat as the trusting eyes of any household pet.

Indeed, each creature favored her with a compelling look as alien to coyotes as anything she could imagine. Their expressions seemed to be *imploring.*

This was so unlikely that she distrusted her perceptions. Yet she thought that she detected a beseeching attitude not only in their eyes but also in their posture and behavior.

She ought to have been frightened by this fanged congregation. Her heart *did* beat faster than usual; however, the novelty of the situation and a sense of the mysterious, rather than fear, quickened her pulse.

The coyotes were obviously seeking shelter, although never previously had Molly seen even one of them flee the tumult of a storm for the protection of a human habitation. People were a far greater danger to their kind than anything they might encounter in nature.

Besides, this comparatively dark and quiet tempest had neither the lightning nor the thunder to chase them from their dens. The formidable volume of the downpour marked this as unusual weather; but the rain had not been falling long enough to flood these stoic predators out of their homes.

Although the coyotes regarded Molly with entreating glances, they reserved the greater part of their attention for the storm. Tails tucked, ears pricked, the wary beasts watched the silvery torrents and the drenched forest with acute interest if not with outright anxiety.

As still more of their wolfish kind slouched out of the night and onto the porch, Molly searched the palisade of trees for the cause of their concern.

She saw nothing more than she had seen before: the faintly radiant cataracts wrung from a supersaturated sky, the trees and other vegetation bowed and trembled and silvered by the fiercely pummeling rain.

Nonetheless, as she scanned the night woods, the nape of her neck prickled as though a ghost lover had pressed his ectoplasmic lips against her skin. A shudder of inexplicable misgiving passed through her.

Rattled by the conviction that something in the forest returned her scrutiny from behind the wet veil of the storm, Molly backed away from the window.

The computer monitor suddenly seemed too bright—and revealing. She switched off the machine.

Black and argentine, the mercurial gloom streamed and glimmered past the windows. Even here in the house, the air felt thick and damp.

The phosphoric light of the storm cast shimmering reflections on a collection of porcelains, on glass paperweights, on the white-gold leafing of several picture frames. . . . The study had the deep-fathom ambience of an oceanic trench forever beyond the reach of the sun but dimly revealed by radiant anemones and luminous jellyfish.

Molly was struck by a disorienting sense of *otherness* that was familiar from dreams but that had never before overcome her while she remained awake.

She backed farther from the window. She edged toward the study door that led to the downstairs hall.

A creeping disquietude stole through her, nerve to nerve. She was anxious not about the coyotes on the porch but about something she couldn't name—a threat so primal that reason was blind to it and instinct revealed only its rough contours.

Counseling herself that she was too mature to succumb to the easy fright of childhood and adolescence, she nevertheless retreated to the stairs, intending to return to the bedroom and wake Neil.

For perhaps a minute, she stood with one hand on the newel post, listening to the drumming rain, considering what to say after rousing him from sleep. Everything that occurred to her sounded to one degree or another hysterical.

She was not concerned about looking foolish in Neil's eyes. During seven years of marriage, each had been a fool often enough to have earned the lasting forbearance of the other.

She nurtured an image of herself, however, that sustained her during difficult times, and she strove always to avoid compromising it. In this self-portrait, she was tough, resilient, tempered by terror at an early age, seasoned by grief, qualified by experience to handle whatever fate threw at her.

At eight, she had endured and miraculously survived an episode of extreme violence that might have left any other child in therapy for decades. Later, when she was just twelve, an invisible thief called lymphoma, with quiet violence, stole the life from her mother.

For most of her existence, Molly had not shied from a truth that most people understood but diligently suppressed: that every moment of every day, depending on the faith we embrace, each of us continues to live either by the merciful sufferance of God or at the whim of blind chance and indifferent nature.

She listened to the rain. The downpour seemed not indifferent, but purposeful and determined.

Leaving Neil to his sleep, she turned away from the stairs. The windows remained faintly luminous, as if with the reflected glow of the aurora borealis.

Although her disquiet slowly gathered the force of apprehension, just as a revolving hurricane spins ever greater winds around its dead-calm eye, Molly crossed the foyer to the front door.

Flanking the door were tall, French-paned sidelights. Beyond the sidelights lay the porch onto which she had looked from her office.

The coyotes still gathered in that shelter. As she drew near the door, some of the animals turned once more to gaze in at her.

Their anxious panting painted pale plumes on the glass. From behind this veil of smoking breath, their radiant eyes beseeched her.

Molly was inexplicably convinced that she could open the door and move among them without risk of attack.

Whether or not she was as tough as she believed herself to be, she was not impulsive or reckless. She didn't possess the fatalistic temperament of a snake handler or even the adventurousness of those who rode rafts over white-water rapids.

The previous autumn, when a wildfire churned up the eastern face of the mountain, threatening to cross the crest and sweep westward to the lake, she and Neil had been, at her insistence, the first among their neighbors to pack essential belongings and leave. Her acute awareness of life's fragility had since childhood made of her a prudent person.

Yet when writing a novel, she often shunned prudence, trusting her instinct and her heart more than she did intellect. Without risk, she could get nothing on the page worth reading.

Here in the foyer, in this false-aurora glow, under the anxious gaze of the gathered canines beyond the French panes, the moment had a mystical quality, more like fiction than reality. Perhaps that was why Molly considered hazarding onto the porch.

She put her right hand on the doorknob. Rather, she found her hand on the knob without quite recalling when she had put it there.

The roar of the rain, escalating from a cataclysmic chorus until it became the very voice of Armageddon, and the witchy light together exerted a mesmerizing effect. Nevertheless, she knew that she wasn't falling into a trance, wasn't being lured from the house by some supernatural force, as in a bad movie.

She'd never felt more awake, more clearheaded. Instinct, heart, *and* mind were synchronized now as they had rarely been in her twenty-eight years of experience.

The unprecedented September deluge and everything about the odd behavior of the coyotes, not least of all their uncharacteristic meekness, argued that the usual logic didn't apply. Here, providence required boldness rather than caution.

If her heart had continued to race, she might not have turned the knob. At the *thought* of turning it, however, she felt a curious calm descend. Her pulse rate declined, although each beat knocked through her with jarring force.

In some Chinese dialects, the same word is used to mean either *dan-*

ger or *opportunity.* In this instance, as never before, she was in a Chinese frame of mind.

She opened the door.

The coyotes, perhaps a score of them, neither attacked nor growled. They did not bare their teeth.

Amazed by their behavior and by her own, Molly crossed the threshold. She stepped onto the porch.

As if they were family dogs, the coyotes made room for her and seemed to welcome her company.

Her amazement still allowed a measure of caution. She stood with her arms crossed defensively over her chest. Yet she felt that if she held a hand out to the beasts, they would only nuzzle and lick it.

The coyotes nervously divided their attention between Molly and the surrounding woods. Their rapid and shallow panting spoke not of exhaustion after a long run, but of acute anxiety.

Something in the rain-swept forest frightened them. Evidently, this fear was so intense that they dared not respond to it with their customary snarls, raised hackles, and counterchallenges.

Instead, they trembled and issued soft mewls of meek submission. Their ears were not flattened to signal an aggressive response, but remained pricked, as if they could hear the breathing and the subtle footfalls of a fierce predator even through the crash of rain.

Tails tucked between their legs, flanks trembling, they moved ceaselessly back and forth. They seemed ready, at any moment, to drop as one to the plank floor and submissively expose their bellies in an attempt to forestall an attack by some ferocious enemy.

Brushing against Molly as they swarmed the porch, the coyotes appeared to take as much comfort from contact with her as they did from their pack mates. Although their eyes were strange and wild, she saw in them some of the hopeful trust and need for companionship that were qualities common to the eyes of the gentlest dogs.

Her amazement gave way to astonishment as a humbling flood of emotions never experienced before—or never experienced this strongly—swelled in her. A sense of wonder, childlike in its intensity. An almost pagan feeling of being one with nature.

The humid air thickened with the odor of damp fur and with the smoky ammonia scent of musk.

Molly thought of Diana, Roman goddess of the hunt, whom artists often depicted in the company of wolves, leading a pack in pursuit of prey, across moonlit fields and hills.

A profound awareness of the interconnectedness of all things in Creation seemed to arise not from her mind, not even from her heart, but from the smallest structures of her being, as if the microscopic tides of cytoplasm in her billions of cells responded to the coyotes, the unusual storm, and the forest in much the way that Earth's oceans were influenced by the moon.

This extraordinary moment was supercharged with a mystical quality so supremely grand in character and so formidable in power, so unlike anything Molly had known before, that she was overcome by awe and trembled with a peculiar exhilaration that was almost joy. Her breathing became quick and shallow, and her legs grew weak.

Then, as one, the coyotes were seized by a greater terror than the fright that had driven them from the woods. With thin, desperate bleats of panic, they fled the porch.

As they swarmed past her, their wet tails lashed her legs. A few looked up entreatingly, as though she must understand the cause of their fear and might be able to rescue them from the enemy, real or imagined, that had chased them from their dens.

Fast down the steps, into the storm, they traveled in a tight defensive pack, not hunting now, but hunted.

Their rain-soaked coats clung to them, revealing lean forms of bone, sinew, and stringy muscle. Always before, coyotes had looked aggressive and formidable to her, but these seemed lost, unsure of their purpose, almost pitiable.

Molly crossed to the head of the porch steps and stared after them. Although irrational and disturbing, the urge to follow was difficult to resist.

As the coyotes descended through the night, the forest, and the queerly luminescent rain, they frequently glanced back, past the house and toward the top of the ridge. Suddenly seeming to catch the scent of a pursuer, they whidded among the pines, as swift and silent as gray spirits. And were gone.

Chilled, hugging herself, Molly let out a pent-up breath that she'd not been aware of holding.

She waited, tense and wary, but nothing followed the pack.

In these mountains, coyotes had no natural enemies capable of challenging them. The few remaining bears foraged on wild fruits, tubers, and tender roots; they stalked nothing bigger than fish. Although bobcats had survived human encroachment in greater numbers than had the bears, they fed on rabbits and rodents; they would not chase down another predator for food and certainly not for sport.

The musky scent of the coyotes hung on the air after they departed. Indeed, the odor didn't diminish but seemed to ripen.

Standing at the head of the steps, Molly held a hand out past the protection of the roof. In this cool autumn night, the glimmering rain slipping through her fingers proved to be unexpectedly warm.

The phosphoric water limned the wrinkles of her knuckles.

She looked at her palm. Head line, heart line, and lifeline shone brighter than the rest of her hand, suddenly scintillating with mysterious meaning, as if some previously unknown Gypsy heritage had manifested in her, complete with the ability to foretell the future from creases in her skin.

When she withdrew her hand from the rushing rain and sniffed it, she detected even more strongly than before the scent that she had attributed to the coyotes. Although not appealing enough to be called a fragrance, it was not unpleasant, either, and was as rich with subtleties as the air in a spice market.

She had never before experienced such a scent. Yet within the intricate matrix of this unique smell, she detected a tantalizingly familiar substance, simple in its nature. The more determinedly she strove to identify this core odor, the more its slippery name eluded her.

Although it smelled like a complex mélange of essences and exotic oils, the rain had the character and consistency of ordinary water. She rubbed it between thumb and fingertips, feeling nothing unusual.

Gradually Molly realized that she was lingering on the porch in the hope that the coyotes would return. Standing among them, like a lamb among lions, trembling on the brink of some revelation, had been such an awesome experience that she longed to repeat it.

When the coyotes did not reappear, an ineffable sense of loss overcame her. With it arose anew the feeling of being watched that earlier had stirred the fine hairs on the back of her neck.

Sometimes the forest appeared to her as a green cathedral. The massive pine trunks were columns in a vast nave, and the spreading boughs formed groin vaults and fan vaults high overhead.

Now, with the reverential hush of the woods replaced by the din of the downpour, the gloom coiling among the trees seemed to be of a different character from that on any previous night. The god of *this* cathedral was the lord of darkness.

Disquieted again, Molly backed across the porch, retreating from the steps. She did not for one moment look away from the encircling forest, half convinced that something would fly at her from out of the pines, something that would be all teeth and temper.

Inside, she closed the door. Engaged the deadbolt. Stood there for a moment, trembling.

She continued to be surprised and disturbed by her emotionalism. Driven by a kind of instinct, less of the mind than of the heart, she felt reduced from womanhood to the overwrought reactions of a girl—and she didn't like it.

Eager to wash her hands, she hurried to the kitchen.

Approaching the open door, she saw that the light above the cooktop was still on, as she had left it when she'd heated the mug of milk.

At the threshold, she hesitated, suddenly expecting someone to be in the kitchen. Someone who had come in the back door while she had been distracted by the coyotes.

More emotionalism. Foolish. No intruder waited for her.

She crossed the kitchen directly to the back door, and tried it. Bolted. Secure. No one could have gotten in that way.

Coruscating curtains of radiant rain silvered the night. A thousand eyes might have watched from behind that sequined veil.

She lowered the pleated shade over the window beside the breakfast table. She dropped the shade at the window above the sink, as well.

After turning on the water and adjusting it to the hottest temperature that she could tolerate, she lathered her hands with liquid soap from the built-in dispenser. The soap smelled like oranges, a gratifyingly clean scent.

She had not touched any of the coyotes.

For a moment she did not understand why she was scrubbing her hands so determinedly. Then she realized that she was washing away the rain.

The curiously aromatic rain had left her feeling . . . unclean.

She rinsed her hands until they were red, half-scalded. Then she pumped more soap and lathered up a second time.

Within that mélange of subtle but exotic scents had been a vaguely familiar odor, smoky and ammoniac, that Molly had not quite been able to identify. Although she had flushed the smell from her hands, it now returned to her in memory, and this time she was able to name it: semen.

Under that spice-market variety of exotic aromas, the rain had exuded the fecund scent of semen.

This seemed so unlikely, so absurdly Freudian, that she wondered if she might be asleep. Or sliding into a neuropsychotic episode.

The inexplicable luminescence, the seminal rain, the cowering coyotes: From bed to foaming faucet, every step and moment of the experience had a hallucinatory quality.

She turned off the faucet, half expecting silence when the water stopped gushing. But the tremendous roar of the unseasonable rain was there, all right—either real or the soundtrack of a singularly persistent dream.

From elsewhere in the house, a sharp cry sliced through the monotonous drone of the storm. Upstairs. It came again. Neil. Her calm, composed, unflappable husband—crying out in the night.

With too much experience of violence dating from the age of eight, Molly reacted with alacrity, snatching the handset from the nearby wall phone. She keyed 9-1-1 before realizing that she hadn't gotten a dial tone.

Over the open line came an audial tapestry of eerie, oscillating electronic tones. Low-pitched pulses of sound, high-pitched whistles and shrieks.

She hung up.

They owned a gun. Upstairs. In a nightstand drawer.

Neil cried out again.

Molly glanced at the locked door, felt again the desire to flee with the coyotes into the night. Whatever else she might be—insane or as foolish and hysterical as a girl—she was not a coward.

She went to the knife drawer and drew the most wicked blade from its sheath.

3

MOLLY WANTED LIGHT, A GREAT BRIGHT DAZZLE OF it, but she didn't touch a switch. She knew the house better than any intruder could know it; in these rooms, darkness would be her ally.

Kitchen to hall to stairs, she cleaved the gloom with the point of the butcher knife and followed in its wake.

Some of the treads creaked, but the rumble of the downpour masked the sounds of her hurried ascent.

Upstairs, the storm still painted luminous galaxies on the skylights. Faint images of those patterns crawled the hallway floor.

Approaching the bedroom, she heard a groan followed by a softer cry than those that had preceded it.

Her heart clenched tight, knocked hard against its caging ribs.

As she pushed open the door and entered the dark bedroom, the butcher knife twitched and bobbed like a dowsing rod, as if divining the location of a hostile intruder, seeking not water but bad blood.

The mercurial light of the radiant rain, eddying through the room with a watery inconstancy, failed to illuminate every corner. Shadows shivered, throbbed; some of them might have been more than mere shadows.

Nevertheless, Molly lowered the knife. At this close range she realized that her husband's groans and cries resulted from a struggle with nothing more threatening than a nightmare.

Neil's sleep was usually as untroubled by narrative as it was deep and reliable. When slumber brought him a story, the plot was soothing, even comic.

She had sometimes watched him smiling in his sleep. On one occasion, without waking, he had laughed out loud.

As with everything else about the early hours of this Wednesday morning, the past did not serve as a guide to the present. Neil's dream clearly was different from others he had experienced during the seven years that Molly had shared a bed with him. His panicked breathing and cries of dread suggested that he raced desperately through the forests of sleep, pursued by a terror that relentlessly gained ground on him.

Molly switched on a nightstand lamp. The sudden flush of light didn't wake her husband.

Sweat darkened his brown hair almost to black. Wrung by anxiety, his face glistened.

Putting the knife on the nightstand, she said, "Neil?"

His name, softly spoken, didn't break the spell of sleep.

Instead, he reacted as if he had heard the close, rough voice of Death. Head tossing, neck muscles taut, twisting fistfuls of the sheet as if it were a binding shroud in which he'd been prematurely buried, he took shallow, panicked breaths, working himself toward a scream.

Molly put a hand on his shoulder. "Honey, you're dreaming."

With a choked cry, he sat up in bed, seizing her wrist and twisting her hand away from his shoulder as though she were a dagger-wielding assassin.

Awake, he nevertheless seemed to see the menace from his dream. His eyes were wide with fright; his face had been broken into sharp new contours by the hammer of shock.

Molly winced with pain. "Hey, let go, it's me."

He blinked, shuddered, released her.

Taking a step backward, rubbing her pinched wrist, she said. "Are you all right?"

Throwing off the covers, Neil sat up, on the edge of the bed.

He was wearing only pajama bottoms. Although not a big man—five feet ten, and trim—he had powerful shoulders and muscular arms.

Molly liked to touch his arms, shoulders, chest. He felt so solid, therefore reliable.

His physique matched his character. She could depend on him, always.

Sometimes she touched him casually, with innocent intention—and passion followed as urgently as thunder in the wake of lightning.

He had always been a confident but quiet lover, patient and almost shy. The more aggressive of the two, Molly usually led him to bed instead of being led.

After seven years, her boldness still surprised and delighted her. She had never been that way with another man.

Even in this unnerving night, in spite of the roof-punishing rumble of radiant rain and the disquieting memory of the coyotes, Molly felt a certain sensual response at the sight of her husband. His tousled hair. His handsome, beard-stubbled face; his mouth as tender as that of a boy.

He wiped his face with his hands, pulling off cobwebs of sleep. When he looked up at her, his blue eyes seemed to be a deeper shade than usual, almost sapphire. Darker shadows moved in the blue, as if a nightmare memory of poisonous spiders still scurried across his field of waking vision.

"Are you all right?" Molly repeated.

"No." His voice was rough, as though cracking from thirst and raw with exhaustion after a desperate chase across the fields of sleep. "Dear Jesus, what was *that*?"

"What was what?"

He got up from the bed. His body had a coiled-spring tension, every muscle taut. His dream had been a hard-turned key that left him as stressed as overwound clockworks.

"You were having a nightmare," she said, "I heard you shouting in your sleep."

"Not a nightmare. Worse." With anxious bewilderment, he turned to survey the room. "That sound."

"Rain," she said, and pointed at a window.

Neil shook his head. "No. Not just rain. Something behind it . . . above it."

His demeanor further unsettled Molly. He seemed to be half in a trance, unable fully to shake off his nightmare.

He shuddered. "There's a mountain coming down."

"Mountain?"

Tipping his head back, studying the bedroom ceiling with evident anxiety, the initial roughness in his voice smoothing into a solemn silken tone of mesmerizing intensity, he said, "Huge. In the dream. Massive. A mountain, rock blacker than iron, coming down in a slow fall. You run and you run . . . but you can't get out from under. Its shadow grows ahead of you faster . . . faster than you can hope to move."

Soft-spoken, yet as sharp as a harpist's plectrums, his words plucked her nerves.

Intending to lighten the moment, Molly said, "Ah. A Chicken Little dream."

Neil's stare remained fixed on the ceiling. "Not just a dream. Here. Now." He held his breath, listening. Then: "Something behind the rain . . . coming down."

"Neil. You're scaring me."

Lowering his gaze, meeting her eyes, he said, "A crushing weight somewhere up there. A growing pressure. You feel it, too."

Even if the moon itself had been falling, she would have been reluctant to acknowledge that its gravitational influence stirred powerful new tides in her blood. Until now, she had been a rider who kept tight reins on life, letting emotion break into full gallop only in the pages of her books, saving the drama for fiction.

"No," she said. "It was just the sound of the rain getting to you in your dream, and your mind spun it into something weird, made a mountain of it."

"You feel it, too," he insisted, and he padded barefoot to a window.

The low amber light from the nightstand lamp was insufficient to disguise the luminous nature of the torrents that tinseled the forest and silvered the ground.

"What's happening?" he asked.

"Unusual mineral content, pollution of some kind," she replied, resorting to the explanations that she had already considered and largely rejected.

The curiosity and wonder that earlier compelled her to venture among the coyotes had curdled into trepidation. With uncharacteristic timidity, she yearned to return to bed, to shrink among the covers, to sleep away the freak storm and wake by the light of a normal dawn.

Neil disengaged the latch on the casement window and reached for the handle to crank it open.

"Don't," she warned with more urgency than she had intended.

Half turning from the window, he faced her.

She said, "The rain smells strange. It feels . . . unclean."

Only now he noticed her robe. "How long have you been up?"

"Couldn't sleep. Went downstairs to write. But . . ."

He looked at the ceiling again. "There. Do you feel that?"

Maybe she felt something. Or maybe her imagination was building mountains in the air.

His gaze tracked across the ceiling. "It's not falling toward us anymore." His voice quieted to a whisper. "It's moving eastward . . . west to east."

She didn't share his apparently instinctual perception, though she found herself wiping her right hand on her robe—the hand that she had held out in the rain and had later washed so vigorously with orange-scented soap.

"As big as two mountains, three . . . so huge," whispered Neil. He made the sign of the cross—forehead to breast, left shoulder to right—which she had not seen him do in years.

Suddenly she felt more than heard a great, deep, slow throbbing masked by the tremulous roar of the rain.

". . . sift you as wheat . . ."

Those words of Neil's, so strange and yet disturbingly familiar, refocused her attention from the ceiling to him. "What did you say?"

"It's huge."

"No. After that. What did you say about wheat?"

As if the words had escaped him without his awareness, he regarded her with bewilderment. "Wheat? What're you talking about?"

A flickering at the periphery of her vision drew Molly's attention to the clock on her nightstand. The glowing green digits changed rapidly, continuously, as though racing to keep pace with time run amok.

"Neil."

"I see it."

The numbers were sequencing neither forward toward morning nor backward toward midnight. Rather, they resembled the streaming mathematics of high-speed computer calculations rushing across a monitor.

Molly consulted her wristwatch, which was not a digital model. The hour hand swept clockwise, counting off a full day in half a minute, while the minute hand spun counterclockwise even faster, as though she were stranded on a rock in the river of time, with the future flowing away from her as swiftly as did the past.

The mysterious deep pulses of sound—almost below the threshold of human hearing but felt in blood and bone—seemed to swell her heart as they pushed through it.

The mood and moment were unique, like nothing that she had previously experienced, but the atmosphere was as unmistakably hostile as it was unprecedented.

With the coyotes, Molly's instinct had seemed to divorce itself from her common sense. She had acted on the former, recklessly stepping onto the front porch.

Now instinct and common sense were married again. Both intuition and cold reason counseled that she and Neil were in serious trouble even though they could not yet grasp the nature of it.

In his eyes, she saw the recognition of this truth. During their years together, serving alternately as confessor and redeemer to each other, they had arrived at an intimacy of mind and spirit that often made words superfluous.

At her nightstand, she withdrew the 9-mm pistol from the drawer. She always kept it loaded; nevertheless, she ejected the magazine to confirm that it lacked no rounds. The gleam of brass. Ten cartridges.

After locking in the magazine again, she put the weapon on the vanity, beside her hairbrush and hand mirror, within easy reach.

Across the room, on the dresser, stood a collection of half a dozen antique music boxes inherited from her mother. Spontaneously, a steely plink-and-jangle issued from them: six different melodies woven into a bright discordance.

On the lids of two boxes, clockwork-driven porcelain figurines suddenly became animated. Here, a man and woman in Victorian finery danced a waltz. There, a carousel horse turned around, around.

The cacophony of brittle notes abraded her nerves and seemed to cut like a surgical saw through her skull bone.

These familiar objects, a part of her life since childhood, became in an instant strange, disquieting.

Neil stared at the tiny dancers for a moment, at the circling horse, and appeared to be unsettled by them. He made no attempt to switch off the music boxes.

Instead, he turned to the window once more, but he didn't crank it open, as he had been prepared to do a minute ago. He engaged the latch that previously he had unlocked.

4

AS THEY HURRIEDLY DRESSED IN JEANS AND SWEAT-
ers, Molly told him about the coyotes.

The somber drone of the rain, the manic plinking of the music boxes,
and the almost subliminal pulsation of unknown source served as a musical score, without coherent melody, that made the adventure on the
front porch seem far more ominous in the telling than it had been in actual experience. She tried—but knew that she failed—to convey to Neil
the sense of wonder and the reverential awe that had characterized the
incident.

Seated on the vanity bench, striving to describe the bond with nature
that she had felt as she'd stood among the coyotes, she worked her feet
into a pair of waterproof walking shoes. Her hands trembled. She fumbled with the laces, finally managed to tie them.

Still talking, she picked up, by habit, the brush that lay beside the pistol. Although she realized the absurdity of trying to deny the weirdness of
the moment by resorting to mundane tasks, she turned to the mirror to
assess the state of her hair.

Her reflection was as it should be, but everything else in the mirror
was *wrong*. Behind her lay not the lamplit and cozy bedroom, neat except
for the disarranged bedclothes; instead, she saw filth and ruin.

Her voice broke off in midsentence, and she dropped the hairbrush.

She swung around on the bench to confirm that the room had changed. It was as it had always been.

In reality, only the bedside clock was out of order. A chaos of radiant green numbers continued to spill across the readout window.

In the mirror, however, stained walls were textured by moss or mold. One lamp remained, the shade cocked and rotting. Across the headboard of the broken-down bed crawled vines too succulent to be native to these California mountains; gray-green and glistening with moisture, the leaves hung like a host of panting tongues.

She was tempted again to believe that she had never risen from bed and gone downstairs, that instead she had been asleep through these events—and still slept. The rain and all the strangeness that began with it—from the coyotes to this mirror—made more sense if they were the fantasies of sleep.

Drawn to her side, Neil reached out to touch the vanity mirror, as though he expected to find that the image in it was not merely a flat reflection, but a three-dimensional reality, a world *beyond* the mirror.

Irrationally, Molly stayed his hand. "No."

"Why?"

"Because . . ."

She had no credible reason to stop him, only a superstitious fear of what would happen when his fingertips met the silvered surface of the looking glass.

With his free hand, he touched the mirror, which proved to be solid.

Then, in that *other* bedroom, something moved. A shadow proved not to be a shadow, after all, but a figure sinuous and dark, darting so fast across the mirror's breadth of view and out of sight that it might have been a man in a cloak, a man with membranous wings—or not a man at all.

With a gasp of surprise, Neil snatched his hand back as if the entity on the other side surely had the power to reach through the mirror as he himself could not.

In the same instant, Molly spun off the bench, exploded to her feet, crazily certain that something had crossed over, through the veil of glass and quicksilver. But no unwanted visitor had entered the bedroom.

She glanced at the clock just as the sideways scroll of numbers abruptly halted. The time was 2:44.

Checking her wristwatch, she discovered that the hour and the minute hands had stopped spinning. Her timepiece agreed with the digital clock—2:44.

The music boxes fell silent.

The miniature carousel horse went from gallop to full stop in a *plink*, and the dancing figurines froze in midwaltz.

Molly felt suddenly relieved of the real or imagined weight that had been suspended overhead like a giant sword of Damocles.

The half-heard, fully felt, deep pulsations of sound stopped throbbing through her.

"The mirror," Neil said.

The reflection that it now offered was of the room in which they stood. No ruins, no mold-textured walls, no crawling vine.

Neil shifted his attention from the mirror to the ceiling. Then he went to a window. He peered less at the surrounding forest than at the obscured night sky from which rain poured in great cascades.

"Gone," he said.

"I felt something," she admitted. "But . . . what was it?"

"Don't have a clue."

He was not being candid with her, nor she with him.

They had been formed by a culture drunk with the yearning for intergalactic contact, the bedrock of a new faith in which God was but a supporting player. Everyone knew the doctrines of this quasi-religion better than most people remembered the words of the Lord's Prayer: *We are not alone . . . watch the skies . . . the answer is out there. . . .* They had been Spielberged and Lucased and Shyamalaned. A thousand movies and TV shows, ten thousand books, had convinced the world that the new magi would be scientists riding not to Bethlehem on camels but to a UFO landing site in mobile labs with satellite dishes on the roofs, and that the salvation of humanity would come from another planet rather than from a higher realm.

Molly knew the signs as prophesied by Hollywood and by science fiction writers. Neil knew them, too.

This September night lay deep inside the Close Encounter Zone. In this territory, alien technology was the only font of miracles.

She didn't want to put this understanding into words, however, and apparently neither did Neil. A pretense of bewilderment felt safer than candor.

Perhaps their reticence had its roots in the fact that on this subject Hollywood offered two familiar scenarios—one in which the extraterrestrials were benign gods, one in which they were full of wrath and cruel judgment. Thus far, these recent events lacked the sweetness and the twinkle of G-rated family entertainment.

Turning away from the window and from his inspection of the rain-choked sky, Neil said, "Not that we'll need it . . . but I'll get the shotgun."

Recalling the half-glimpsed, sinuous figure that had flashed darkly across the moldering room in the mirror, Molly retrieved her handgun from the vanity and said, "I'll get some spare cartridges for this."

5

ON THE KITCHEN TABLE LAY THE SHOTGUN AND A box of shells. Beside it were the pistol, a spare magazine, and a box of 9-mm cartridges.

Pleated window shades in the kitchen and the adjacent family room held back the night and the sight—though not the omnipresent sound—of the luminous rain.

Molly couldn't shake the feeling that the surrounding forest, previously a friendly woods, now harbored unknown hostile observers. Neil apparently shared her paranoia; he had helped her lower the shades.

They both intuited that the mysterious forces at work in this drenched night were not restricted to these mountains. Simultaneously they reached for the TV remote, and Neil got it first.

They stood in front of the big screen, watching, too agitated to settle into chairs.

Television reception was not what it should be. Some channels were so afflicted with electronic snow that only ghostly images could be seen through the blizzard. Broken voices spoke distorted words.

One of the twenty-four-hour cable-news networks offered better sound and a relatively clear picture that rolled and flickered only occasionally.

The young woman—Veronica something—anchoring the news desk was as lovely as any movie starlet. Her eyes were avaricious, her smile as genuine as that of a mannequin.

She traded unscripted commentary with a young man, Jack, who might have been a successful underwear model for Calvin Klein if he had not gone to journalism school and majored in broadcasting. His smile, quick to come and quick to falter, revealed bleached-white teeth as square as those of a cow.

War, politics, crime, and even the doings of Hollywood royalty had been washed entirely off the news wires by freakish weather of an unprecedented nature and ferocity.

During the night, unpredicted, the largest continuous storm front ever recorded had formed at sea with impossible speed. It had moved ashore along the entire west coast of the Americas—South, Central, and North.

Reports of a curiously scented rain falling at the rate of four, five, and even six inches an hour had been received, corroborated. Within a few hours, low-lying cities all the way from Argentina to Alaska had begun suffering various degrees of flooding.

Live satellite feeds from both exotic and familiar metropolitan areas, sometimes distorted or grainy, showed cars and trucks afloat in city streets that resembled canals. Families on the roofs of their half-submerged houses. Soggy hillsides sliding away in rivers of mud.

Through every image, like pure-silver threads subtly woven in a tapestry, the luminous rain glimmered, so that Argentina and Alaska, and every point between, seemed unreal, revealed by dream light.

Molly had never been a fan of catastrophic news. She found neither enlightenment nor entertainment value in watching disaster befall others. Usually she would have turned away from the TV, half sick with pity. In this case she sensed that her future was tied to the fate of the strangers on the screen.

More recently, torrential rains had begun falling across Europe. Asia.

Africa. From the arid Middle East, even from the parched sands of Saudi Arabia, came reports of rain in unprecedented volume. Video was expected shortly.

Nothing in the breaking news warranted a smile. Manning their anchor desk, Veronica and Jack were nevertheless guided by the first rule of electronic journalism: Establish rapport with the audience; ingratiate yourself and make yourself welcome in their homes; be authoritative but *nice*, dignified but *fun*.

Neither of them could entirely conceal the excitement of being junior talent, consigned to the graveyard shift, yet suddenly on-air as a huge story began breaking. Minute by minute, their audience was growing from maybe a hundred thousand insomniacs to perhaps millions of riveted viewers. You could almost hear them calculating the boost their careers would receive from this lucky timing.

Although the precise nature and the seriousness of the current crisis remained unclear, field reports compensated with dramatic content for what they lacked in coherency.

Six hours earlier, prior to the arrival of the rain along the coastline of the Americas, the crew of a French marine-research ship had witnessed the sudden birth of a spectacular waterspout three hundred miles southwest of Tahiti. The twister spun down from a cumulonimbus mass about three miles off the ship's starboard flank, and grew with astonishing rapidity until the funnel point, sucking at the ocean, broadened to an estimated six hundred meters, more than a third of a mile.

Digital video, shot by a crew member and uploaded through the vessel's satellite link, revealed a formation of daunting size. A scientist aboard the research ship estimated that the tornado-like form measured three miles in diameter where the highest point of the vertical updraft disappeared into the clouds.

"Sweet Jesus," Neil whispered.

In these scenes, neither the sea nor the massive column of water churning into the sky was touched by the mysterious luminescence.

Nevertheless, the extraordinary rain, now drumming beyond the blinded windows, must somehow be related to this gigantic waterspout videotaped earlier in the far reaches of the South Pacific. Although Molly couldn't understand the connection, the worldwide character of these events sharpened her anxiety.

On TV, the raging Pacific vortex spun off mean weather. The day darkened rapidly, as if God had applied a heavy finger to a celestial rheostat. Great claws of lightning tore at the ocean.

If the video frame had included any object with which to compare the funnel, the scale of the phenomenon would have been not merely breathtaking but terrifying. She could sense the cameraman's fear when the twister began to move toward his ship.

As if rocked with anger and pain as the lightning slashed its great dark hide, the sea thrashed and heaved. The ship dropped into a fearsome trough, a chasm.

The bow dug into the floor of the trough. Tons of water broke over the railing and churned across the deck.

Battered by this surge, the cameraman's legs were nearly swept out from under him. He kept his balance and staggered off the open deck as the ship abruptly shuddered and rose along the steep face of a colossal swell.

The starlet reporter, Veronica, appeared on the screen again to say that following the transmission of the preceding video, the French ship had not been heard from again.

Jack, her co-anchor, expressed concern for the crew and then, with mindless conviction, concluded that they were certainly safe because "those marine-research guys really know their way around the sea."

Through a smile as constant as that of a ventriloquist's wooden partner, Veronica revealed that she had spent one semester of college aboard a sailing vessel in an at-sea learning program.

Molly wanted to scream at them, as if her voice might travel back along a microwave path to New York City or Washington, or to wherever they were located. She wanted to rock them out of their self-satisfied journalistic detachment, which always seemed to her to be merely smug superiority and emotional indifference masquerading as professionalism.

Additional video had been recorded and transmitted via satellite by military personnel aboard the USS *Ronald Reagan,* an aircraft carrier currently under way three hundred miles due west of Japan. This tape documented the astonishingly swift development of a dense cloud cover out of a previously clear sky.

Subsequently, at three points of the compass, within sight of observers aboard the aircraft carrier, waterspouts had formed. The diameter of their funnels grew rapidly until each was larger than the single twister captured on video by the French. An officer aboard the carrier, unable to keep either the awe or the tremor of fear out of his voice, added narration to the incredible visuals.

Again, neither the sea nor the spinning funnels revealed any trace of the scintillation that characterized the falling rain.

Impossibly, reports of giant waterspouts were also coming in from ships in the Atlantic Ocean and the Mediterranean Sea, though these were not supported by video.

Obviously reading from a TelePrompTer, in a pedantic but still ingratiating tone, Veronica said, "Although waterspouts appear to be twisting tubes of solid water, they consist of mist and spray, and are not as formidable as they look."

"However," Jack chimed in, "relying on sophisticated computer analysis of Doppler-radar images, technicians aboard the *Ronald Reagan* determined that the spouts under their observation did not conform to any known models of the phenomenon. These *are* nearly solid forms, and Dr. Randolph Templeton, a meteorologist with the National Weather Service, who joined us in the studio just a short while ago, estimates that each of these funnels is drawing water from the sea at the rate of a hundred thousand gallons per minute."

"More," said Templeton when he came on-screen. "Twice that, at least." He had the good sense not to smile.

In the meteorologist's eyes, Molly saw the measured fear of an informed intelligence.

Needing to touch Neil, she put a hand on his shoulder, and was less reassured than usual by his solid physique.

With furrowed brow, in a solemn voice, Jack asked Dr. Templeton if these phenomena were the result of global warming.

"The vast majority of meteorologists don't believe there is any global warming," Templeton replied with a note of impatience, "at least not any that isn't natural and cyclical."

Jack and Veronica both appeared dumbfounded by this statement, and before a producer could murmur a suitable comeback question in their earpieces, they both looked simultaneously at the ceiling of the broadcast studio.

"A very hard rain has just begun falling here in Washington," said Veronica.

"Remarkably hard," Jack agreed. Apparently, the producer at last whispered in his earpiece, for Jack turned to the meteorologist. "But Dr. Templeton, everyone knows the effect of greenhouse gases—"

"What everyone knows is bunk," Templeton said, "and if we're going to get a handle on this, what we need right now is analysis based on *real* science, not—"

Neil thumbed the remote control repeatedly until he found one of the three major networks, which had belatedly risen to the crisis like a shark to a swimmer.

The anchorman was older than the pair on cable news, and famous. He preened with self-importance as he interviewed a specialist in satellite-data analysis.

According to the bio line on the bottom of the screen, the expert was Dr. Sanford Nguyen. He worked for the same government agency that employed Randolph Templeton, who was at that moment debating global warming with Jack and Veronica on another channel.

The anchorman was surely being fed questions by an unseen producer and a first-rate team of researchers, but his inquiries rolled off his golden tongue as though he himself were a maven of orbital data-recovery systems.

Dr. Nguyen made the unsettling revelation that three hours prior to the observation of the extraordinary waterspouts, all orbital assets of the National Weather Service and other federal agencies had gone blind. Evidently, industry-owned satellites with high-resolution photographic capability were out of commission, as well. No high-altitude photographic, infrared, or radar images of the waterspouts were available to suggest why and how these phenomena had occurred.

"What about military satellites, the missile trackers?" Molly wondered. "What about spy satellites?"

"They'll have been blinded, too," Neil predicted.

On the TV, the anchorman asked Dr. Nguyen if a burst of cosmic radiation or perhaps unusually intense sunspot activity could have fried the circuitry in all those eyes in the sky.

"No," Nguyen assured him. "That can't be the explanation. Besides, it's too coincidental. Neither cosmic radiation nor magnetic pulses could have precipitated the calamitous weather we're seeing, and I'm sure that whatever blinded our satellites is the cause also of those waterspouts and these storms."

Puckering his face into his most solemn of all expressions, the network anchorman said, "Dr. Nguyen, are we seeing at last the terrible consequences of global warming?"

Nguyen's expression suggested contempt but also sudden bewilderment at the unanswerable question he must have been asking himself: *What the hell am I doing here?*

Molly said, "Why would only observation satellites be out of commission?" She gestured toward the TV. "Obviously, communications satellites are still functioning."

"Probably they prefer we don't see them," Neil said, "but they want us to know what's happening with the weather because fear debilitates. Maybe they want us frightened, cowering, and pliable."

"They?"

He didn't reply.

She knew what he meant, and he knew that she understood. Yet both of them were reluctant to express the truth that they suspected, as if to name the enemy would be to unleash in themselves a terror that they could not tame.

Neil put down the remote control, turned from the TV, and headed out of the family room into the adjoining kitchen. "I'm going to make coffee."

"Coffee?" she asked with a note of disbelief.

This domestic task seemed to be evidence of total psychological denial, a reaction unworthy of the unshakeable, eternally competent man whom she had married.

"We haven't had a full night's sleep," he explained. "We might need to stay awake, keep our wits about us, for a long time. Coffee will help. I better make it while we still have electrical service."

Molly glanced at the TV, at the lamps. She hadn't thought the power might go off.

She was chilled by the prospect of having no light except the eerie luminosity of the unclean rain.

"I'll gather all the flashlights," she said, "and whatever spare batteries we have."

Flashlights were distributed throughout the house, continually charging in wall outlets. They were to provide guidance in the event that an earthquake imposed darkness in rocked rooms filled with avalanched furniture.

He turned to her, paler than he'd been a moment ago. "No, Molly.

From now on, neither of us goes anywhere alone. We'll collect the flashlights later, together. Right now, let's brew some coffee. And make sandwiches."

"I'm not hungry."

"We'll eat anyway."

"But Neil—"

"We don't know what's coming. We don't know when we'll have a chance to eat again . . . in peace."

He held out a hand to her.

He was the most beautiful and appealing man whom she had ever known. The first time that she'd seen him, more than seven years ago, Neil had been standing in a complicated geometry of multicolored light, smiling warmly, his face so perfect and his eyes so kind that she briefly mistook him for Saint John the Divine.

She gripped his hand, shivering with fear and inexpressibly grateful that fate had combed her and him from the tangle of humanity, and that love had braided them together in marriage.

He drew her into his arms. She held fast to him.

One ear against his chest, she listened to his heart. The beat was strong, at first quickened by anxiety, but then growing calmer.

Molly's heart slowed to match the pace of his.

Steel has a high melting point, but higher still when it is alloyed with tungsten. Cashmere is a strong fabric, as is silk; however, a cashmere-and-silk blend will be more durable and will provide more warmth to the wearer than will either fabric alone.

Alone, she had learned at a young age to carry all the weight the world piled on her. As long as she had Neil, she could endure not just the terrors of this world but also those that might come from beyond it.

6

ALTHOUGH THE KITCHEN AND FAMILY ROOM WERE redolent of the rich aroma of coffee, Molly thought that she could detect the faint but singular odor of the rain penetrating the walls from the saturated night.

She and Neil sat on the floor in front of the TV, the shotgun and pistol within easy reach, eating chicken sandwiches and potato chips.

Initially she had no appetite. On first bite, however, she discovered that she was ravenous.

No food had ever tasted as delicious as this. The chicken proved juicier, the mayonnaise creamier, the pickles more tart, and the chips crispier than any she had eaten before. Every flavor was exquisitely enhanced.

Perhaps any prisoner on death row, savoring his last meal before being given a lethal injection, experienced the flavors and textures of food this intensely.

On television, silvery-blue snow fell in the French Alps, in the mountains of Colorado, on the streets of Moscow. Each scene appeared to have been dusted with Christmas-card glitter.

The domes and minarets of the Kremlin had never before looked so magical. Every glimmering shadow in those twinkling boulevards and sparkling plazas seemed to harbor elves, pixies, and other fairy folk who might momentarily spring into sight, dancing and performing aerial acrobatics in exuberant celebration.

The ethereal beauty of the sequined blue snow suggested that whatever might be happening could not be entirely without a positive aspect.

In Denver, although dawn had not yet broken, children were frolicking in the streets, tossing snowballs, drawn from their homes by the novelty of a blue, luminous blizzard.

Their delight and their musical laughter inspired a hopeful yet uncertain smile from the on-scene network reporter. He said, "And another remarkable detail about this extraordinary phenomenon—the snow smells sort of like vanilla."

Molly wondered if the newsman had a sufficiently sensitive nose to be able to detect a far less appealing underlying scent if one existed.

"Vanilla laced with the fragrance of oranges," he continued.

Perhaps here in the San Bernardino Mountains, the rain no longer smelled as it had when Molly stepped onto the porch with the coyotes. Maybe, as in Colorado, the night now offered the olfactory delights of a confectioner's kitchen.

Turning, encouraging the cameraman to pan with him, the reporter indicated the wintry panorama: the mantled street, the evergreen boughs laden with fluffy masses of sapphire flocking, the warm amber lights of houses huddled cozily in the blue impossible.

"It's indescribably beautiful," he said, "like a scene out of Dr. Seuss, a street in Whoville, the glitter without the Grinch."

The hundred-eighty-degree sweep of the camera came to a stop, zooming in on a group of children who were bundled for winter play.

A girl of perhaps seven held a snowball in her gloved hands.

Instead of throwing it at anyone, she licked it, as if it were one of those treats made with shaved ice and flavored syrup, sold at carnivals and amusement parks. She grinned at the camera with blue-tinted lips.

An older boy, inspired by her example, took a bite from his snowball. The taste seemed to please him.

This image disturbed Molly so much that if she had not already consumed her sandwich, she would have put it aside, unfinished.

She remembered the unclean feel of the rain. She would never have turned her face to the sky and opened her mouth to imbibe this storm.

Evidently, the sight of the children eating snow dismayed Neil no less than it did Molly. He picked up the remote, surfed for news.

7

UNABLE TO PRESS FROM HER MIND THE IMAGE OF THE children feeding on the tainted snow, Molly paced and drank too much coffee.

Neil remained seated on the floor, using the TV remote.

Up and down the broadcast ladder, more channels than before were too poorly received to be watchable. And more than previously were out of service altogether.

Twice they encountered signals that manifested on the screen as coruscating patterns in vibrant colors. Although reminiscent of the symmetrical displays that dazzled at the bottom of a kaleidoscope, these designs had no sharp edges; they were all curves and sinuous forms, apparently infinite in variety, yet suggestive of meaning.

Accompanying the patterns were the oscillating electronic tones that Molly had heard on the telephone: shrieks followed by low pulses of sound, followed by piercing whistles . . .

Government officials were suddenly all over the tube, sounding authoritative—but looking at best disquieted and confused, at worst frightened. The Secretary of the Department of Homeland Security, various officials from the Federal Emergency Management Agency . . .

Weather-related crises were springing up by the dozens every hour, all because of the unprecedented volume of rain, now estimated at seven inches an hour in many locations. With frightening rapidity, rivers overflowed their banks. Dams filled faster than floodgates could relieve the growing pressure; already, in Oregon, only a few hours after the rains had begun, a dam had burst, and several small towns had been washed away.

Incredibly, when the entire world might be at risk, Molly worried about the stability of their one piece of real estate. "What about mud slides?"

"We're safe," Neil assured her. "We're on bedrock."

"I don't *feel* safe."

"We're so high . . . two thousand feet above any possible flood plain."

Irrationally, she felt that they might somehow ride out even the end of the world as they knew it if only their home remained intact, as if the Sloan residence were a bubble universe sufficient unto itself.

While they had eaten sandwiches and watched the world falling into tumult on TV, Neil had moved the family-room telephone from the end table beside the sofa, where it usually stood, to the floor at his side. From time to time, he had tried to call his brother, Paul, in Hawaii.

Sometimes he got a dial tone; Paul's cell phone rang out there on Maui, but no one answered. At other times, when he picked up the handset, he got the oscillating electronic tones that accompanied the colorful patterns on TV.

On the seventh or eighth attempt, a connection was made. Paul answered.

The sound of his brother's voice clearly lifted Neil's spirits. "Paulie. Thank God. Thought you might be just crazy enough to catch some waves in this."

Paul surfed. The ocean was his second passion.

Molly grabbed the remote control, muted the TV.

Into the phone, Neil said, "What?" He listened. "Yeah, we're okay. Here at the house. It's raining so hard maybe we need gopher wood and plans for an ark."

Molly knelt in front of her husband, reached to the phone, and pressed the button labeled SPEAKER.

From the north shore of Maui, Paul said, "—seen a lot of tropical rains, but nothing like this."

"TV says seven inches an hour."

"Worse than that here," Paul said. "Much worse. Rain so thick, you can almost drown on your feet. If you gasp for breath, you get more water than air. The rain—it's a heavy *weight*, wants to drive you to your knees. We've gathered in the courthouse. Almost four hundred of us."

"The courthouse?" Puzzlement furrowed Neil's brow. "Not the church? The church is on higher ground."

"The courthouse has fewer and smaller windows," Paul explained. "It's more easily fortified and defended."

Defended.

Molly glanced at the pistol, the shotgun.

On the muted television, spectacular video from some far city showed buildings burning in spite of quenching masses of falling rain.

On the phone, Paul said, "*First Peter,* chapter four, verse seven. Does it feel that way to you, little brother?"

"Truth? It feels like *Close Encounters* to me," Neil admitted, at last putting into words the thought that neither he nor Molly had been willing to express. "But where it's ultimately going—who knows?"

"I know," Paul said, his voice firm and calm. "I've accepted with good will all the anguish, pain, and sorrow that might come."

Molly recognized his stilted words as a paraphrasing of Acceptance of Death, one of the Church's evening prayers.

She said, "It's not going to be like that, Paulie. There's something . . . I don't know . . . something positive about this, too."

"Molly, I love your sweet voice," Paul said. "Always the one to see a rainbow in a hurricane."

"Well . . . life's taught me to be optimistic."

"You're right. Death is nothing to fear, is it? Just a new beginning."

"No, I don't mean that." She told him about the coyotes on the porch.

"I walked among them. They were so docile. It was miraculous, Paul, exhilarating."

"I love you, Molly. You've been a godsend to Neil, made him happy, healed his soul. That first year, I said hurtful things—"

"Never," she disagreed.

Neil took her hand, squeezed it gently.

On the TV, in yet another city, no buildings were afire, but looters smashed store windows. The cascades of shattered glass glittered no more brightly than the spangled rain.

To Molly, Paul said, "This is no time for lies, kiddo. Not even the polite kind meant to spare feelings."

Initially Paul had not approved of their marriage. Over the years, however, he adjusted to it, eventually embraced it. He and Molly had become fast friends, and until now they had never spoken about his early antagonism.

She smiled. "All right, Father Paul, I confess. There were times you really pissed me off."

Paul laughed softly. "I'm sure God felt the same way. I asked His forgiveness long ago—and now I'm asking yours."

Her voice thickened. She wanted to hang up. She despaired over the inescapable implications of this conversation. They were saying goodbye. "Paulie . . . you're my brother, too. You can't know . . . how I treasure you."

"Oh, but I know. I do. And listen, kiddo, your last book would have made your mother proud."

"Sweet melody, good rhythm," she said, "but in the service of shallow observations."

"No. Stop beating yourself up. It rang with the same wisdom as Thalia's best work."

Tears blurred Molly's vision. "Remember . . . this is no time for lies, Paulie."

"Haven't told any."

Silently, a rain-drenched, wild-eyed mob raced toward and past the TV camera. They appeared to be fleeing in terror from something.

From the phone, Paul said, "Listen . . . I have to go. I don't think there's much time left."

"What's happening there?" Neil worried.

"I finished saying Mass a few minutes before you called. But not everyone gathered here is a Catholic, so they need a different kind of comforting."

On the screen, the cameraman was knocked over by the panicked throng. The point of view swung wildly, crashed down to pavement level, revealing running feet that splashed up luminous sprays from darkly jeweled puddles.

Holding tightly to the handset even though the speakerphone feature was engaged, as though he were keeping his brother on the line sheerly by the intensity of his grip, Neil said, "Paulie, what did you mean—the courthouse can be more easily defended? Defended from who?"

Interference distorted the reply incoming from Hawaii.

"Paulie? We didn't hear that. The line broke up a little. Who're you expecting to defend against?"

Although audible again, Paulie sounded as if he were speaking from the bottom of a deep pit. "These are mostly simple people, Neil. Their imaginations may be working overtime, or they might see what they expect to see rather than what really is. I haven't seen one myself."

"One what?"

Static fizzed and crackled.

"Paulie?"

Among the broken, twisted words issuing from the speaker, one sounded like *devils.*

"Paulie," Neil said, "if this line goes, we'll call you right back. And if we can't get through, you try calling us. Do you hear me, Paulie?"

On TV, in a city now identified by caption—*Berlin, Germany*—the last of the soundless, running feet chased across the streaming pavement, past the fallen videocam.

Suddenly out of distant Maui, as clear as if originating from the adjacent kitchen, Paul Sloan's voice once more swelled loud in midsentence: ". . . chapter twelve, verse twelve. Do you remember that one, Neil?"

"Sorry, Paulie, I didn't catch the book," Neil replied. "Say it again."

In Berlin, captured blurrily through a wet lens, legions of luminous raindrops marched across the puddled street, casting up a spray more glittery than diamond dust.

A prescient awareness of pending horror kept Molly's attention riveted on the muted TV.

The action seemed to be over, the mob having moved on to other territory, but she assumed that the accompanying audio must be telling an important story. Otherwise, the network would have cut away from Berlin when the camera struck the pavement and was not at once snatched up again.

She still held the remote. She didn't press MUTE and summon the sound again because she didn't want to risk blotting out anything that her brother-in-law might say.

On the phone, Paul's voice fell into an abyss, but just as Neil was about to hang up, the connection proved intact, and Paul rejoined them briefly again: " '. . . having great wrath because he knows that he hath but a short time.' "

The line finally went dead, transmitting not even the click and scratch of static.

"Paulie? Paulie, can you hear me?" Neil pumped the disconnect bar in the phone cradle, trying without success to get a dial tone.

On the TV, as silent as a bubble drifting into frame, a human head, perhaps that of the luckless cameraman, precisely cleaved in half from brow through chin, dropped to the pavement, landing flat-side down, one dead terror-brightened eye peering along the microwave pipeline from Berlin to California.

8

UNTIL NOW, MOLLY HAD NEVER FELT A NEED TO TAKE
a loaded pistol to the bathroom.

She put it on the yellow ceramic tiles beside the sink, the muzzle toward the mirror. The presence of the weapon gave her no comfort, but
made her bowels quiver.

In the quick, when either you had the heart for justice or you didn't,
Molly could squeeze the trigger without hesitation. She'd done it once
before.

Nevertheless, the prospect of having to shoot someone half sickened
her. She was a creator, not a killer.

On her porcelain prie-dieu with flusher handle, she prayed that regardless of what might transpire in the hours ahead, she would not have
to defend herself against other human beings. She wanted only enemies
so alien that, after the shooting, there could be no cause for doubt, no
reason for guilt.

Although acutely aware of the multiple ironies and absurdities of both
her position and her prayer, she sent each word to God with sincerity, in
a fever of mind and bone. The humor of the moment was too bitter to
tease from her even a wretched laugh.

She had chosen the windowless half-bath off the kitchen. From beyond the door, through the white noise of the rain on the roof, came the

clink and clatter of Neil packing two insulated coolers full of provisions to take with them in the SUV.

Each of his two careers had required that he think ahead. These days he worked as a cabinetmaker. He knew the importance of having good plans and precise measurements before making the first cut.

He worried that they would grow hungry before they were ready to come home. Worse, events might prevent them from returning home at all.

More monk than adventurer, Diogenes to his Columbus, Molly regretted the need to leave. Her preferred strategy was to bar the doors, board the windows, press sleep from lidless eyes, and wait for trouble to knock. And hope that it never would.

She knew, however, that Neil's argument for action was the wiser course. Whatever might be coming in the rain or on the wake of it, they would be more vulnerable alone than they would be in the company of their neighbors.

Before she washed her hands, she lowered her face to the sink and warily breathed the steam rising from the gushing water. She could not detect any trace of the scent of the rain.

The tainted storm had not yet found its way into the public water system. Or if it *had* found its way, it traveled now in this bland disguise, undetectable.

Before picking up the cake of soap, she transferred the pistol from the counter to the toilet tank—beyond the grasp of anything that might reach through the mirror.

With such bizarre precautions already second nature only hours into this new reality, Molly wondered if she would know when she had gone mad. Perhaps she had already left sanity behind. Perhaps she had journeyed so far from rationality that Neil could never pack enough hampers of provisions to feed her during a return trip.

She washed her hands.

She remained the only presence in the mirror, not stained and ruined and grown over with strange vines, nor cleaved through the face from brow to chin, but still so young, and bright-eyed with a desperate hope.

Coolers filled with food, a case of bottled water, and basic first-aid supplies had been loaded aboard the SUV in the garage. They were prepared for travel where the ways were deep and the weather sharp.

Molly had also packed her mother's books, and the four that she herself had written, plus her current uncompleted manuscript. Worlds might perish but, in her view, never the written word.

Gathering courage to depart, she and Neil stood side by side in the family room, watching TV.

Channel by channel, chaos had expanded its domain. More than half of the microwave highways were clogged with snow, scintillation, flare, woomp, and third-generation ghosts of people and objects unidentifiable.

Another third carried the pulsing, serpentine, kaleidoscopic patterns of intense color. These were accompanied by the humming, hissing, blurping, wow-wows, squeals, whistles, and birdies that also rendered the telephone useless.

They could find no news, no meaningful information.

A handful of channels continued to broadcast clear signals: sharp pictures, surprisingly pristine sound. Every one of these was devoted to entertainment programming.

For a minute, they watched an old episode of *Seinfeld*. An audience, real or virtual, laughed and laughed.

Neil changed channels, found a game show. For a quarter of a million dollars and a chance to go on for half a million, name the author of *Old Possum's Book of Practical Cats*.

"T. S. Eliot," Molly said.

She was right, but she suspected that one week from now a quarter of a million dollars might have no more value than last week's newspaper.

On another channel, in the black-and-white Casablanca night, Bogart said good-bye to Ingrid Bergman as total war descended on the world.

Neil knew the dialogue so well that he could recite it word for word. His lips moved to match those of the actors, though he made no sound.

He switched channels: Here, Cary Grant, with exquisite comic timing, grew increasingly flustered in the face of Katharine Hepburn's nonstop screwball patter.

And here, Jimmy Stewart wisecracked with an invisible, six-foot-tall rabbit.

At first Molly didn't understand why Neil watched these old films with such shining-eyed intensity. Only moments ago he'd been determined to seek out the company of their neighbors as quickly as possible.

Soon she realized that he expected never to have the opportunity to enjoy these movies again, or any other, if all of Earth fell under the rule of an alien people clutching their new gods.

Greedily, then, she watched Gary Cooper walk the dusty streets of a Western town under the high-noon sun. Watched Tom Hanks gumping his way through a life charmed by virtue of simplicity. Watched John Wayne sweep Maureen O'Hara off her feet.

Repeatedly she found herself holding her breath, a sweet pain in her breast. What had once been mere time-filling entertainment now seemed inexpressibly beautiful and profound.

Neil surfed out of old movies and into a contemporary program—one of those orchestrated geek fests mislabeled "reality TV," which celebrated cruelty, championed ignorance, lured viewers with the promise of degradation, and never quite faded from popularity. A female contestant was eating a plateful of pale, squirming slugs.

Here, a more recent film. A beautiful, lithe blonde executed impossible martial-arts maneuvers, wielding a sword, beheading a series of adversaries, stabbing them in the eyes, eviscerating them with delight, prettier than a Barbie doll and just as heartless.

Suddenly the remote control seemed no longer to be an instrument allowing random selection, seemed instead to be programmed to seek out atrocities. Channel after channel, blood burst, blood sprayed, blood spattered across the screen.

Pay-per-view pornography—to which they had not subscribed, and which therefore they should not be able to receive—filled the screen with an explicit scene of violent gang rape. The victim was shown to be enjoying her vicious brutalization.

Shrill comedians telling mean jokes drew meaner laughter from braying audiences.

No crafted piece of propaganda could have mocked the pretensions of humanity more effectively than this apparently random selection of cruel entertainment.

Neil pressed the POWER button on the remote, but the TV did not switch off. He tried again, without success.

Under the control of some taunting entity, the screen swarmed with rapidly changing scenes of violent sex and horrendous murder. Here unspooled a chilling montage of humanity in its most debased and savage condition.

"This is a lie," Neil said through half-clenched teeth. "This isn't what we are. It isn't *all* we are."

The unseen master of the airwaves chose to disagree, and the images of primitive lust and blood hunger surged across the screen, tides of cinematic sewage.

Molly remembered reading about one of the Nazi death camps—Auschwitz or Bergen-Belsen, or Dachau—in which the Jewish prisoners had been subjected to propaganda that portrayed their heritage as a deformed tree watered with lies, feeding on the labor of others, its branches twisted by greed. Their tormentors wanted them first to embrace this false history of their people and then to renounce it before accepting execution as their proper reward.

Even the architects of genocide, their hearts sold to Evil and their souls already held in the portfolio of Hell, feel the need to justify their abuse of power. They wish to believe that their victims, at the penultimate moment, acknowledge guilt and recognize the justice of mass murder—which suggests that, even if unconsciously, the executioners know how far they themselves have fallen.

Molly turned from the hideous spectacle on the TV. She glanced anxiously at the blinded windows, at the ceiling that seemed to press lower under a roof-crushing weight of roaring rain.

She sensed that death trains, or their equivalent, were being marshaled now in railroad yards. Long chains of cattle cars were waiting to be packed with human cargo and hauled to mass graves where the remains of millions, plowed over, would eventually fertilize vast, lush meadows for the pleasure of creatures that were deaf and blind to the beauties wrought by untold human generations.

High in the house, something thumped loudly. Rattled. Then subsided into silence.

Perhaps a broken tree branch had dropped onto the roof. A loose chimney stone, sluiced from its mortar bed by the rain, might have rolled along the shingles.

Or some unimaginably strange visitor had entered by the attic, and now explored the space under those cobwebbed rafters, searching for the trapdoor and spring-loaded ladder that would give it access to the second floor.

"Time to go," Neil said.

PART TWO

"Waste and void. Waste and void. And darkness on the face of the deep."

T.S. Eliot, *Choruses from "The Rock"*

9

FOR ONCE UNCONCERNED ABOUT NEXT MONTH'S
electrical bill, they left lights on rather than allow darkness to take up residence in the house during their absence.

In the utility room, they quickly donned rubber boots and black raincoats. The deep tread of the rubber soles squeaked on the tile floor.

Beyond the utility room, the garage was chillier than the house. The humid air smelled of damp wood, moist Sheetrock; but as yet the rain had not worn a leak in the roof.

The Ford Explorer stood ready, loaded. Although worried about the size of the monthly payments, they had recently traded up from their ten-year-old Suburban. Now Molly was glad to have this newer and more reliable vehicle.

She took two steps toward the SUV before Neil drew her attention to his workbench. Thirty or forty mice had gathered on that surface. Because the rodents were silent and for the most part as still as ceramic figurines, Molly had not at once noticed the infestation.

Field and forest mice, some brown, some gray, had fled their natural habitat for the refuge of this garage. As many of them congregated under the workbench as perched on top of it.

In groups, mice huddled in the corners and along the walls. On the lids of the two trash cans. Atop a row of storage cabinets.

They numbered more than a hundred, perhaps over two hundred. Many stood on their hind feet, alert, trembling, whiskers quivering, pink noses testing the air.

Under ordinary circumstances, the mice would have scattered when Molly and Neil entered. These didn't react. The cause of their fear lay outside, in the storm.

Although Molly had always been squeamish about rodents and had taken more than the usual precautions to keep them out of the house, she didn't recoil at the sight of these timid invaders. As with the coyotes, she recognized that men and mice lived under a common threat in this perilous night.

When she and Neil got into the Explorer and closed the doors, Molly said, "If their instinct is to come inside, should we be going out?"

"Paul and his neighbors are gathered in that courthouse on Maui because its architecture makes it more defensible. Our house, with all the windows, the simple locks . . . it can't be defended."

"Maybe no place can be."

"Maybe," he agreed.

He started the SUV.

The mice did not react to the noise of the engine. Their eyes shone red and silver in the blaze of headlights.

Neil locked the doors of the Explorer with the master switch. Only then did he use the remote to raise the garage door.

Molly realized that she had not locked the house. Keys and deadbolts no longer seemed to offer much security.

Behind the Explorer, the segmented garage door rolled upward. She could barely differentiate the rumble of its ascent from the unrelenting voice of the rain.

She was overcome by the urge to bolt from the vehicle and return to the house before the crouching night could be entirely let into the garage.

A desperate domestic fantasy gripped her. She would make hot tea and serve it in a mug. Oolong, with its distinctive fragrance, grown in the distant Wu-I Mountains of China.

She would drink it in the cozy parlor, eating butter cookies. Warmed by an afghan. Reading a love story of eternal passion and timeless suffering.

When she turned the last tear-stained page, the rain would have stopped. The morning would have come. The future would no longer be bleak and impenetrable, would instead be revealed by an invisible light too bright for mortal eyes.

But she did not open the passenger door and pursue that fantasy of tea and cookies and easy happy endings. Dared not.

Neil popped the brake, shifted into reverse, and backed out of the garage, into the windless storm. The rain fell straight down with such judgmental force that the Explorer seemed to quiver in every joint, to strain at every weld, from the impact.

Less out of concern for their property than in consideration of the frightened mice, Molly pressed the remote and closed the garage door.

In the headlights, the formerly muted fluorescence of the rain brightened, seething with scintillating reflections.

The cedar siding of the house, quaintly silvered by time, was more brightly silvered by the luminous wet. Along the roof line, from long lengths of overflowing rain gutters spilled shimmering sheets that veiled whole aspects of the structure.

Neil turned the Explorer around and drove uphill toward the two-lane county road. The ascending driveway funneled a descending stream through which slithered great swarms of false serpents, more sinuous luminosities.

When the SUV reached the top of the driveway, Molly peered back and down, through the rush of rain and the steadfast trees. All lights aglow, their house looked welcoming—and forever beyond reach.

The shortest route into town was south on the county road.

The two-lane blacktop remained passable because it followed the ridge crest around the lake, shedding rain from both shoulders. Here and there the pavement was mantled with a thick slippery mush of dead pine needles beaten from the overhanging trees by the storm, but the SUV had all the traction needed to proceed unimpeded.

Even at high speed, the windshield wipers couldn't cope with the downpour. Sluicing rain blurred their view. Neil drove slowly and with caution.

To the east, the forest—portions burned out in the previous autumn's fire—descended toward treeless but grassy hills, which in turn gave way to more-arid land and eventually to the Mojave. Only a few houses had been built in that territory.

On the west face of the ridge, residences were numerous, though widely separated. The nearest neighbors to the south were Jose and Serena Sanchez, who had two children, Danny and Joey, and a dog named Semper Fidelis.

Neil turned right at their mailbox and halted at the top of the driveway, headlights focused on the house below.

"Wake them?" he wondered.

An indefinable quality of the house, something other than the lack of lights, troubled Molly.

If the Sanchez family had been home, surely the unprecedented power of this rain would have awakened them. Curiosity stirred, they would have risen from bed, turned on the TV, and thereby discovered the fate of the world.

Molly recognized the monotonous drone of the rain as the voice of Death, and now it seemed to speak to her not from the heavens but from the house at the foot of the driveway.

"They're gone," she said.

"Gone where?"

"Or dead."

"Not them," Neil hoped. "Not Jose, Serena . . . not the boys."

Molly was a mystic only to the extent that she was a writer, not to the extent that she suffered visions or premonitions. Yet she spoke with the certainty of unwanted intuition: "Dead. All dead."

The house blurred, clarified, blurred, clarified. Perhaps she saw movement behind the lightless windows; perhaps she did not.

She imagined a sinuous and winged figure, like the mysterious thing they had glimpsed beyond the mirror, flitting now through the rooms of the Sanchez house, from corpse to corpse, capering with dark delight.

Though she spoke in a tremulous whisper, her voice carried to Neil above the chanting rain. "Let's get out of here. Now. Quickly."

10

SOUTH OF THE SANCHEZ PROPERTY, THE WIDOWER, Harry Corrigan, had lived alone since the previous June, when his beloved Calista had died at the foot of an ATM.

This stone house, with a hipped and gabled roof, stood much nearer to the county road than did Neil and Molly's place. The driveway was shorter and less steep than theirs.

These were the lights that she had seen when she had first gotten out of bed and gone to the window to assess the violence of the storm. They had looked like the running lights of a distant ship on a mean and swelling sea.

Every pane appeared to be lit, as if Harry had gone room to room, searching for his lost wife, and had left every lamp aglow either with the hope of her return or in her memory. No shadows loomed or swooped beyond the glass.

If Harry was here, they needed to join forces with him. He was a friend, dependable.

At the foot of the driveway, in the turnaround, Neil parked facing out toward the county road. He switched off the headlights.

As Neil reached for the key in the ignition, Molly stayed his hand. "Leave the engine running."

They didn't have to discuss the danger or the wisdom of going together into the house. Wise or not, they earlier had established that henceforth they went nowhere alone.

Their raincoats featured hoods. They pulled them up, and were transformed into monkish medieval figures.

Molly dreaded getting out of the SUV. She remembered how vigorously she had scrubbed her rain-dampened hand with orange-scented soap . . . and had nevertheless felt unclean.

Yet she could not sit here eternally, paralyzed by the weight of fear or by a lack of faith. She could not sit here, shape without form, gesture without motion, waiting for the world to end.

The 9-mm pistol nestled in a pocket of her coat. She kept her right hand on it.

She got out of the Explorer and closed the door quietly, though a slam would not have carried far in the drumming deluge. Discretion seemed advisable even during an apocalypse.

The tremendous force of the downpour staggered her until she planted her feet wide and moved with conscious attention to her balance.

The rain was no longer ripe with the scent of semen. She could identify a faint trace of that odor, but it was now masked by new and sweet fragrances, reminiscent of incense, hot brass, lemon tea. She detected, as well, smoky essences for which she could think of no familiar comparisons.

She tried to avert her face, but rain found its way past the hood of her coat. The pelting drops were no longer warm, as they had been earlier.

Unthinkingly, she licked her lips. The taste proved to be not salty with the memory of the sea, but faintly sweet, pleasant.

When she thought of the children eating blue snow, however, she gagged and spat, only to drink in more rain.

The driveway drain had been blocked by fallen pine needles and wads of sycamore leaves. A pool of water, six inches deep, churned around their boots, brightened by silver filigrees of dancing eldritch light.

Neil had unzipped his raincoat to be able to carry the shotgun under it. With his left hand, he clutched the front panels of the garment, holding them closed as best he could.

A sloped flagstone walkway led from puddled pavement to front steps.

Sheltered by the porch roof, Molly threw back her hood. She drew the pistol from her coat. Neil held the shotgun with both hands.

The door of Harry Corrigan's house stood ajar.

An orange spot of light on the casing indicated the illuminated bell push, but these were not circumstances that recommended the customary announcement. With one boot toe, Neil gingerly nudged the door inward.

While it arced wide, they waited. Studied the deserted foyer for a moment. Entered the house.

They had frequently been here as invited guests before Calista's murder in Redondo Beach, and a few times since. When the kitchen had been remodeled four years ago, Neil had built the new cabinetry. Yet now this familiar place seemed strange, nothing exactly as Molly remembered it, nothing quite in its place.

The first floor offered much evidence of a simple life conducted in longstanding routines: comfortable furniture well used, landscape and seascape paintings, here a pipe left in an ashtray, here a book with the reader's place marked by a candy-bar wrapper, houseplants lovingly tended and lush with glossy leaves, purple plums ripening in a wooden bowl on a kitchen counter . . .

They saw no indications of violence. No sign of their friend and neighbor, either.

In the foyer once more, standing at the foot of the stairs, they briefly considered calling out to Harry.

To be heard above the fierce cataracts crashing upon the roof, however, they would have to raise their voices. Someone or something other than their neighbor might come in answer to a shout, a prospect that argued for continued silence.

Neil led the way to the second floor. Molly ascended sideways, keeping her back to the wall, so she could look both toward the top and the bottom of the stairs.

In the upper hallway, the solid-oak door to the master bedroom had been wrenched off its hinges. Cracked almost in half, it lay on the hall floor. Bright fragments of the lock were scattered across the carpet.

Each of the two substantial hinges remained anchored to the jamb by its frame leaf, although each leaf—a quarter-inch steel plate—had been bent by the fearsome force that had ripped away the door. The barrel knuckles joining the frame leaf to the center leaf of each hinge were also deformed, as was the steel pivot pin that connected them.

If Harry had taken refuge behind the locked bedroom door, the barrier hadn't stood for long.

Not even a steroid-pumped bodybuilder with Herculean slabs of muscle could have torn the door off its hinges without a winch and tackle. The task, accomplished barehanded, would have defeated any mortal man.

Expecting slaughter or an outrage so inhuman in nature that it could not be anticipated, Molly hesitated to follow Neil into the bedroom. When she crossed the threshold, however, she saw no signs of violence.

The walk-in closet stood open. No one in there.

When Neil tried the closed door between the bedroom and the adjacent bath, he found it locked.

He glanced at Molly. She nodded.

Putting his face close to the bathroom door, Neil said, "Harry? Are you in there, Harry?"

If the question had been answered, the reply had been too soft to be audible.

"Harry, it's me, Neil Sloan. You in there? Are you all right?"

When he received no answer, he stepped back from the door and kicked it hard. The lock was only a privacy set, not a deadbolt, and three kicks sprung it.

How curious that whatever had wrenched off the sturdier door to the bedroom had not torn this one away, as well.

Neil stepped to the threshold, then recoiled and turned away, the features of his face knocked out of true by a seismic jolt of visceral horror and revulsion.

He tried to prevent Molly from seeing what he had seen, but she refused to be turned away. No sight could be worse than some that she had endured on that terrible day in her eighth year.

Eyeless, his head hollowed out as completely as a jack-o'-lantern, Harry Corrigan sat on the bathroom floor, resting against the side of the bathtub. He had sucked on a short-barreled, pump-action, pistol-grip shotgun.

Sickened but not shocked, Molly turned at once away.

"He couldn't stop grieving," Neil said.

For an instant, she didn't understand what he meant. Then she realized that in spite of all he had thus far witnessed, he remained to some degree in denial.

She said, "Harry didn't kill himself because of Calista. He retreated to the bathroom and blew his brains out to avoid coming face-to-face with whoever tore down the bedroom door."

The directness of "blew his brains out" caused Neil to flinch, and his face, paper-pale since he'd seen the dead man, shaded to a penciled gray.

"And when they heard the shotgun," she continued, "they knew what he had done—and had no further interest in him."

"They," he said thoughtfully, and looked to the ceiling as if remembering the enormous descending mass that he had sensed earlier in the night. "But why not use the shotgun on . . . them?"

Suspecting that the answer might await discovery elsewhere in the house, Molly didn't reply, but instead led the way back into the hall. A further search of the second floor turned up nothing of interest until they reached the back stairs.

This single narrow flight descended to a mud room adjacent to the kitchen. Molly knew that the lower chamber led also to the backyard.

Apparently Harry Corrigan had first encountered his unwanted visitors down there. He had been armed with the shotgun and had used it more than once on these stairs. Buckshot had gouged and pocked the walls, had chopped chunks and splinters from the wooden stairs.

Backing toward the second floor, firing down on the intruders, he could not have missed any target in that tightly confined space, considering the spread pattern of a shotgun. Yet there were no dead bodies on the stairs or at the foot of it. No blood.

Standing at the top of the stairwell with Molly, sharing her reluctance to enter that narrow flight, Neil wondered, "What was he shooting at—ghosts?"

She shook her head. "It wasn't any ghost that tore the bedroom door off its hinges."

"But what could walk through shotgun fire unscathed?"

"I don't know. And maybe I don't want to find out." Molly turned away from the back stairs. "Let's get out of here."

They retraced the route they had taken from the front stairs, and as they were stepping around the fallen door in the hall outside the master bedroom, the lights flickered and went out.

II

WINDOWLESS, THE HALLWAY LACKED EVEN THE UN-
earthly glow of the luminous rain. Here ruled the absolute black of corri-
dors in death dreams, of final resting places underground.

Still learning the necessary tactics to weather doomsday, Molly had
unthinkingly left her flashlight in the Explorer.

In this blind domain rose a rustle separate from the susurrant chorus
of the rain, a rustle like the unfurling, flexing, furling of featherless, membranous wings. She insisted to herself that it must be the sound of Neil
searching his raincoat.

The sudden beam of his flashlight proved her right. She let out her
pent-up breath.

The gloom in the hallway seemed not like ordinary darkness, subject
to the laws of physics, but like Darkness Visible, the sooty essence of a
palpable evil. The light carved a swath less revealing than she would
have liked, and when the beam moved, the murk returned in eager leaps
and swoops.

They negotiated the fallen door, but had gone only a few steps farther
when a presence in the surrounding shadows recited a line by one of her
favorite poets, T. S. Eliot.

"I think we are in rats' alley—"

He spoke in a stage whisper, not in a shout, but somehow the words carried through the insistent tattoo of the rain, and Molly recognized the voice of Harry Corrigan, dead Harry, who had done to himself what a thug had done to his wife for the gain of only two hundred dollars.

Whipping, darting, arcing, the flashlight beam probed left, right, behind them. No one.

Neil passed the flashlight to Molly, freeing both of his hands for the shotgun.

Wielding light and handgun, she aimed the pistol with the beam. A half-open door to a guest bedroom on her right. The barely cracked door of a study to her left. Another door: a flare of porcelain in a bathroom beyond.

Harry or the grotesquery that had been Harry, or the thing that pretended to be Harry, might lurk in any of the three rooms. Or in none of them.

And now came the line from "The Waste Land" that in fact followed the one already spoken:

"—*Where the dead men lost their bones.*"

Molly couldn't deduce the voice's point of origin. The words twisted around her with serpentine deception, seeming to arise from first one side, then from another.

Her galloping heart stampeded, knocking so hard against her ribs that it seemed fire must have flared in her blood as surely as iron-shod hooves would have struck sparks from cobblestones.

First the palm of her right hand, then the checked grip of the pistol grew slick with sweat.

The stubborn dark, the cloying dark, the inadequate light, doors to both sides poised as tensely as the spring-loaded lids of pop-up toys, and forty feet to the head of the stairs.

Now thirty.

Twenty.

Near the stairs, a figure stepped out of a doorway or out of a wall, or through a portal between worlds; she couldn't tell which and was prepared to believe anything.

The jittering light first revealed his shoes, the cuffs of his corduroy pants.

On the floor in his splattered bathroom, Harry had slumped in flannel shirt and corduroy pants. Corduroy of precisely this tan shade.

Molly's knees weakened at the prospect of seeing again the hollow-pumpkin head, the empty sockets of the jack-o'-lantern eyes, the teeth broken jagged by the bucking barrel of the 12-gauge.

Yet what she wanted to see and what her determined hand intended to show her were different things. She raised the flashlight to his knees, belt buckle, flannel shirt, grizzled chin. . . .

Mercifully, Neil stepped past her, fired his shotgun, pumped a new round into the breach as the funhouse figure blew back, reeled back, into shadows. He said urgently, "Go, Molly, go, get out."

The concussion had rung off the hallway walls; and still the echo tolled through surrounding rooms, through rooms below, as if the house were a many-chambered bell.

The unthinkable was there in the darkness between her and the stairs, just a lunge away from her: the dripping thing, the hangman, the eternal Footman, the Stranger who comes to everyone's door sooner or later, and knocks and knocks and will not go away, now here for her in the impossible form of dead Harry, her lost friend.

She ran behind the wildly leaping light, toward the inconstant light, toward the polished mahogany newel post marking the way down, and she didn't look to her left, where the resurrected neighbor had fallen backward into shadows.

It must have risen, moved, approached, because Neil fired again. The flare from the muzzle chased a flurry of shadows, like a flock of bats, through the hallway.

Molly reached the stairs, which seemed markedly steeper in the descent than they had been in the ascent. Flashlight in one hand, pistol in the other, she was not able to clutch at the railing, but owed her balance to sheer luck. She plunged down steps as unforgiving as ice-crusted ladder rungs, headlong, stumbling, flailing her arms, and landed, staggered, on both feet in the foyer, in a billow of raincoat.

The front door stood open. As a third shotgun blast rocked the house, she fled those dry rooms for the questionable sanctuary of the radiant storm.

She hadn't pulled up her hood. Torrents of rain washed her face, her hair, and a trickle at once found its way down the nape of her neck, under her collar, along her spine, into the cleft of buttocks, as if it were the questing finger of a violator taking advantage of a moment of vulnerability.

She sloshed across the flooded turnaround, to the driver's door of the Explorer. Soft lumpish objects bumped against her boots.

The flashlight revealed dead birds—twenty, thirty, forty, more—beaks cracked in silent cries, eyes glassy, bobbing in the silvered pool, as if they had been drowned in flight and washed down from the flooded sky.

Neil rushed out of the house, toward the idling SUV. Nothing pursued him, at least not immediately.

Climbing behind the wheel of the Explorer, Molly dropped the flashlight in the console cup-holder, put the pistol between her legs, and released the hand brake.

With the Remington smelling of hot steel and expended gunpowder, Neil came aboard as Molly shifted out of park. He pulled his door shut after they had begun to roll.

Out of the feathered pool, up the driveway that appeared to be paved in the glistening black-and-silver scales of serpents, to the county road, they escaped that haunted precinct of the cataclysm and drove into another.

12

IN THIS NIAGARA, ON PAVEMENT AS SLICK AS A BOB-
sled chute, speed was worse than folly; speed equaled madness. Nevertheless, Molly drove too fast, eager to reach town.

Here and there, weak and sodden tree branches cracked loose, fell to
the roadway. Layered veils of rain obscured the way ahead, and often she
couldn't see obstacles until she was nearly upon them.

Cold terror made of her an expert driver, and a keen survival instinct
improved her judgment, honed her reaction time to a split-second edge.
She piloted the Explorer through a slalom course of storm debris, wheeling into every slide, jolting through chuckholes that made the steering
wheel stutter in her hands, powering out of a near stall when a flooded
swale in the pavement proved to be deeper than it looked.

When she saw a gnarled, clawlike evergreen limb too late to avoid it,
those broken fingers of pine tore at the undercarriage, scratched, scraped,
knocked, as though some living creature were determined to get at them
through the floorboards. The branch got hung up on the rear axle, rapping
noisily for a quarter of a mile before it finally splintered and fell away.

Chastened, Molly eased up on the accelerator. For the next quarter of
a mile, she glanced repeatedly at the fuel gauge, worried that the gas tank
might have been punctured.

The indicator needle held steady just below the FULL mark. No instrument-panel lights appeared to indicate falling oil pressure or a loss of any other vital fluid. Her luck had held.

At this slower speed, less intently focused on her driving, she could think more clearly about the grisly episode at the Corrigan place. No matter how hard she mulled it over, however, she could not understand it.

"What was *that,* damn, what happened back there?" she asked, recognizing a scared-girl note in her voice, neither surprised nor embarrassed to hear her words strung on a tremor.

"Can't get my mind around it," Neil admitted.

"Harry was dead."

"Yeah."

"Brains all over the bathroom."

"That's a memory maybe even Alzheimer's couldn't erase."

"So how could he be up on his feet again?"

"Couldn't."

"And talking."

"Couldn't."

"But he did, he was. Neil, for God's sake, I mean, what does something like that have to do with Mars?"

"Mars?"

"Or wherever they're from—the other side of the Milky Way, another galaxy, the end of the universe."

"I don't know," he said.

"This isn't like ETs in the movies."

" 'Cause this isn't the movies."

"Doesn't seem to be real life, either. The real world runs on logic."

Having fished spare shells from his raincoat pockets, Neil reloaded the shotgun. He didn't fumble the ammunition. His hands were steady.

Never in her memory had his hands been otherwise, or his mind, or his heart. Steady Neil.

"So where's the logic?" Molly asked. "I don't see it."

Half as big as pineapples, two objects dropped from overhead, bounced off the hood of the Explorer.

Molly braked before she realized they were pine cones. They resembled hand grenades as they ricocheted off the windshield and arced away into the night.

"Parasites," Neil said.

She brought the Explorer to a full stop, half on the road, half on the graveled shoulder. "Parasites?"

"They might be parasites," he said, "these things from the far end of the universe or the dark side of the moon, or wherever they're from. Parasites—that's an old theme in science fiction, isn't it?"

"Is it?"

"Intelligent parasites, capable of infecting a host body and controlling it as if it were a puppet."

"What host body?"

"Anything, any species. In this case, Harry's corpse."

"You call that logic?"

"Just speculation."

"But how does this parasite—I don't care if it's smarter than the entire membership of Mensa combined—how does it control a host that's *blown out its brains*?"

"The corpse still has a jointed skeleton, musculature, intact nerve pathways below the brainpan," he said. "Maybe the parasite plugs into all that and can manipulate the host, brain or no brain."

Her anxiety ebbed just enough to allow for a small amazement. "You sure don't sound like a guy who was schooled by Jesuits."

"Oh, but I do. They value nimbleness of thought, imagination, and open-mindedness."

"And evidently they watch old *Star Trek* episodes too much. The parasite theory doesn't qualify as logic in my book."

For a moment, Neil studied the dripping, silvered forest, which dar-kled to a black void in the distance. With evident uneasiness, he surveyed the rain-washed county road ahead and behind them.

"Let's keep moving," he said. "I think we're more vulnerable when we're sitting still like this."

13

BY VIRTUE OF ITS EXTRAORDINARY VOLUME, ITS numbing roar, and its fearsome spectacle, the ceaseless rain inspired curious psychological reactions. The monotony of the phenomenon and its oppressive force had the power to depress and disorient.

As she drove slowly across the storm-swept western ridge line above Black Lake, toward the town of the same name, Molly Sloan was able to resist depression and disorientation. But she felt that something essential in herself was gradually being washed away.

Not hope. She would never lose hope; like calcium, hope was part of the structure of her bones.

The certainty of purpose that characterized her approach to life seemed, however, to be less firm than usual, turning soggy under the influence of this deluge, so quickly washed thin and bleached of its former intensity.

She didn't know where she was going, other than to town, or why, other than to seek sanctuary with neighbors. She had always planned her life not a month ahead, not even just a year ahead, but a decade or more in advance, setting goals and striving ever toward them. Now she was unable to see as far as the coming dawn, and without a clear purpose, without a long-term plan, she felt adrift.

She wanted to survive, of course. But survival had never before been enough for her, and it wasn't enough now. To be motivated, she needed a more profound purpose and greater meaning.

Pages crystallizing into chapters, chapters accreting into books: The story-painting, spell-casting, truth-telling work of a novelist had seemed to be a lifelong purpose. Her mother had taught her that talent is a gift from God, that a writer has a sacred obligation to her Creator to explore the gift with energy and diligence, to polish it, to use it to brighten the landscape of her readers' hearts.

In her haste to pack food, weapons, and other essentials for whatever perilous journey might be ahead of them, Molly had forgotten to bring her laptop. She had always written on a computer; she didn't know if her talent would flow as easily, or at all, from the point of a pen.

Besides, she had brought no pen, no pencil. She hadn't included any paper in her provisions, either, only the pages of her current, unfinished manuscript.

Perhaps purpose and meaning and ambitious plans would elude her until she better understood the current situation and, based on more hard facts than she now possessed, could begin to imagine what future might await them.

If understanding was to be achieved, questions needed to be answered.

Although driving at only ten miles per hour through the dismal downpour, she didn't look away from the road when she said to Neil, "Why T. S. Eliot?"

"What do you mean?"

"What Harry . . . the thing that used to be Harry . . . what it said to me. 'I think we are in rats' alley, Where the dead men lost their bones.' "

"Eliot is one of your favorites, right? Probably Harry would know that."

"Harry's body was there in the hall when he spoke to me, but his brains were in the bathroom, all the memories blown out of them."

Literally riding shotgun and wary of the night, Neil offered neither an explanation nor even a supposition.

Molly pressed: "How would your alien parasite have tapped the contents of Harry's mind if Harry didn't *have* a mind anymore?"

Scattered across the roadway were more fallen birds. Although they were clearly dead, she tried her best to drive around rather than over them.

Grimly, she wondered how soon she would encounter human cadavers heaped in similar numbers.

"Some sci-fi writer," Neil said at last, "I think it was Arthur C. Clarke, suggested that an extraterrestrial species, hundreds or thousands of years more advanced than us, would possess technology that would appear to us to be not the result of applied science but entirely supernatural, pure magic."

"In this case, black magic," she said. "Evil. What practical purpose could they have for turning a dead man into a marionette—except to terrorize?"

Ahead in the luminous storm, a separate light arose, and grew brighter as they approached it.

Molly slowed further, allowed the SUV to coast forward.

Out of the torrents loomed a blue Infiniti, standing in their lane, facing the same direction that they were traveling, but dead still. The lights of the car blazed. Three of its four doors hung open wide.

Molly rolled to a stop ten feet behind the vehicle. The engine was running: Pale exhaust vapor issued continuously from the car's tailpipe, but the skeins of rain washed the plume away before it could attain much length.

From this angle, Molly could see no driver, no passengers.

"Keep moving," Neil encouraged.

She swung the Explorer into the northbound lane and slowly drove around the Infiniti.

No one, either dead or alive, was slumped inside below the level of the windows.

The car had not failed its occupants, yet they had abandoned it and had chosen to continue on foot. Or had fled in panic. Or had been taken.

On the pavement in front of the Infiniti, illuminated by its headlights, lay three objects. A baseball bat. A butcher knife. A long-handled ax.

"Maybe they didn't have guns," Neil said, expressing Molly's very thoughts, "and had to arm themselves with whatever they could find."

During the confrontation that occurred here, the occupants of the Infiniti must have discovered that their weapons were useless and must have discarded them. Or perhaps they had been forcibly disarmed by something that was unimpressed by clubs and blades.

"Maybe we'll meet up with them somewhere on the road ahead," Neil suggested.

Molly didn't think that would happen. Those people were gone forever: to where, unknown; to what hideous end, unguessable.

14

AS THE ABANDONED INFINITI'S HEADLIGHTS FADED into the rain behind them, Neil switched on the radio, perhaps to forestall further disturbing speculation about the missing occupants of that car. The fate of those travelers might be the fate of all who ventured into the storm, in which case no credible argument could be advanced for continuing to town.

Across the FM and AM bands, quarrels of static and electronic screeching alternated with silences where voices and music had once crowded the airwaves. At a small number of frequencies, words coalesced out of the cacophony, a few sentences at a time.

In two instances, reporters or government spokesmen seemed to be reading official advisories. These lacked concrete facts and for the most part consisted of empty assurances.

Some guy on a station in Denver spoke directly to his wife and son, expressing his love in simple but piercing words. Obviously, he did not expect to see either of them again.

Out of some far place, through the turbulent ether of this momentous night, came music: the classic sad song "I'll Be Seeing You."

In ordinary times, those exquisitely melancholy lyrics, that melody so full of yearning, could pierce Molly's heart. In these extraordinary circumstances, this song about lost love became a surprisingly poignant metaphor for the greater loss of an entire society, a civilization, for the sudden end of peace and hope and promise.

Throughout her lifetime, the world had been shrinking, made ever smaller by television, by satellite communications, by the Internet. Now, in mere hours, all those bonds had been cut, and the compressed world had expanded to the size that it had been more than a century ago.

The man speaking to his wife and son in Denver had sounded as if he were broadcasting from another continent. And now this song, written just prior to World War II and resonant with the uncertainties of that troubled age, brought with it through the night a quality of distance, as if it had been broadcast not merely from faraway Europe but from the Europe of another era, traveling across both half a world and more than half a century.

Tears blurred Molly's vision.

Her sense of loss, sharpened by every note of the song, grew painful, a knife of emotion twisting in her breast. Yet she remained loath to ask Neil to switch off the radio and thereby deprive them of this tenuous connection to a civilization that seemed to be dissolving rapidly around them in the caustic waters of the preternatural storm.

Either aware of her reaction to the song or sharing it, Neil pushed the SCAN button, searching for another station.

After squawk, squall, and too many frequencies marked by ominous silence, the radio pulled in a clear voice. A disc jockey, a talk-show host, a newsman: Whoever he was, whatever he was, he sounded angry and scared.

He was obsessing about audio transmissions from the crew of the International Space Station high in orbit above Earth, messages that had been sent early in the night, simultaneously with the appearance of the gigantic waterspouts on the planet's oceans. "I've played this ten times before, and I'll play it ten times more, a hundred times, hell, I'll play it until we lose power and can't broadcast anymore, until something breaks down the door and just kills us all. Listen to this, America, listen close and hard to this, and *know your enemy.* This is not global warming, sunspots, cosmic radiation, this is not some inexplicable spasm in the planet's climate. This is *the war of the worlds.*"

Either the transmissions had been received in broken segments or they had been edited for this news broadcast. They began with surprise, excitement, even wonder. Soon the tone changed.

First, a crew member speaking English with a Russian accent reported that following a failure of exterior cameras, their computer recorded the successful docking of an unknown craft with the space station. This came as a surprise, because radar had not detected an approaching mass of any kind, neither orbiting space junk nor a UFO exhibiting controlled flight.

The communications officer, Wong, had been unable to raise a response from the visitors. "Are we really sure something's docked with us?"

"Positive," said the Russian.

"Not a computer malfunction, a false docking report?"

"*Nyet.* I *felt* it, so did you, we all did."

Another crew member, straight out of Texas, declared that from a porthole with a partial view of the docking module, he was unable to make a direct visual confirmation of the visiting spacecraft. "Momma taught me not to be profane but, Christ, from here I oughta be able to see a piece of that puppy, shouldn't I?"

The Russian again: "Heads-up, everyone! Computer shows outer air-lock hatch cycling open."

Another American, this one with a Boston accent, said, "Who the hell gave the go signal for that?"

"No one," the Russian said. "They now control our systems."

"They who?"

The Texan said, "Maybe Jamaica has a space program nobody knew about," but he didn't get a laugh.

Molly had let the Explorer's speed fall below five miles an hour because the drama high above the earth distracted her so much that she could not concentrate adequately on the rain-curtained roadway.

Evidently having returned from the porthole that provided a partial view of the docking module, perhaps studying various interior cameras on a bank of monitors, the Texan said, "Lapeer, is that you I see inboard of the airlock?"

"Yes, it's me, Willy," replied a woman with a French or perhaps Belgian accent. "I'm here in reception with Arturo. Instruments show positive pressure in the airlock. In fact, it's almost up to full atmosphere."

The Russian again: "Better get out from there, Emily. You, too, Arturo. Retreat, get secured bulkheads between them and you, until we understand situation."

Excited, Emily Lapeer laughed, if nervously. "It's a new dawn, Ivan. Not a time for old fears."

Another voice, female, perhaps German, said urgently, "Lose the idealism, Emily. Think. Boarding protocols ought to be universal. This is too aggressive. It feels hostile."

"That's a xenophobic interpretation," Lapeer protested.

The German disagreed: "That's common sense."

The Texan said, "I agree, Lapeer. Pull back, seal hatches as you go. Haul ass out of there."

Lapeer said, "This is history."

The Russian had more bad news: "Airlock cameras gone blind. If visitors boarding, can't see what they look like."

"We can hear noises in the airlock," Lapeer reported.

The Texan said, "Sonofabitch, Lapeer, the cameras inboard of the airlock just died, too. This sucks like a sump pump. We can't see *you* anymore, either."

Startled if not alarmed, Lapeer spoke in rapid French, then reverted to English: "Something impossible is happening here—"

Maybe it was Arturo who said, "What the shit—?"

Lapeer said, "—not opening the inner airlock hatch, but just, just phasing *through* it—"

"Say *what?*"

"—materializing *right out of the steel*—"

The Russian said, "Computer shows that hatch closed."

Sudden overwhelming terror reduced Emily Lapeer to the urgent, tremulous petitions of a frightened child: *"Sainte Marie, mère de Dieu, non, non, bénie Marie, non, sauvez-moi!"*

Down there in the reception chamber of the space station, inboard of the airlock, Arturo began to scream in wordless horror—then in agony.

"Mère de Dieu, sauvez-moi! Bénie Marie, non, non, NON—"

Abruptly, Emily Lapeer's desperate prayer gave way to screams that matched the intensity of Arturo's.

Although she and Neil might be safer if they kept moving, Molly could not drive. Her ability to focus was stolen from her not by fear but by empathy, by pity. She braked to a stop and sat shaking.

Neil at once reached out to her. Grateful that she was not alone, grateful beyond expression, Molly seized his hand and held it tightly.

High above Earth, from various chambers of the space station, the crew shouted to one another over the open intercom system. At times they spoke English, and at times they reverted to their native tongues, but no matter what language they spoke, their questions and pleas were the same:

What's happening? where are you? can you hear me? are you there? what are they? what're they doing? why, where, how? keep them out! brace the door! no! help me! somebody! help me, God, help me! God! please, God, NO!

Then only screaming.

Maybe because the screams were twice removed—transmitted from orbit, recorded on tape or disc, replayed by the radio station—Molly was aware of subtle nuances of terror and agony and dread that she would not have heard if she had been present at the slaughter itself. The cries were first shrill and piercing, sharp with disbelief and denial, then grew more hoarse and terrible, before finally becoming wet, raw, the essence of misery. These were the tortured shrieks and sobs of men and women being slowly torn limb from limb, eviscerated by a patient evil that wanted time to savor its work.

After the invaders had progressed chamber by chamber from one end of the space station to the other, after every luckless member of the crew had been reduced to the wretched squeals of animals in the dung-splattered vestibule of a slaughterhouse, the victims fell silent, one by one, until the voice of a single astronaut cried down from that highest throne of human technology. His cry came through vacuum and strato-sphere, through the last good day on one side of the planet and through the beginning of the longest night, through the gathering storm that, at the time of his suffering, had not yet begun to drown the earth, and his wail of agony came as a warning to the world, a clarion bell and bell ves-per that tolled the final hour.

His lonely voice rang out one last time.

Silence followed, reverberant with the memory of terror.

Listening, Molly had been able to breathe only in quick shallow shud-ders, and now she held her breath entirely, head cocked, ear bent closer to the radio.

Out of the dead space station came a new voice—deep, silken, strange—with all the riveting power of a Presence summoned by forbid-den incantations to a candle-encircled pentagram drawn with lamb's blood. It spoke in a language that perhaps had never before been heard on Earth.

"Yimaman see noygel, see refacull, see nod a bah, see naytoss, retee fo sellos."

In addition to a love of words and a passion for poetry, Molly pos-sessed the ability to memorize verse with ease, as a piano prodigy can hear a song just once and thereafter play it note for note. Those alien words had a rhythm reminiscent of poetry, and when the inhuman voice on the radio repeated what it had said, she murmured along with it:

"Yimaman see noygel, see refacull, see nod a bah, see naytoss, retee fo sellos."

Although she knew nothing of their meaning, she sensed arrogance in those words: arrogance sharp with a sense of triumph, bitterness, blackest hatred, and rage beyond the capacity of the darkest of human hearts, rage beyond all understanding.

"Yimaman see noygel . . . see refacull . . . see nod a bah . . . see naytoss . . . retee fo sellos," Molly said once more, though this time she spoke alone.

On the radio, dead air gave way to the voice of the agitated newsman: *"War of the worlds,* America. Fight back, fight hard. If you have guns, use 'em. If you don't have guns, get 'em. If anyone out there in the government can hear me, for God's sake break out the nukes. There can be no surrender—"

Neil switched off the radio.

Rain. Rain. Rain.

Dead astronauts above and the tempest below.

Four miles to town—if the town still existed.

If not the town, then how far to fellowship, how far to people gathered in mutual defense?

"God have mercy on us," Neil said, for he had been schooled by Jesuits.

Letting off the brake, driving once more, Molly refrained from praying for mercy because her faith had been sullied by primitive superstition: She feared that perverse fate would deny her what she asked for, and give her only what she did not request.

Yet, as was her nature, she still had hope. Her heart clenched like a fist around a nugget of hope; and if not as much as a nugget, then at least a pebble; and if not a pebble, a grain. But around a single grain of sand, an oyster builds a pearl.

Rain. Rain. Rain.

15

THE SECOND ABANDONED VEHICLE, A LINCOLN NAVI-
gator, stood in the northbound lane, facing the Explorer as it traveled
southbound. The engine was idling, as had been the case with the Infiniti, and none of the tires was flat, suggesting that the SUV had in no
way failed its driver.

The headlights were doused, but the emergency flashers flung off
rhythmic flares, with stroboscopic effect, so that the million tongues of
rain appeared to stutter, stutter in their fall.

On the Infiniti, three of four doors had stood open, but in this case
only one. The rear door on the driver's side admitted rain and offered a
view of the backseat illuminated by the Lincoln's interior lights.

"Neil, my God."

Molly braked, stopped, as Neil said, "What?"

The smeared glass in her door, the blurring rain, and the metronomic
dazzle of the flashers all combined to deceive the eye, yet Molly knew
what she saw, and knew what she must do.

"There's a child," she said, shifting the Explorer into park. "A baby."

"Where?"

"On the backseat of that Navigator," she said, and threw open her
door.

"Molly, wait!"

If the rain was toxic, she had been poisoned beyond the hope of anti-dote when they had fled Harry Corrigan's house. Another dose could do no worse injury than the damage she had already sustained.

As if the rain were warmer than it was, the beaten blacktop sweated oil and made slick the path beneath her feet.

Molly slipped, slid, almost went down. Regaining her balance, she was gripped by the conviction that something watched her, some crea-ture in hiding, and that if she had fallen, the nameless thing would have slithered out of the wet gloom, would have seized her in cruel jaws, and in an instant would have carried her off the pavement, over the crest of the ridge, into trees and weeds and brambles, down into the thorny belly of the night.

Reaching the open door of the Navigator, she discovered that the abandoned child—not an infant but a barefoot little girl in pink pedal pushers and a yellow T-shirt—was a large doll, only a couple of inches shorter than two feet. Its chubby jointed arms were extended as if in sup-plication or in hope of an embrace.

Molly looked into the front seat, then into the cargo space at the back of the SUV. No one.

The child to whom the doll belonged had gone wherever her parents had gone. To shelter, perhaps.

And what is the most enduring place of shelter if not death?

Rebelling against that thought, Molly pressed through the rain to the back of the Navigator.

Neil called worriedly to her. She turned and saw that he had got-ten out of the Explorer and stood, shotgun in both hands, giving her cover.

Although she couldn't quite hear his words, she knew that he wanted her to get behind the wheel once more and drive them into town.

Shaking her head, she went around behind the Navigator and then to the passenger's side. She wanted to be sure that the child, the owner of the doll, had not crouched behind the vehicle, hiding from whatever menace might come along the highway, from whatever evil might have taken her parents.

No child huddled there. Nor under the SUV, either, when Molly dropped to her knees and searched that low space.

The shoulder of the road was narrow. Spalled-off asphalt and gravel and the sparkling shards of tossed-away bottles and the bright aluminum ring-pulls from uncounted beverage cans dimly reflected the luminous rain, a meaningless mosaic in an unstable bed of mud.

When Molly rose to her feet again, she thought that the woods, already crowding the highway before she dropped to her hands and knees, had grown closer while her back was turned. The saturated boughs of the looming evergreens hung like sodden vestments—capes and robes, cassocks and chasubles.

Unseen but acutely felt, alert observers watched her from the hooded cowls of those pines, creatures less ordinary than owls and raccoons, and less clean.

Frightened but sensing that a show of fear would invite attack, she did not at once retreat. Instead, she rubbed her muddied hands together, rinsing them in the downpour, though she would not feel clean again until she could wash off the rain itself.

Counseling herself that the hostile presences she sensed in the forest were only figments of her imagination, but knowing that her counsel was a lie, she continued unhurriedly around the Navigator, returning to the driver's side with a nonchalance that was pure performance.

Before retreating to the Explorer, she snatched the doll from the backseat of the Lincoln. Its shaggy blond hair, blue eyes, and sweet smile reminded her of a child who had died in her arms a long time ago.

Rebecca Rose, her name had been. She was a shy girl who spoke with the faintest lisp.

Her last words, whispered in delirium and making no apparent sense, had been, *"Molly . . . there's a dog. So pretty . . . how he shines."* For the first time in her life, there at the end of it, she had not lisped at all.

Having failed to save Rebecca, Molly saved this rough image of her, and when Neil got in the Explorer after her, she gave him the doll for safe-keeping.

She said, "We might encounter the girl and her parents on the road into town."

Neil did not remind her that the Navigator had been traveling in the opposite direction when abandoned. He knew that she recognized this as clearly as he did.

She said, "It'll be nice to have the doll to give her. I'm sure she didn't intend to leave it behind."

Intellectually, she knew that the war of the worlds, if indeed it had begun, would not spare children.

Emotionally, however, she refused to acknowledge that no degree of innocence could guarantee immunity in a plague of genocide.

On one rainy afternoon long ago, Molly had saved some children and been unable to save others. But if the fine grain of hope in her heart were to be the foundation of a pearl, she must believe that no child would ever again suffer in her presence and that those who came under her care would be safe, protected, until she herself died defending them.

As the Explorer rolled forward and they resumed their journey into town, Neil said, "It's a beautiful doll. She'll be happy to see it again."

Molly loved him for always understanding precisely what words she needed to hear. He knew what motivated her at all times and in all cir-cumstances, even in these.

16

THEY HAD NOT DRIVEN FAR FROM THE ABANDONED
Navigator when Molly realized belatedly that the rain had been imbued
with less scent than at any time since she'd stepped onto the porch
among the coyotes. The underlying semenlike odor had faded altogether,
and the mélange of other fragrances had been only a fraction as intense
as they were at the Corrigan house.

Neil confirmed her observation. "Yeah. And it's also not quite as radiant."

The goblin night still appeared to stream with Christmas tinsel; however, the rain was a few lumens dimmer than it had been earlier, though
it fell in undiminished volume.

Perhaps these changing conditions should have given Molly heart. Instead they troubled her. Evidently the first phase of this strange war was
drawing to an end. The second would soon begin.

"I half remember," Neil said, "your Mr. Eliot wrote something famous
about doomsday."

"Yeah. He said we've become hollow men, stuffed men, heads filled
with straw, no convictions or higher purpose . . . and for hollow men, the
world will end not with a bang but a whimper."

Leaning forward in his seat, squinting up toward the drowned sky,
Neil said, "I don't know about you, but I'm expecting the bang."

"Me too."

Just a minute later, how the world would end, with what noise and degree of violence, suddenly concerned Molly less than she would have imagined possible. The sight of a hiker, walking at a brisk pace in the northbound lane, turned her thoughts away from planetary catastrophe to the more intimate cataclysm that had changed her life at the age of eight and had shaped it every day thereafter.

You couldn't accurately call him a mere pedestrian. There were no sidewalks along the county road, no encouragement whatsoever for any- one to travel the ridge line on foot. Besides, he walked with a determined stride, with the purpose of an enthusiast.

Molly first thought he must be one of those who calculated that if he walked often enough and far enough, and never dared to eat a spoon of ice cream, he would live forever—barring, of course, the threats that self- denial could not affect, such as runaway trucks, crashing airplanes, and alien invasions.

In utter disregard of the weather, he wore no rain gear. His pale-gray slacks and matching shirt, suggestive of a uniform, were soaked.

He must have been miserable, but he soldiered on, his pace hardly if at all affected by sodden clothes and other discomforts. Indeed, because poor visibility and caution and a fear of what she might find in town caused Molly to hold the Explorer to little more than coasting speed, the hiker seemed to be walking north almost as fast as the Explorer cruised south.

His thick dark hair was plastered to his skull. He kept his head down, the better to net each wet breath from the vertical ocean.

As the Explorer closed on him, the hiker looked up, across the two- lane blacktop.

Even through the blur of the storm, his features were bold and clean. He would have seemed movie-star handsome to Molly if she hadn't known that the mind behind that charming face was monstrous, corrupt, and cunning.

The hiker was Michael Render. Her father. The murderer.

She hadn't seen him face-to-face in almost twenty years.

At once she looked away from him, less because she worried that he would know her than because, even at this distance, she feared the power of his eyes, the magnetism of his gaze, the vortex of his personality.

"What the hell?" Neil said, shocked, turning around in his seat to look out the tailgate window as Molly accelerated. "He's supposed to be locked up."

Her husband's instant confirmation of the man's identity prevented Molly from taking refuge in the hope that her imagination had run away with her and that the hiker was in fact a stranger with only a vague resemblance to Render.

Usually, she thought of him not as her father but only by his surname, which as a girl she had dropped in favor of her mother's maiden name. When occasionally he appeared in her dreams, he had no name, but the skull was visible beneath his skin, and his hands were scythes, and in his broad grin, his teeth were broken tombstones.

She worried, "Did he . . ."

"What? Recognize you?"

"You think he did?"

"I don't know."

"We recognized him."

"Because of the headlights. Harder for him to see you."

"Has he changed directions, is he coming behind us now?"

"He's just standing there, I think. I can't really tell. He's almost out of sight."

"Shit."

"It's all right."

"The hell it is," she said sharply. "You know where he was going."

"Maybe."

"What else would he be doing out here?" she asked. "He was going to our place. He was coming for me."

"He doesn't know where you live."

"Somehow he found out."

She shuddered when she realized what would have happened if they had chosen to ride out this storm at the house, mistaking home for security.

"I can't see him anymore," Neil said. "I think . . . he continued north, the way he was going."

In the rearview mirror, Molly saw only falling rain and clouds of backspray from the tires.

With a successful plea of insanity skillfully supported by a clever attorney, Render had avoided prison. He had spent the last twenty years in a series of mental institutions. The first had been a maximum-security facility, but with each transfer, he had moved to a less restrictive environment, and been allowed more amenities.

Therapy and medications had helped him take slow steady steps out of his mental darkness. So the psychiatrists said, though their reports were written in circumlocutions and obfuscatory jargon meant to conceal that their conclusions were mere opinions unsupported by facts.

They claimed that he'd come to regret his actions, which by their way of thinking merited more relaxed living conditions and more frequent therapy sessions. If eventually he progressed from regret to remorse, he might then be viewed as rehabilitated and, under certain circumstances, might even be judged to have been cured.

The previous summer, his case had come up for mandatory review. The evaluating psychiatrists differed in their analyses of Render's condition. One recommended that he be released under supervision, but two opposed that recommendation, and he was remanded to the care of mental-health authorities for an additional two years.

"What've the idiots done?" Molly wondered, and in her agitation, she accelerated too much.

She half believed that the rearview mirror would sooner rather than later reveal Render in the backspray, running after her with inhuman balance and agility, with superhuman speed.

"If they've let him loose," she said, "the crazy bastards are as sick as he is."

"We don't know what's happening beyond these mountains, out in the wider world," Neil reminded her, "except that everything seems to be falling apart, breaking down. Not every last crewman on every sinking ship stays at his post."

"Every man for himself," Molly said. "We've come to that now—if we haven't always been there."

The pavement was greasy with oil, water. She felt the tires skating, but could not find the courage to slow down. Then gnawing tread bit blacktop, found purchase, and the four-wheel drive staved off a slide.

Neil said, "This latest institution he was transferred to . . . It's not exactly a stone-cell, steel-door, straitjacket sort of place."

A short bitter laugh escaped her. "Television in every room. Porn on demand, for its therapeutic value. High tea every afternoon, croquet on the south lawn. Maid service for those who promise, under penalty of the most severe disapproval, not to rape and kill the maids."

She was in a dark humor that was new to her and, she sensed, dangerous to indulge.

"If the staff skipped," Neil said, "and surely they *did* skip, the inmates wouldn't let ordinary locked doors and wire-glass windows hold them in for long."

" 'We don't call them inmates,' " Molly said, quoting one of the psychiatrists. " 'We call them patients.' "

"But the most recent place they were keeping him—it's far up north."

"Two hundred fifty miles from here," she confirmed.

"The storm, this nightmare—it didn't begin so long ago."

Indeed, when Molly considered the swiftness with which the usual order seemed to have given way to chaos, a jittering terror crawled the

darker hallways of her mind. Could human civilization crumble signifi-
cantly, worldwide, in a matter of hours, in but a quarter of a day, as suddenly as the planet itself might convulse if struck by an asteroid the size
of Texas? If their as yet unseen adversary, come down from the stars,
could topple centuries-old kingdoms and overturn all of history so
swiftly, without meaningful resistance, then surely it was easy to foresee—and impossible to prevent—the eradication of every human life, in
every low habitation and high redoubt on Earth, in just twenty-four
hours.

If the technology of a greatly advanced extraterrestrial race would
seem like purest magic to any civilization a thousand years its inferior,
then the masters of that technology would be as gods—but perhaps gods
with enigmatic desires and strange needs, gods without compassion,
without mercy, offering no redemption, no viaticum, and utterly unre-
sponsive to prayer.

Neil said, of Render, "He couldn't have broken out and gotten here so
quickly. Not even with a fast car and your address, not in these driving
conditions, with plenty of roads washed out or flooded between here and
there."

"But there he was, and walking," Molly said.

"Yes, there he was."

"Maybe there's nothing impossible tonight. We're down the hole to
Wonderland, and no White Rabbit to guide us."

"If I remember correctly, the White Rabbit was an unreliable guide,
anyway."

In a few miles, they came to the turnoff to Black Lake, both the body
of water and the town. Molly turned right, leaving the ridge, and followed
the descending road, into the steadily darkening rain, its luminosity
nearly spent, between massive trees that rose in black ramparts, toward
the hope of fellowship and the disquieting expectation of new terrors.

PART THREE

"Through the dark cold and the empty desolation ..."

T.S. Eliot, *East Coker*

17

MOLLY EXPECTED THAT THE POWER GRID WOULD have failed by now and that the town would stand in darkness. Instead, the glimmer of shop lights and streetlamps was amplified by the refracting rain, so Black Lake looked as if it were the site of a festival.

With a year-round population of fewer than two thousand, the town was much smaller than Arrowhead and Big Bear, the two most popular destinations in these mountains. Lacking ski slopes, Black Lake didn't enjoy a winter boom, but in summer, campers and boaters outnumbered locals two to one.

The lake was fed by an artesian well, by a few small streams, and now by the deluge. Instead of mixing with the existing lake and being diluted by it, the accumulating rain seemed to float atop the original body of water, as oil would, its luminosity compounded by its volume, shining as if the moon had fallen here.

With inflow substantially exceeding the floodgate outflow, the lake already had risen beyond its banks. The marina was under water, the boats tethered to cleats on submerged docks, the belaying ropes stretched taut.

Silver fingers of water explored with blind patience among the shoreline buildings, learning the lay of the unfamiliar land, probing for weaknesses. If the rain continued unabated, within hours the houses and the businesses on the lowest street would disappear under the rising tide.

Molly had no doubt that during the coming day, the people of Black Lake would face worse threats than flooding.

With most houses brightened by lamplight in every window, the citizens were clearly alert to the dangers at their doorstep and to the momentous events in the world beyond these mountains. They knew that darkness was coming, in every sense of the word, and they wanted to press it back as long as possible.

Black Lake's residents were different from the former flatlanders and the vacation-home crowd drawn to the more glamorous mountain communities. These folks were at least third- or fourth-generation highlanders, in love with altitude and forests, with the comparative peacefulness of the San Bernardinos high above the overpopulated hills and plains to the west.

They were tougher than most city people, more self-sufficient. They were more likely to own a collection of firearms than was the average family in a suburban neighborhood.

The town wasn't big enough to have a police force of its own. Because of inadequate manpower spread over too much territory, the county sheriff's response time to a call from Black Lake averaged thirty-two minutes.

If some hopped-up loser, desperate for drug money or violent sex, broke into your house, you could be killed five times over in thirty-two minutes. Consequently, most of these people were prepared to defend themselves—and with enthusiasm.

Molly and Neil saw no faces at any windows, but they knew that they were being monitored.

Although they had friends throughout Black Lake, neither of them was keen to go door-knocking, partly because of all those guns and their anxious owners. They were also wary of walking into a situation as bizarre as that at the Corrigan place.

In the unrelenting downpour, the cozy houses with their lamplit windows appeared welcoming. To the hapless insect, of course, the Venus'sflytrap offers a pretty sight and an alluring scent, while the two-lobed leaves wait, jaws cocked and teeth poised.

"Some will have kept to their own homes," Neil said, "but not all. The more strategically minded have gathered somewhere, pooling ideas, planning a mutual defense."

Molly didn't inquire how even the most rugged individualists among these mountain rustics—or an army, for that matter—might be able to defend themselves against technology that could use weather as a weapon on a planetary scale. As long as the question remained unasked, she could pretend there might be an answer.

Black Lake had no grand public buildings that could serve as a nerve center in a crisis like this. Three elected councilmen, who shared the title of mayor on a rotating basis, held their meetings in a booth at Benson's Good Eats, one of only two restaurants in town.

No schoolhouse, either. Those kids who weren't home-schooled were bused to out-of-town schools.

Black Lake had two churches, one Catholic and one evangelical Baptist. When Molly cruised by them, both appeared deserted.

At last they found the master strategists on Main Street, in the small commercial district, safely above the steadily rising lake. They had gathered in the Tail of the Wolf Tavern.

A dozen vehicles were parked in front of the place, not along the curb, where the gutters overflowed, but almost in the middle of the street. They faced out from the building, forming an arc, as if they were getaway cars ready to make a fast break.

Under an overhanging roof, protected from the rain, two men stood watch outside the tavern. Molly and Neil knew them.

Ken Halleck worked at the post office that served Black Lake and a few smaller mountain towns. He was known for his smile, which could crease his rubbery face from muttonchop to muttonchop, but he was not smiling now.

"Molly, Neil," he said solemnly. "Always thought it would be the nut-case Islams who did us in, didn't you?"

"We aren't done yet," said Bobby Halleck, Ken's son, raising his voice higher than necessary to compete with the rain. "We got the Marines, Army Rangers, Delta Force, we got the Navy Seals."

Bobby was seventeen, a high-school senior and star quarterback, a good kid with a gee-whiz spunkiness like that of a character from a 1930s or '40s football movie with Jack Oakie and Pat O'Brien. He seemed not too young to be standing guard but certainly unseasoned, which was probably why his father, armed with a rifle, had given Bobby a pitchfork, which seemed an inadequate deterrent to alien storm troopers although less likely to be accidentally discharged.

Bobby said, "TV's gone kerflunk, so we aren't hearing about them, but you can bet the U.S. military is kicking ass."

Ken watched his son with affection that it was his nature to express openly and often, but now also with a grief that he would never dare put into words for fear that sadness would soon thicken into unrelieved de-spair, robbing their last hours or days together of what small joys they might otherwise share.

"The President's holed-up inside some mountain somewhere," Bobby said. "And we got secret nukes in orbit, I'll bet, so the bastards won't be as safe high up in their ships as they think they are. You agree, Mr. Sloan?"

"I'd never bet against the Marines," Neil told the son, and put a hand consolingly on the father's shoulder.

"What's happening here?" Molly asked Ken, indicating the tavern.

"The idea is mutual defense," he said. "The reality . . . I don't know. People have different ideas."

"About whether they want to live or die?"

"I guess they don't all see the situation that starkly." Of her disbelief, he said, "Molly, you know, folks in this town are still who've always lived here . . . except, as people, they aren't always the same as they used to be. Sometimes I think we'd be better off if the TV had gone kerflunk fifty years ago and never come back on."

The cold gray stone exterior of the tavern promised less warmth than the interior in fact delivered: worn mahogany floors, polished mahogany walls and ceiling, photographs of the town's early residents in that time, a century previous, when the streets were shared by automobiles and horses.

The air was redolent of stale beer spilled through the years, of fresh beer recently drawn from taps, of onions and peppers and the limy corn-tortilla fragrance of nachos, of damp wool and cotton clothing slowly steamed dry by body heat—and of a faint sour scent that she imagined might be the odor of communal anxiety.

Molly was dismayed to find only about sixty people, perhaps twenty of whom she knew. The bar held twice that many on an average Saturday night; it could have accommodated four times that number in this emergency.

Only six children were present, which worried her. She expected that families with kids would have been among the first to organize a community defense.

She had brought the doll with her, hoping that the girl who'd left it in the abandoned Navigator might be among those sheltering here. None of the children reacted to the sight of the doll, so Molly put it on the bar.

There was always a chance that the doll's owner would still arrive here, out of the storm. Always hope.

All six children were gathered at a large corner booth, but the adults had settled in four distinct groups. Molly sensed at once that they were divided by four different ideas about how best to respond to the crisis.

She and Neil were greeted by those they knew and studied by those they didn't know with a calculation that was almost wariness, as if they were viewed, first, not as allies by the simple virtue of being neighbors, but instead as outsiders to be greeted with greater warmth only when their opinions and loyalties were known.

More than anything else, the dogs surprised her and Neil. She'd once been to France, where she had seen dogs in both drab working-class bars and the finest restaurants. In this country, however, health codes confined them to open patios, and most restaurateurs did not even tolerate them in an al fresco setting.

She saw four, six, eight dogs at first count, in every corner of the room. There were mutts and purebreds, mid-size and larger specimens, but no lap dogs. More canines than children.

Almost as one, the dogs rose to their feet and turned their heads toward her and Neil: some comic faces, some noble, all solemn and alert. Then, after a hesitation, they did a peculiar thing.

18

FROM ALL OVER THE TAVERN, BY DIFFERENT ROUTES, the dogs came to Molly. They didn't approach in the exuberant romp that expresses a desire to play or with the tail-tucked caution and the wary demeanor that is a response to an unfamiliar and vaguely troubling scent.

Their ears were pricked. Their tails brushed the air with slow tentative strokes. They were clearly drawn to her by curiosity, as if she were something entirely new in their experience—new but not threatening.

Her first count had been one short. Nine dogs were present, not eight, and each was intrigued by her. They circled, crowding against her, busily sniffing her boots, her jeans, her raincoat.

For a moment she thought they smelled the coyotes on her. Then she realized that when she had ventured onto the porch among those beasts, she had been in pajamas and robe, not in any of the clothes she currently wore.

Besides, most domesticated dogs had no sense of kinship with their wild cousins. They usually reacted to the scent of a coyote—and certainly to the cry of one in the night—with raised hackles and a growl.

When she reached down to them, they nuzzled her hands, licked her fingers, welcoming her with an affection that most dogs usually reserved for those people with whom they had enjoyed a much longer acquaintance.

From behind the bar, the owner of the tavern, Russell Tewkes, said, "What've you got in your pockets, Molly—frankfurters?"

The tone of his voice didn't match the jokey nature of the question. He spoke with a heavy note of insinuation that she didn't understand.

With the build of a beer barrel, the haircut and the merry face of a besotted monk, Russell was the image of a friendly neighborhood barkeep. For the woebegone, he had a sympathetic ear to rival that of any child's mother. Indefatigably good-natured, at times he came dangerously close to being jolly.

Now a squint of suspicion narrowed his eyes. His mouth set in a grim line. He regarded Molly as he might have reacted to a hulking Hell's Angel who had the word *hate* tattooed on both fists.

As the dogs continued to circle and sniff her, Molly realized that Russell was not alone in his distrust. Others in the bar, even people she knew well, who had a moment ago greeted her by name or with a wave, watched her not with the previous political calculation, but with unconcealed suspicion.

Suddenly she understood their change of attitude. They were as familiar with those alien-invasion movies as she and Neil were, and the creepshow currently playing in the theaters of their minds was one of those they-walk-among-us-passing-for-human tales, perhaps *Invasion of the Body Snatchers* or John Carpenter's *The Thing*.

The singular behavior of the dogs suggested that something about Molly must be different. Even though the nine members of this furry entourage wagged their tails and licked her hands, and seemed to be charmed by her, most if not all of the people in the tavern were no doubt wondering if the dogs' actions ought to be interpreted as a warning that something not of this earth now walked among them in disguise.

She could too easily imagine what their reaction would have been if all of the dogs—or even just one mean-tempered specimen—had greeted her with growls, hackles raised, ears flattened to their skulls. Such a display of hostility would have received but one interpretation, and Molly would have found herself in the position of an accused witch in seventeenth-century Salem.

In at least two places in the large room, rifles and shotguns leaned against the walls, arsenals within easy reach.

Many of these would-be defenders of the planet surely were packing handguns, as Molly was. Among them would be a few, wound tight by dread and frustrated by their powerlessness, who would be relieved, even beguiled, to have a chance to shoot something, someone, *anyone.*

In this fever swamp of paranoia, if the shooting started, it might not stop until every shooter had himself been shot.

Molly turned her attention toward the back of the room, where the children were gathered. They looked scared. From the moment that Molly had seen them, they had struck her as terribly vulnerable, and now more than ever.

"Go," she said to the dogs, "shoo, go."

Their reaction to her command proved as peculiar as their unanimous attraction to her. Instantly compliant, as if all nine of them had been trained by her, they retreated to the places they had been when she had entered.

This remarkable exhibition of obedience only sharpened the suspicion of the sixty people gathered in the tavern. But for the grumble of the rain, the room had fallen silent. Every stare made the same circuit: from Molly to the retreating dogs, and back to Molly again.

Neil broke the spell when he said to Russell Tewkes, "This is one strange damn night, weirdness piled on weirdness. I could use a drink. You doing business? You have any beer nuts?"

Russell blinked and shook his head, as though he had been in a *trance* of suspicion. "I'm not selling the stuff tonight. I'm giving it away. What'll you have?"

"Thank you, Russ. Got Coors in a bottle?"

"I only sell draft and bottled, no damn cans. Aluminum causes Alzheimer's."

Neil said, "What do you want, Molly?"

She didn't want anything that might blur her perceptions and cloud her judgment. Surely survival depended on sobriety.

Meeting Neil's eyes, however, she knew that he wanted her to drink something, not because she needed it but because most of the people in the tavern probably thought that under the circumstances she *ought* to need a drink—if she was merely human like them.

Survival would also depend on flexibility.

"Hit me with a Corona," she said.

While Molly had to study people and brood about them to arrive at a useful understanding of their natures, much in the rigorously analytic fashion that she built the cast of players in her novels, Neil formed an instinctive understanding of anyone he met within moments of the first introduction. His gut reactions were at least as reliable as her intellectual analysis of character.

She accepted the Corona and tipped it to her lips with an acute awareness of being the center of attention. She intended to take a small sip, but surprised herself by chugging a third of the beer.

When she lowered the bottle, the level of tension in the tavern dropped noticeably.

Inspired by Molly's thirst, half the assembled crowd lifted drinks of their own. Many of the teetotalers watched the drinkers with disapproval, worry, or both.

Having won their acceptance by such a meaningless—if not downright absurd—test of her humanity, Molly doubted that the human race could survive in even the most remote bunker, behind the most formidable fortifications, if in fact the invaders could assume convincing human form.

So many people had difficulty acknowledging the existence of unalloyed evil; they hoped to wish it away through positive thinking, to counsel it into remorse through psychotherapy, or to domesticate it with compassion. If they could not recognize implacable evil in the hearts of their own kind and could not understand its enduring nature, they were not likely to be able to see through the perfect biological disguise of an extraterrestrial species capable of exquisitely detailed mimicry.

From their various posts around the tavern, the dogs still watched her, some openly, others furtively.

Their continued scrutiny suddenly struck chords on that operatic pipe organ of paranoia that stands front and center in the theater of the human mind: She wondered if the dogs had rushed to greet her, grateful for human contact, *because everyone else in the tavern was an imposter, even the children, all alien presences masquerading as friends, as neighbors.*

No. The dogs hadn't reacted to Neil as they had to her, although Neil was unquestionably Neil and nothing else. The reason for their interest in Molly remained mysterious.

Pretending indifference, they were acutely alert to her every move, their lustrous eyes seeming to adore her, as if she were the still point of the turning world, where past and future are gathered, exalted beyond ordinary mortal status, the only thing in Creation worthy of their rapt attention.

19

MOLLY AND NEIL CIRCULATED THROUGH THE TAV-
ern, listening to the experiences of others, seeking information that
would allow them to better assess the situation both here in town and in
the world beyond Black Lake.

Everyone at the Tail of the Wolf had seen the apocalyptic images on
television. Perhaps they would be the last in human history to witness
world-shaking news through the communal medium of the tube.

After the TV channels had filled with blizzards of electronic snow or
with the enigmatic pulsations of color, some people had turned on their
radios and had caught scraps of AM and FM broadcasts from cities far
and near. Newsmen had spoken of terrifying presences in the streets—
variously referred to as *monsters, ETs, aliens, demons,* or simply *things*—
though often they were too consumed by horror to fully describe what
they saw or else their reports abruptly ended in screams of terror, pain.

Molly thought of the man whose head had been cleaved in half, falling
to the pavement on a street in Berlin, and she shuddered at the memory.

Others in the tavern had sought information on the Internet, where
they had encountered such a raveled tapestry of wild rumor and fevered
speculation that they had been more confused than informed. Then the
phones—landline and cellular—had failed, as had cable service, where-

upon the Internet had deconstructed as abruptly as a plume of steam in a gust of wind.

As Molly and Neil had seen clocks behaving oddly, mechanical devices—like the music boxes—running of their own accord, and impossible reflections in mirrors, so had numerous others among those gathered in the Tail of the Wolf. Battery-powered carving knives had suddenly buzzed and rattled in closed kitchen drawers. Computers switched themselves on, while across the screens scrolled hieroglyphs and ideograms from unknown languages. Out of CD players had come exotic and discordant music like nothing on the discs that were loaded in the machines.

They had stories of remarkable encounters with animals much like Molly's experience with the coyotes, and with the mice in the garage. All the fauna of this world seemed to recognize that the present threat was unearthly, supplanting all previous and familiar dangers.

In addition, *everyone* had sensed something ominous overhead in the rainy night, what Neil called "a mountain coming down," a mass of colossal size and crushing weight that first descended, then hovered, then moved east.

Norman Ling, who owned the town's only food market, recounted how his wife, Lee, had awakened him with a cry of "the moon is falling."

"I almost wish it had been the moon," Lee said now, with a solemnity that matched the expression in her dark, anguished eyes. "It would all be over now if it had been the moon, all of us gone—and nothing worse to come."

Nevertheless, though this cross-section of humanity had shared the same experiences and had drawn from them approximately the same conclusions—that their species was no longer the most intelligent on the planet and that their dominion of Earth had been usurped—they could not come together to devise a mutually agreeable response to the threat. Four philosophies divided the occupants of the tavern into four camps.

The drunks and those who worked diligently at becoming drunk made the smallest group. To their way of thinking, the most desirable comforts of human civilization were already lost beyond all hope of recovery. If they could not save the world, they would drink to the memory of its glories—and hope that when one kind of brutal death or another came to them, they would be unconscious, courtesy of Jack Daniel's or Absolut.

More numerous than the drunks were the peace lovers, the meek who styled themselves as prudent and reasonable. They remembered movies like *The Day the Earth Stood Still,* in which well-meaning aliens, bringing gifts of peace and love to the people of Earth, are willfully misunderstood and become the targets of mindless human violence.

To this crowd, with or without benefit of liquor, the unfolding worldwide catastrophe was not proof of bad intentions, but rather a tragic consequence of poor communication, perhaps even the result of some unspecified, precipitous, and typically ignorant human action. These prudent, reasonable citizens were convinced—or pretended to be—that the current terrors would be satisfactorily explained in time, and rectified, by the benign ambassadors from another star.

In these circumstances, *The Day the Earth Stood Still* had less relevance to Molly than an old episode of *The Twilight Zone* in which aliens arrived with solemn promises to alleviate all human want and suffering, guided by a sacred volume whose title translated as *To Serve Man.* Too late, the sheepish people of Earth realized that the sacred volume was a cookbook.

Of the four groups, more numerous than the drunks and the peace lovers combined were the fence-sitters, who could not decide if the current crisis would best be addressed by a violent response or by peace overtures and songs of love—or perhaps even by consuming disabling quantities of alcoholic beverages. They claimed to need more information before they could make up their minds; they would no doubt be patiently awaiting further information even as a meat lover from Andromeda was basting them in butter.

Molly was dismayed to see friends among the fence-sitters. She would have had more respect for them if they had embraced either pacifism or inebriation.

The fourth group, only slightly less numerous than the fence-sitters, were those who preferred to stand up and fight, regardless of the odds against them. Among them were as many women as men, folks of all ages and persuasions. Angry, energized, they had brought most of the guns and were eager to strike back.

They pulled up two more chairs and welcomed Molly and Neil, inferring from the shotgun and the pistol that they might be like-minded. This spirited group had put half a dozen tables together to form a U, the better to jointly speculate on all the possible what-ifs, as well as to discuss strategy and tactics for each contingency.

Because they knew next to nothing about their enemy, all their theorizing and planning amounted to little more than blue-sky war gaming. Their discussions provided them with a sense of purpose, however, and purpose was at least a partially effective antidote to fear.

While they might dread the coming confrontation, they were also frustrated that the invaders had not yet shown themselves, at least not in Black Lake. Although they were willing to fight and ready to die if necessary in the struggle, they couldn't battle an invisible adversary.

Molly felt at home among them—and glad that she and Neil at last had comrades.

The unofficial leader of this live-free-or-die faction appeared to be Tucker Madison, a former Marine, currently a deputy with the San Bernardino County Sheriff's Department. His composure, his calm voice, his clear direct gaze reminded Molly of Neil.

"The only thing that worries the skin off me," Tucker said, surely understating the number of his concerns, "is that they won't soon or often come out where we can see them. With the ability to control the weather all around the world, what reason do they have to risk our gunfire, even if our weapons probably are primitive by their standards?"

"Some of the godless bastards are apparently showing up in the cities," said a squint-eyed, sixtysomething woman with sun-toughened skin, reminding Tucker of the news reports. "They'll come here, too, eventually."

"But none of us has actually seen one," Tucker said. "Those things on the news might be just reconnaissance machines, drones, robots."

Vince Hoyt, a history teacher and coach of the regional high school's football team, had features as bold and commanding as those on ancient marble busts of the more iron-willed Roman emperors. His jaws looked strong enough to crack walnuts, and when he spoke in his gravelly voice, he sounded as if he had swallowed the shells.

"The big question is, what happens if this rain doesn't stop for a week, two weeks, a month? Our homes won't stand up to that kind of deluge. I already have leaks at my place, major damage, and no safe way to get on the roof to fix it in this downpour. They might think they can drown our will to resist, wash the fight right out of us."

"If rain, why not wind?" asked a young man with curly blond hair, a gold ring in his left ear, and a red tattoo of a woman's puckered lips on his throat. "Tornadoes, hurricanes."

"Targeted lightning," the sun-baked woman suggested. "Would that be possible? Could they do that?"

Molly thought of the enormous and evidently *artificially generated* waterspout churning up from the Pacific, sucking hundreds of thousands of gallons per minute from the sea. Targeted lightning didn't sound as far-fetched as it would have yesterday.

"Maybe even earthquakes," said Vince Hoyt. "Before any of that happens, we've got to decide on a headquarters where we can maybe consolidate an arsenal, food, medicines, first-aid supplies—"

"Our market already has plenty of food," said Norman Ling, "but it's on a lower street. If the rain keeps up, the place will be underwater by this time tomorrow."

"Besides," Tucker Madison said, bringing his Marine experience to bear, "the market isn't a defensible structure, not with all those big plate-glass windows. And I hate to mention this, but it's not just ETs we have to worry about. With the collapse of communications, civil authority is breaking down out there. Maybe it's already been swept away. I haven't been able to get in touch with the sheriff's office over in the county seat. No police. Maybe no National Guard, no coherent command-and-control systems to make proper use of the military . . ."

"Chaos, anarchy," Lee Ling whispered.

As calmly as anyone could have discussed this terrifying aspect of civilization's collapse, Tucker said, "Believe me, there are lots of bad people who'll take advantage of chaos. And I don't mean just outsiders. We've got our own thugs and creeps right here in town, thieves and rapists and violence junkies who'll think anarchy is paradise. They'll take what they want, do what they want to anyone, and the more they indulge their sickest fantasies, the sicker and more savage they're going to become. If we're not ready for them, they'll kill us and our families before we ever come face-to-face with anything from the other end of the galaxy."

A solemn silence settled over the group, and Lee Ling looked as if she were wishing again for a falling moon.

Molly thought of Render, the murderer of five children and the father of one, last seen walking north on the ridge road.

He would not have been the only monster freed from captivity this night. When prison and asylum staffs abandoned their posts, perhaps they had left the doors open behind them, either because they were careless or were motivated by misguided pity for the incarcerated. Or maybe in the chaos, the inmates seized control and freed themselves.

This was the Halloween of all Halloweens, six weeks early on the calendar, with no need of jack-o'-lanterns and cotton-bedsheet ghosts when the night was patterned with the pus trails of so many suppurating evils.

"The bank," Neil suggested.

Eyes turned to him, blinking, as if each person at the table, like Molly, had been roused from a waking nightmare by his words.

"The bank," Neil said, "is poured-in-place concrete clad in limestone, built in 1936 or '37, when the state first enforced earthquake-resistant building codes."

"And they made things to last in those days," Molly said.

Tucker liked the idea. "The bank was designed with security in mind. One or two entrances. Not many windows, plus they're narrow."

"Barred, too," Neil reminded him.

Tucker nodded. "Plenty of space for people and supplies."

Vince Hoyt said, "I never coached a single game where I ever thought a loss was inevitable, not even in the final quarter when the other team had us by four touchdowns, and I have no intention of trading that attitude for a loser mentality now. Damn if I will. But there is one other good thing about the bank. The vault. Armored walls, thick steel door. It'll make a hell of a final bolt-hole if it comes to that. If they want to tear the door off and come in after us, we'll make a shooting gallery of them, and take a slew of the bastards with us."

20

WITH THE CALCULATED CARRIAGE OF A DIGNIFIED
landlubber trying to cross the deck of a yawing ship without making a
fool of himself, Derek Sawtelle traveled from the camp of the swillpots to
Molly's chair among the fighters. He bent close to her. "Dear lady, even
under these circumstances, you look enchanting."

"And even under these circumstances," she said affectionately,
"you're full of horseshit."

"Might I have a word with you and Neil?" he asked. "In private?"

He was a genteel drunk. The more gin and tonic that he consumed,
the more mannerly he became.

Having been a casual friend of Derek's for five years, Molly knew that
he had not been driven to the bottle tonight by the contemplation of civilization's collapse. Managed inebriation was his lifestyle, his philosophy,
his faith.

A long-tenured professor of literature at the state university in San
Bernardino, nearing sixty-five and mandatory retirement, Derek special-
ized in American authors of the previous century.

His novelist heroes were the hard-drinking macho bullies from Hemingway to Norman Mailer. His admiration for them was based partly on
his literary insights, but it also had the quality of a homely girl's secret
crush on a high-school football star.

Lacking an athletic physique, too kind to punch people out in barroom brawls or to cheer the bloody spectacle of a bullfight, or to dangle a wife from a high-rise window by her ankles, Derek could model himself after his heroes only by immersion in literature and gin. He had spent his life swimming in both.

Some professors might have made fine actors, for they approached teaching as a performance. Derek was one of these.

At his request, Molly had spoken to his students a few times and had seen him in action on his chosen stage. He proved to be an entertaining teacher but also an excellent one.

Here with the drums of Armageddon beating on the roof, Derek dressed as if he were soon to enter a classroom or attend a faculty reception. Perhaps mid-twentieth-century academics had never favored wool slacks and tweed jackets, harlequin-patterned sweater vests, foulard handkerchiefs, and hand-knotted bow ties; however, Derek had not only written his role in life but also had designed his costume, which he wore with authority.

When Molly rose from the table and, with Neil, followed Derek Sawtelle toward the back of the tavern, she saw that once more she had the full attention of the nine dogs.

Three of them—a black Labrador, a golden retriever, and a mutt of complex heritage—were roaming the room, sniffing the floor, teasing themselves with the lingering scents of bar food dropped in recent days but since cleaned up: here, a whiff of yesterday's guacamole; there, a spot of grease from a dropped French fry.

Since the rain had begun, this was the first time that Molly had seen animals engaged in any activity that seemed right and ordinary. Nevertheless, while the roaming trio kept their damp noses to the plank flooring, they rolled their eyes to watch her surreptitiously from under their lowered brows.

At the quiet end of the bar, where they could not be overheard, Derek said, "I don't want to alarm anyone. I mean more than they're already alarmed. But I know what's happening, and there's no point in resisting it."

"Derek, dear," Molly said, "no offense, but is there anything in your life that you ever found much reason to resist?"

He smiled. "The only thing I can think of was the disgusting popularity of that dreadful cocktail they called a Harvey Wallbanger. In the seventies, at every party, you were offered that concoction, that abomination, which I refused with heroic persistence."

"Anyway," said Neil, "we all know what's happening—in general if not the specific details."

Gin seemed to serve Derek as an orally administered eyewash, for his gaze was crystalline clear, not bloodshot, and steady. "Before I explain, I must confess to an embarrassing weakness you know nothing about. Over the years, in the privacy of my home, I have read a great deal of science fiction."

If he thought this secret required confession and penitence, perhaps he was drunker than Molly had realized.

She said, "Some of it's quite good."

Derek smiled brightly. "Yes, it is. Undeniably, it's a guilty pleasure. None of it is Hemingway or Faulkner, certainly, but whole libraries of the stuff are markedly better than Gore Vidal or James Jones."

"Now science fiction is science fact," Neil acknowledged, "but what does that have to do with living through tomorrow?"

"In several science-fiction novels," Derek said, "I encountered the concept of terraforming. Do you know what it is?"

Analyzing the word by its roots, Molly said, "To make earth—or to make a place like the planet Earth."

"Yes, exactly, yes," said Derek with the enthusiasm of a *Star Trek* fan recounting a delicious plot twist in his favorite episode. "It means altering the environment of an inhospitable planet to make it capable of supporting terrestrial life forms. Theoretically, for instance, one could build enormous machines, atmosphere processors, to liberate the composite molecules of a breathable atmosphere from the very soil and rock of Mars, turning a nearly airless world into one on which human beings, flora, and fauna would flourish. In such science-fiction stories, terraforming a planet takes decades or even centuries."

Molly at once understood his theory. "You're saying they aren't using weather as a weapon."

"Not primarily," Derek said. "This isn't the war of the worlds. Nothing as grand as that. To these creatures, wherever they may be from, we are as insignificant as mosquitoes."

"You don't go to war with mosquitoes," Neil said.

"Exactly. You just drain the swamp, deny them the environment in which they can thrive, and build your new home on land that no longer supports such annoying bugs. They're engaged in reverse terraforming, making Earth's environment more like that on their home world. The destruction of our civilization is to them an inconsequential side effect of colonization."

To Molly, who believed that life was a gift given with meaning and purpose, the perfect cruelty and monumental horror that Derek was describing could not exist in Creation as she understood it. "No. No, it's not possible."

"Their science and technology are hundreds if not thousands of years more advanced than ours," Derek said. "Literally beyond our comprehension. Instead of decades, perhaps they can remake our world in a year, a month, a week."

If this was true, humankind was indeed the victim of something worse than war, denied even the dignity of enemy status, viewed as cockroaches, as less than cockroaches, as an inconvenient mold to be rinsed out of existence with a purging solution.

When Molly's chest tightened and her breath came less easily than before, when her heart began to race with anxiety, she told herself that her reaction to Derek's premise was not an indication that she recognized the ring of truth in his words. She did not believe that the world was being

taken from humanity with such arrogance and with no fear of the consequences. She *refused* to believe such a thing.

Evidently sensing her innate resistance to his theory, Derek said, "I
have proof."

"Proof?" Neil scoffed. "What proof could you possibly have?"

"If not proof, at least some damn convincing evidence," Derek insisted. "Follow me. I'll show you."

He turned away from them, toward the back of the tavern, but then
faced them again without having taken a step.

"Molly, Neil . . . I'm sharing this out of concern for you. I don't mean
to cause you any distress."

"Too late," Molly said.

"You're my friends," Derek continued. "I don't want to see you waste
your final hours or days in futile resistance to an inevitable fate."

"We have free will. We make our own fate, even if it's figured in the
drift of stars," Neil said, for so had he been taught, and still believed.

Derek shook his head. "Better to seize what pleasure you can. Make
love. Raid Norman Ling's market for your favorite foods before the place
is underwater. Settle into a comforting haze of gin. If others want to go
out with a bang . . . well, let them. But pursue what pleasures are still
available to you before we're all washed into that long, perfect, ginless
darkness."

He turned away from them once more and went to the back of the
tavern.

Watching him, hesitating to follow, Molly saw Derek Sawtelle as she
had never seen him before. He was still a friend but also other than a
friend; he was now the embodiment of a mortal temptation—the temptation to despair.

She did not want to see what he wished to show them. Yet the refusal
to look would be a tacit acknowledgment that she feared his evidence
would be convincing; therefore, refusal would be the first step on a different road to despair.

Only by seeing his evidence could she test the fabric of her faith and have a chance to hold fast to her hope.

She met Neil's eyes. He recognized her dilemma, and shared it.

Pausing at the archway that led to a short hall and the public rest rooms, Derek looked back and promised, "Proof."

Molly glanced at the three lazily roaming dogs, and they looked at once away from her, pretending to be enthralled by the history of dropped food written on the stained wood floor.

Derek passed through the archway, disappearing into the hall.

After a hesitation, Molly and Neil followed him.

21

WHEN DEREK HAD ASCERTAINED THAT THE MEN'S
room was unoccupied, he propped the door open with a trash can and
motioned for Molly and Neil to enter.

A strong piney scent rose from the perfumed cakes in the two urinals.
Under that astringent fragrance, the odor of stale urine persisted.

The room had three inner doors. Two offered access to toilet stalls, and
the third opened on a janitorial closet.

"I had just washed my hands," Derek said, "and realized there were
no paper towels in the dispenser. I opened the closet to look for
some. . . ."

A light came on automatically when the closet door was opened, and
would go off when it was closed.

The closet contained metal shelves laden with supplies. A broom. A
sponge mop and a rag mop. A bucket on wheels.

"I noticed the leak at once," said Derek.

The ceiling Sheetrock at the back of the closet was saturated. A blister
had formed, then broken, and rain had dripped down through the open
metal shelving, gradually saturating the supplies stored there.

When Derek removed the bucket, broom, and mops, the closet proved
large enough to allow the three of them to crowd inside.

At the sight of Derek's promised evidence on the wet tile floor, Molly drew back a step, bumping against Neil. She thought the thing must be a snake.

"It's probably a fungus," said Derek, "or the equivalent, I think. That would be the closest word we'd have for it."

On reconsideration, she realized that a colony of mushroomlike fungi lay before her, fat and round and clustered in such a way that they resembled the coils of a gathered serpent.

"It was the size of a round loaf of bread when I first saw it," Derek said. "That was hardly an hour ago, and already it's half again as big."

The fungus was black overall, as shiny black as oiled rubber, with bright yellow ameboid spots edged in orange. That she could have mistaken it for a snake was no surprise, because it looked poisonous and evil.

"The rain isn't a weapon," Derek said, stooping beside the fungus. "It's an instrument of radical environmental change."

Crouching behind him, peering over his shoulder, Molly said, "I'm not sure I follow you."

"The water is drawn out of the ocean and processed . . . somewhere, I don't know, maybe in hovering ships more immense than we're able to comprehend. The salt must be removed because the rain isn't salty. And seeds are added."

"Seeds?" Neil asked.

"Thousands of millions of tiny seeds," Derek said, "microscopic seeds and spoors, plus the nutrients necessary to nourish them and the beneficial bacteria needed to sustain them—all washing down across the world, on every continent, every mountain and valley, into every river, lake, and sea."

In a near whisper, his voice thickened by a fearful awe, Neil said, "The entire spectrum of vegetation from another world."

"Trees and algae," Derek speculated, "ferns and flowers, grasses and grains, fungi and mosses, herbs, vines, weeds—none of them ever before seen by any human eye, seeded now ineradicably in our soil, in our oceans."

Shiny black with yellow spots. Glistening. Fecund. Infinitely strange.

Had this unwholesome thing indeed grown from a spoor transported with much planning and purpose through the dark cold and the empty desolation of interstellar space?

The chill that spread through Molly was different from any that she had experienced previously. It was not a quivery thing localized along the spine or the nape of the neck, did not shiver through her like a vagrant breath of eternity, but lingered. A coldness seemed to be spawned in the very cavities of her bones, in the red-and-yellow mush of marrow, from which it spread outward to every cell in every extremity.

Derek said, "If these extraterrestrial plants are aggressive—and judging by this creepy specimen, I suspect they're going to be relentlessly incursive—then they will sooner than later crowd out and perhaps even feed upon every species of flora that's native to Earth."

"This beautiful world," Molly murmured as the chill spreading through her carried with it a piercing grief, a sense of loss that she dared not contemplate.

"All of it will vanish," Derek said. "Everything we love, from roses to oaks, elms and evergreens—eradicated."

Black and yellow, the plump fungi coiled upon one another, tubular mushrooms nestled in the form of an eyeless snake. Smooth, glistening with an exuded film of oil. Luxuriant. Proliferous and merciless.

"If by some miracle," Derek continued, "some of us were to survive the initial phase of alien occupation, if we were able to live in primitive communities, furtively, in the secret corners where the world's ruthless new masters wouldn't see us, how soon would we be left without any familiar food?"

Neil said, "The vegetables and fruits and grains of another world wouldn't necessarily be poisonous to us."

"Not necessarily all of them," Derek agreed, "but surely some would be."

"And if they weren't poisonous," Molly wondered, "would we find them palatable?"

"Bitter," Derek guessed. "Or intolerably sour, or so acidic they would sicken us. Even if palatable, would they nourish us? Would the nutrients be in chains of molecules that our digestive systems could break down and utilize? Or would we fill our stomachs with food . . . and nevertheless starve to death?"

Derek Sawtelle's cultured voice, reverberant by nature, rich with dramatic technique polished by decades in the classroom and on the lecture-hall stage, had half mesmerized Molly. She shook herself to shed the bleak spell that his grim words had cast upon her.

"Damn," he said, "I talked myself sober, and I don't like it on this side of the gin curtain. Too scary."

Desperate to refute Derek's vision of their future, Molly said, "We're assuming that this thing, this fungus, is from another world, but we don't really know that. I'll admit I've never seen anything like it . . . but so what? There are lots of exotic funguses I've never seen, some probably stranger-looking than this."

"I've another thing to show you," Derek said, "something much more disturbing—and unfortunately more sobering—than what you've seen so far."

22

ON ONE KNEE IN THE JANITORIAL CLOSET, WITH
Molly crouching more at his side now than behind him, and with Neil
standing over him, Derek withdrew a Swiss Army knife from a pocket of
his tweed sports jacket.

Molly could think of no one less likely to be carrying a Swiss Army
knife than this bow-tied academic. Then she realized that among the
tools included in that clever instrument were a corkscrew and a bottle
opener.

Derek employed neither of those devices but instead extracted the
spear blade. He hesitated with the point of the knife above one of the
clustered fungi.

His hand shook. These tremors weren't the consequence of either in-
toxication or alcohol withdrawal.

"When I did this before," he said, "I was pleasantly soused, full of the
giddy curiosity that makes dipsomania such an adventure. Now I'm
sober, and I know what I'm going to find—and I'm astonished that I had
the courage to do this the first time."

Having steeled himself, he poked the blade into the tubular cap of one
of the fattest of the fungi.

The entire colony, not just the pierced specimen, quivered like gelatin.

From the wound, a puff of pale vapor escaped with an audible wheeze, suggesting that the interior of the mushroomlike structure had been pressurized. The malodorous vapor reeked like a concoction of rotten eggs, vomit, and decomposing flesh.

Molly gagged, and Derek said, "I should have warned you. But it dissipates quickly."

He slit the membrane that he had already punctured, revealing the inner structure of the fungus.

The interior was not solidly meaty, like that of an ordinary mushroom, but a hollow chamber. A graceful architecture of spongy struts supported the surface membrane that Derek had slit.

A wet mass, the size of a hen's egg, lay at the center of this chamber. At first glimpse, Molly thought of intestines because these looked, in miniature, like ropey human guts, but gray and mottled as if corrupted, infected, cancerous.

Then she saw that these coils and loops were slowly moving, sliding lazily over and around one another. The better comparison was to a knot of copulating earthworms.

The reeking vapor lost, the black-and-yellow membrane slit, these worm forms continued their sensuous writhing for only three or four seconds—and abruptly disengaged, bristled to every curve of the chamber. They became a dozen questing tentacles much quicker than worms, connected to something unseen at the bottom of the hollow, as quick and jittery as spider legs, frenziedly probing the knife-torn edges of the ruined canopy.

Molly tensed, shrank back, certain that the repulsive resident of the fungus would spring out of its lair and, loose, would prove to be faster than a cockroach.

"It's all right," Derek assured her.

Neil said, "The fungus is a home to something, like the shell of a conch."

"No, I don't think so." Derek wiped the blade of his knife on his display handkerchief. "You can strain for earthly comparisons, but there

really isn't one. From what I can tell, this squirmy little creepshow is part
of the fungus itself."

The frenetic lashing of the small tentacles subsided. They continued to
move quickly, but now in a more calculated manner.

Molly sensed that they were embarked on some task, though she
could not at once discern their purpose.

"The rapid movement," Neil said, "the ability to flex at will and manipulate appendages . . . those things indicate animal life, not plants."

Molly agreed. "There's got to be muscle tissue involved, which plants
don't have."

Discarding his soiled display handkerchief, Derek said, "On the planet
they come from, there may not be as clear a division between plant and
animal life as we have on this world."

Beginning at both ends of the torn canopy, the tentacles had begun to
repair the gash.

"I'd need to look more closely than I care to," Derek said, "and perhaps with a magnifying glass, to be able to tell exactly how they knit the
wound shut. The tentacles appear to be exuding a bonding material . . ."

Molly could see a pinkish ooze seeping from the tips of some of those
busy appendages.

". . . but I think I also detect microfilaments, as well . . . as if the damn
thing is stitching itself shut much the way a surgeon might close an inci-
sion." He shrugged. "All our knowledge brings us nearer to our ignorance."

With a fascination equal to her disgust and dread, Molly could not
look away from the self-repairing fungus—if that was the right name
for it.

"Imagine," Derek proposed, "a world filled with a variety of hideous
plants that all present a still exterior . . . but teem with secret internal
life."

Molly knew that on the distant world from which it had come, this
fungus had been as natural and unremarkable in its environment as a

dandelion in an earthly field. Reason did not allow her to attribute a moral value to it any more than she could rationally ascribe conscious intention to a carrot.

Nevertheless, judging only by the evidence of her eyes, she felt that this thing was profoundly malignant. On an intuitive level, she *knew* that it harbored malice, that in some strange way it dreamed of violence, as a trap-door spider might dream of sucking the juices from the beetle that sooner or later would fall into its lair, though this thing dreamed of cruelty with a glee that no spider could ever experience, with a ferocity that transcended nature. On a level even deeper than intuition, in that realm of belief that is of the heart rather than of the mind, and might be called faith, she had no doubt whatsoever that this life form, whether fungus or not, whether plant or animal or something between, was not just poisonous but *evil.*

As the repulsive thing finished sewing itself together from the inside, as the squirming gray tentacles disappeared behind the glossy black-and-yellow-spotted skin, it seemed to have no rightful place in a universe created by the God of light, but belonged in another universe than this one, where the divine impulse had been dark and twisted, the divine intention cruel beyond imagining.

Folding the blade of his knife into the handle, pocketing it, Derek looked at Molly. "You still think it might be just an exotic mushroom you've never happened to run across before?"

"No," she admitted.

23

AFTER MOLLY AND DEREK HAD RETREATED FROM the janitorial closet, Neil took one last look at the fungus before switching off the light in there. Closing the door, he said, "If we explored Black Lake right now, we'd find those things all over town, wouldn't we?"

"Those and God knows what else," Derek replied. "Fast-track terraforming. The growing cycle has begun. In the streets and parks, in backyards and alleyways, in school playgrounds, out there in the forests, at the bottom of the lake—oh, everywhere, everywhere—we will find a new world growing, a botanical wonderland of things we've never seen before and that we'll wish we'd never seen at all."

With sudden, devastating understanding, Molly said, "The air."

"I wondered when you'd think of that," Derek said.

Trees, grasses, the vast floating fields of algae in the seas: The flora of Earth filter carbon dioxide from the atmosphere. As a by-product of photosynthesis, they pump out oxygen. Vital, life-sustaining oxygen.

What process, similar to but different from photosynthesis, might this alien vegetation employ? Instead of oxygen, might it produce another gas? The current equation could conceivably be reversed: oxygen in, carbon dioxide out.

"How many days before we notice that we're suffering from oxygen deprivation?" Derek wondered. "If we even do notice. After all, one of the symptoms of oxygen deprivation is delirium. How many weeks before we suffocate like fish flopping on a beach?"

These questions staggered the mind and so oppressed the heart that Molly felt prescient when she remembered how she had earlier thought of Derek Sawtelle as the embodiment of the mortal temptation to despair.

The astringent piney scent of the deodorizing cakes and the more subtle but repugnant effluvium of stale urine seemed to burn in Molly's nostrils and throat. She inhaled shallowly to avoid those unpleasant smells. When that didn't work, and when she found that without conscious volition she had suddenly begun breathing more deeply and rapidly, she recognized an incipient panic attack and strove to repress it.

"Perhaps we should hope to suffocate sooner than later," Derek said, "before the beasts of that other world are set loose among us."

"If news reports can be trusted, they're already in the cities," Neil reminded him.

Derek shook his head. "By 'beasts,' I don't mean the invaders themselves, but all the many animals of their world, the beasts of their fields and forests, the predators and the serpents and the insects. I suspect some of them are going to be more vicious and terrifying than anything the poor damn science-fiction writers have ever dreamed up in their darkest stories."

In a voice thick with sarcasm, Neil said, "Gosh, Derek, I never realized what a fountain of positive thoughts you are."

"It's not pessimism. It's simply the truth," Derek said. "Too much of the truth is never a good idea." He led them out of the men's room, into the hallway. "Which is why I'm inviting you to my table. Cast your fate with the tipplers, the tosspots, and make the best use possible of what time we have left. Come pour down a few glasses of anesthesia. We aren't the cheery lot we usually are, not quick to laugh at all tonight, but shared melancholy can be comforting, even sweet. In place of anxiety and grief and anger, we offer you a great warm gently rolling sea of melancholy."

When Derek tried to take Molly by the arm and escort her back to the main room of the tavern, she resisted him. "I've got to use the rest room."

"You'll forgive me if I don't wait for you," Derek said. "But there's perilous little gin oiling my system at the moment, and I'm afraid that if I don't quickly pour a pint of Gordon's best in my crankcase, this old machine is going to stutter to a stop."

"I wouldn't want to be responsible for your crankshaft freezing up," she said with a thin smile. "You go ahead."

They watched the professor make his way back toward oblivion, and when they were alone in the short hallway, Neil said, "You look . . . gray."

"I *feel* gray. Dear Lord, can it really be as grim as he's painted it?"

Neil had no answer for her. Or perhaps he preferred not to put into words the only answer that seemed honest.

"I wasn't just trying to be shed of him," Molly said. "I really do need to use the bathroom. Wait here for me. Stay close."

When she entered the women's lavatory, she seemed to be alone. The doors on all three stalls were slightly ajar, not fully closed and latched.

The sound of rain swelled louder here, not merely an insistent drumming on roof shingles, but a more intimate gurgle, plink, and splash.

The double-hung window featured panes of frosted glass. The lower sash had been raised, opening the room to the night.

Choruses of rain danced on the windowsill, drizzled off the edge, and formed a shallow puddle on the floor.

The water reflected the ceiling light but didn't appear to be luminous in its own right. It seemed to have no peculiar odor, either, so perhaps the storm had entered a new phase.

Considering what a leak had spawned in the janitorial closet in the men's room, however, Molly moved directly to the window to close it.

As she reached for the bottom rail to pull down the lower sash, she was shaken by the conviction that something lurked in the night just beyond the window. Something waited that she could not see through the doubled panes of frosted glass, a hostile presence that would reach inside and seize her and drag her out into the dark wet or, with razored claws, would slash her open, groin to breast, and eviscerate her where she stood.

So intense and specific was this fear that it had the impact of a paranormal vision, rocking her backward. She stumbled, nearly fell, regained her balance, and chastised herself for allowing Derek to reduce her to the condition of a frightened child.

As she stepped toward the window again, a familiar voice spoke behind her, one that she hadn't heard in many years but that she instantly identified: "Do you have a little kiss for me, sweetheart?"

She turned and discovered Michael Render, murderer of five children and father of one, standing hardly more than an arm's length away.

24

IN RAIN-SOAKED GRAY COTTON PANTS AND MATCH-
ing shirt, Render looked not storm-battered but storm-refreshed, as if this
downpour that had been conjured and concocted to nurture alien vegetation had also nurtured him.

He appeared to have thrived in twenty years of sympathetic custody.
Freed from the worries of work and self-support, granted leisure greater
than that of pampered kings, with the services of an institutional nutri-
tionist and the use of a well-equipped gym, he had stayed slim at the
waist, had added muscle, and had acquired no lines at the corners of his
eyes or mouth. At fifty, he could pass as a man still shy of his fortieth
birthday.

Pleased by the effect that his surprise appearance had on Molly, he
smiled and said, "For heart-rending emotion, nothing quite equals a
father-and-child reunion."

Molly found her voice and was relieved to hear no tremor in it, no reflection of the fact that her thundering heart boomed hard enough to rattle bone on bone in her knees. "What are you doing here?"

"Where else should I be but with my only remaining family?"

"I'm not afraid of you."

"I'm not afraid of you, either, sweetheart."

The 9-mm pistol nestled in her raincoat. She slipped her right hand into that pocket, closed it around the checked grip, and hooked her index finger on the trigger guard.

"Going to shoot me again?" he asked, once more with a note of amusement.

Render was handsome now, as he had always been; and once he had been uncannily charming, too, sufficiently winning in his ways that her mother, who even as a young woman had a keen insight into people, had been seduced by him and swept into marriage.

Thalia had soon learned the consequences of her naiveté. She'd mistaken Render's possessiveness for love. She discovered that what had seemed to be an admirable male desire to cherish and protect had in fact been an almost demonic need to control.

Rain-slicked, rain-beaded, Michael Render stood here in his true persona, reveled in it. But there was something different about him, too, a disturbing change that Molly could sense but not define. His seductive gray eyes had a luster to rival the luminosity of the early rain, as if the storm had filled him to the brim and pooled now within his skull.

"I've given up guns," he assured her. "They're effective but so impersonal. Between the idea and the reality, the thrill is lost, and murder by gun fades in memory too fast. In a year or two, reliving it doesn't even stir an erection."

By the time Molly was two years old, her mother had endured enough of Render's intimidation, his irrational jealousy, his self-pitying tantrums, his threats, and finally his violence. Choosing freedom at the cost of poverty, she had taken nothing from their marriage except her most personal possessions and her daughter.

"And let me tell you, Molly, dear, when a virile man is confined to solitary accommodations in a sanitarium for the criminally insane, even in one of the progressive institutions with all its comforts, he is denied the satisfaction of women, and to achieve relief, he *really needs* all of the erotic memories he can get."

During and following the divorce, Render had initially pursued sole custody of his child, then joint custody. When the legal system proved slow enough to try his short-fuse patience and when judges admonished him for his behavior in their courtrooms, he argued his case in personal confrontations with Thalia, often in public places, red-faced and shouting threats, which resulted in the issuance of restraining orders that diminished his chances of obtaining joint custody. Contempt for the restraining orders had landed him in jail for thirty days and had put an end to even his supervised visitation rights.

"After a year of isolation," he said now, "I'd all but forgotten the feel of your mother—the taste of her mouth, the weight of her breasts. I had cheap whores who stayed in memory better." A smile, a shrug. "Your mother was a boring porcelain bitch."

"Shut up." Molly couldn't summon any volume, only a whisper. As always, Render insisted on dominance, and to her chagrin, Molly was unable to assert herself, as though twenty years had dropped out from under her, plunging her into childhood again. *"Shut up."*

"After two years, the memory of your head-shot, gut-shot little playmates didn't do it for me anymore, either. A bullet is just too impersonal. A bullet isn't a blade, and a blade isn't bare hands. I've found that strangulation stays vivid in the memory. It's much more intimate than merely pulling a trigger. I stiffen even now at the thought of it."

Molly drew the pistol from her raincoat pocket.

"Ah," he said with evident satisfaction, as though the intention behind his visit to the tavern had been to taunt her into precisely this confrontation. "I've come a long way through bad weather to ask you a few questions—but first to tell you a little story, so you'll better understand your dear old dad."

The moment was increasingly surreal. Claustrophobic. Paralytic. Emblematic.

She stood at the vise point between the jaws of the past and the future, both pressing hard and insistently upon her, constraining her breath, denying her mobility, pinching her voice in her throat.

"I've spent twenty years under lock and key. Internal darkness, deprivation. At least you owe me a friendly ear for a moment. Just one little story, and then I'll go."

Twenty years earlier, when he destroyed his last hope of winning legal custody of Molly, Michael Render resorted to the instrument of persuasion that he now claimed to find unsatisfactory: the gun. He had come to her elementary school to take her from her classroom. Having asked to see his daughter on some pretense that the principal had found unconvincing, Render realized that he'd aroused suspicion, whereupon he pulled a pistol and shot the principal dead.

"After five years of treatment," he told her now, "I was sent to a facility with lower security standards. They had large, lovely grounds. The best-behaved patients who had made the most progress in their therapy, who were judged to have reached a point of remorse on a journey to contrition, were encouraged to work in the various gardens if they wished."

With the principal dead, Render had gone in search of Molly's third-grade classroom, killing one member of the faculty en route and wounding two others. He found her room and grievously wounded her teacher, Mrs. Pasternak, and would have abducted Molly if the police had not then arrived.

"In the gardens, we wore an electronic shackle around one ankle, which would trigger an alarm in the security office if we ventured farther than allowed. I made no attempt to escape. There was a fence, after all, and a world outside that knew my face too well. I became something of a horticulturist, specializing in roses."

With the arrival of the police, he had taken Molly and twenty-two other children hostage. He wasn't a stupid man—in fact he had earned two university degrees—and therefore knew that having killed two and wounded three, he could not hope to negotiate freedom for himself. By then, however, his ever-simmering anger, which was the essence of his personality, had grown into a fiery rage, and he determined that if he could not have the control of the daughter that he had for so long pursued, then he would deny other parents the pleasure of their children's company.

"One day, as I worked alone in the rose garden, what should appear before me but a nine-year-old boy with a disposable camera."

Render had killed five of the twenty-two children before Molly shot him. He'd brought two pistols and spare magazines of ammunition. After reloading both guns, he'd reacted with such fury to something he heard from a police bullhorn outside that in his rage he left one weapon lying on the teacher's desk, and turned his back on it.

His voice these twenty years later, colored by something darker than his usual anger, mesmerized her: "On a dare, to prove his courage to his pals, the boy had cut a hole in a far corner of the fence, distant from the actual sanitarium buildings, and had crept across the grounds, hoping to photograph one of the infamous patients as evidence of his nerve."

Although only eight years old and unfamiliar with firearms, Molly had picked up the second pistol from the teacher's desk. Gripping it with both hands, she squeezed off three shots. Rocked and terrified by the recoil, she still managed to hit Render twice—first in the back, then in the right thigh—and fortunately harmed no one with the third shot, which lodged in a wall.

"The infamous patient the boy chanced to come across was me," said Render. "He was skittish, but I charmed him, mugged for the camera, and let him take eight photographs there among the roses."

When Render, having been shot twice, crashed to the schoolroom floor, the seventeen surviving children fled. In their wake, a SWAT team entered to find Molly weeping at the side of her badly wounded teacher, who would spend the rest of her life in a wheelchair.

"By the end of our little photo shoot, the boy had let down his guard. I hit him very hard in the face, and hit him again, and then strangled him there among the roses. The experience would have been even more satisfying if he'd been a young girl, but you have to work with what you're given."

Later on that bloody day, twenty years before this current encounter, Molly had wondered how she could have wounded him twice with three shots even though she had never handled a gun before, though she had been shaking with terror, though three times the punishing recoil had nearly knocked her off her feet. That she had been able to stop him seemed a miracle.

"Not far from the rose garden was an old cistern, an enormous stone-walled underground tank. They'd once had a complex rainwater-collection system that funneled runoff into the cistern to be used for maintenance of the landscaping in dry months."

Molly had told her mother that some spirit had been with her on that awful day, an angel that could have no influence with Render but could guide her and steady her to do what must be done.

"The cistern hadn't been used in sixty years. They left it there because the cost of tearing it out was prohibitive."

Thalia had assured young Molly that she—and she alone—deserved the credit for her courage, for what she'd done. Angels, Thalia said, didn't work their miracles with guns.

"Using gardening tools, I pried off the cistern lid and dropped the boy into that hole. So dark in there, and such a stench. Shallow water far below. He landed with a splash, and a chorus of rats squeaking in fright."

In spite of her mother's well-meaning counsel, Molly believed then, and to this day, that some guiding spirit had been with her in that school-room.

She felt no spirit now, however, and was inexpressibly grateful for the pistol in her hand.

"I buried his little disposable camera at the foot of a rosebush. It was the Cardinal Mindszenty rose, so named because of its glorious robe-red color."

Render moved, not toward her—and risk being shot—but around her, slowly circling away from the toilet stalls, in the direction of the sinks.

"Police came looking for the boy, of course, but they took some time to find him. The rats had done their work. But better yet, the bottom of the cistern had cracked and broken out ages ago. The boy had settled into a natural limestone catacomb under the cistern. His condition, when they discovered him, didn't give the CSI techies much to work with."

Slowly Render moved past the first sink, then past the second.

Molly turned, tracking him with the pistol.

"Suspicion fell on another patient. Edison Crain, his name was. A plump, sweaty little man. Ten years before, he had raped a young boy and strangled him to death—his only known act of violence."

Second by second, the lavatory seemed less real to Molly, while simultaneously Render grew more vivid, commanding her attention, as hypnotic as a weaving cobra.

"Crain had lived ten blameless years since then, had been a model patient, and it was thought that his cure was well advanced, that he would be eligible for medically supervised release in a year or so. But the poor troubled thing must still have been eaten with guilt over the boy he *did* kill, and must not have trusted his own sanity. Because when suspicion fell on him, he cracked and broke, confessed to the murder of the camera boy."

Having circled a hundred eighty degrees of the room, Render stood with his back to the window, his feet in the puddle of rain.

"They transferred Crain to a maximum-security hospital, and I . . . well, I escaped all consequences. That was fifteen years ago, but still, when I'm lying alone in bed at night, between the desire and the spasm, the memory of strangling the boy excites me no less than the first time I resorted to it for stimulation."

Molly had been aware of a difference in him, the nature of which for a while eluded definition; but now she understood it. Render's characteristic anger was not in evidence. His hot temper had cooled.

New to him was a self-satisfied air approaching smugness. And the intense focus of a predator. The dark amusement in his voice. A glimmer of wicked merriment in his eyes.

Twenty years in the care of psychiatrists had resulted in the maturation of his raw anger into sociopathic contempt and psychotic glee; the wine of rage had become a more sophisticated, well-aged venom.

"And now my questions," he said. That smile again. Almost a smirk. "Is your mother still dead?"

Molly couldn't grasp Render's purpose in coming here. If he had meant to harm her, he could have struck her from behind instead of announcing his presence.

"Does anyone still read the dumb slut's books?"

Unreality chased surreality, round and round. Why would he travel so far only to tell the story of the strangled boy when he knew that Molly could not loathe him more than she already loathed him, or to disparage her mother when he knew that she would dismiss his slurs and insults with contempt?

"Are any of her books even in print? She was as bad a writer as she was a bad hump."

His taunting seemed designed to goad Molly into shooting him, but that made no sense. His matchless arrogance and his capacity for cruelty surely meant that he was incapable of grief or guilt. His passion was homicidal, not suicidal.

"Are any of *your* books in print, sweetheart? After tonight, what does it matter that you've written anything? Or that you've existed at all? You're a failed writer, a barren woman, an empty hole. Dark, dark, dark—they all go into the dark. You, too. And soon. To avoid the horrors that are coming, have you thought about turning that pistol on yourself?"

She sensed that he was about to slip out through the open window. "Don't try to leave," she warned.

He raised his eyebrows. "What—you think you can ring up the sanitarium and they'll quick send out some white-coat types with a straitjacket? The gates are open, sweetheart. Don't you realize what's happened? The gates are open. There's no authority anymore. It's dog eat dog, and every man a beast."

When he stooped to the window, the curious spell that he had cast over her was broken by his clear intent to leave.

She moved toward him. "No. Damn you, stop."

That grin again: sardonic, full of appetite and devoid of humor. "You know the story of the flood, the ark, the animals loaded two by two—all that Old Testament bullshit. But do you know *why*? Why the world had to end, why the judgment, the big flush, and then a whole new start?"

"Get away from the window."

"It's pertinent, sweetheart. You did the right thing once, but now your head is stuffed with twenty years of learning, which means doubts and equivocations and confusions. Now you can either shoot me in the back—again—or suck on that pistol and blow your own brains out."

Render ducked his head, hunched under the raised sash, and slid across the sill, as Molly shouted, *"Neil!"*

The outer rest-room door slammed open, and Neil rushed into the room as Molly reached the open window. "What's happening?"

Stooping to the window, one hand on the wet sill, pistol ready in the other, she said, "We can't just let him go."

"Who? Where?"

She leaned out of the window, head in the rain, and looked left along the alleyway, then right: the night, the storm, the suspicion of monstrosities growing nearby in secret shadows, and Render already gone.

PART FOUR

*"The corpse you planted last year in your garden,
Has it begun to sprout? Will it bloom this year?"*

T.S. Eliot, *The Waste Land*

25

AT THE BAR AGAIN, WHEN MOLLY DISCOVERED THAT strong coffee was available, she ordered a mug of it. Hot, black, thick, fragrant, it had the power, if anything did, to wake her from this dream if she were dreaming.

From the table of the tosspots, Derek waved at her. She ignored him.

Neil took coffee with her, suggesting answers to some of the things that puzzled her, though he had none of substance for the questions that were the most profound and therefore most urgent.

"So he recognized us when we passed him on the ridge road," she said. "But how did he find us here?"

"The Explorer's parked out front. He recognized it."

"If he didn't come to kill me, *why* did he come?"

"From what you've said, it sounded like he was . . . throwing down a challenge to you."

"Challenging me to what—kill him? What sense does that make?"

"None," Neil admitted.

"He called me a barren woman. How could he know?"

"There's ways he could've found out we don't have kids."

"But how could he know that we've tried so hard for seven years and that . . . I *can't*."

"He couldn't know."

"But he *did.*"

"He was just guessing," Neil said.

"No. He knew, all right. He knew. He stuck the knife in exactly where it would hurt the most. The crude bastard called me 'an empty hole.' "

Her thoughts seemed muddled, maybe because she'd had too little sleep or because this night had been filled with too much event to process. The coffee hadn't clarified her mind yet, and perhaps even a pot of it wouldn't bring her thinking up to speed.

"Funny but . . . I'm glad now we didn't have children," Neil said. "I couldn't handle being unable to protect them from all this."

His left hand rested on the bar. She covered it with her right. He had such strong hands but had used them all his life in gentle pursuits.

"He quoted T. S. Eliot," she said, coming now to the thing that most mystified and most disturbed her.

"Are we back at Harry Corrigan's place?"

"No. I mean Render. He said 'between the idea and the reality' and later 'between the desire and the spasm.' They were wrapped up in his other crazy rantings, but they're lines from 'The Hollow Men.' "

"He could know Eliot is one of your favorites."

"How could he know?"

Neil considered a moment but had no answer.

"Just before he left, he said 'Dark, dark, dark—they all go into the dark,' which is more Eliot. The thing that used to be Harry Corrigan . . . and now Render."

She sensed that she was circling an elusive insight that, once seized and opened, would unfold into a stunning revelation.

"That lurching, head-shot Harry Corrigan wasn't really Harry," she said. "So I wonder . . . was my father, in the rest room, really my father?"

"What do you mean?"

"Or maybe he was really Render . . . but not *only* Render."

"I'm still chasing you and losing ground."

"I don't know what I mean, either. Or maybe I know down on a subconscious level, where I can't get my hands around it . . . because right now, the hairs are quivering on the back of my neck."

Too little sleep, too little coffee, too much terror. Layered veils of weariness and confusion hid the truth from her if in fact she was close to any truth at all.

Deputy Tucker Madison, chief strategist of those who were determined to resist the taking of their town and their world, joined Molly and Neil at the bar.

"A few of us are remaining here in case new recruits show up," he informed them, "but most of us are forming task groups and heading out. One squad to inspect the bank and find ways to better fortify it. Another to truck food out of the market before it floods. A third to procure more weapons from Powers' Gun Shop. Are you with us?"

Molly thought of the yellow-spotted black fungus squirming with repulsive inner life, growing rapidly in the janitorial closet, the harbinger of a new world, a changed world, and even if no other choice might be as sensible as to fortify the bank and hunker down, the effort seemed futile.

"We're with you," Neil assured Tucker. "But there's this . . . situation we have to deal with first."

Molly glanced across the room at Derek Sawtelle and his group of fugitives from reality. Just as she feared before submitting to his macabre little show-and-tell, he had been an agent of despair.

"We'll meet you at the bank in a little while," Molly told Tucker.

Futility is always in the eye of the beholder. Her fate was in her own hands. With hope, all things were possible.

That was what she had always believed. Until tonight, however, she had operated automatically on that philosophy and had not found it necessary to remind herself of it or to argue herself into that conviction.

Derek hadn't been the only agent of despair she'd encountered in the past few hours. The first had been whatever entity controlled the corpse of Harry Corrigan.

The third had been Render. What reason could he have had for his bizarre performance if not to leave her shaken, frightened, and despairing?

Once more, she felt that enlightenment lay within her reach, waited just around the next turn in the twisty coils of logical deduction.

With a start, Neil put down his mug so hard that coffee slopped onto the bar. "Here it comes again."

For a moment, Molly didn't know what he meant—and then she felt the heavy, rhythmic pulses of pressure that were not accompanied by sound, that had no visible effect on anything in the tavern, but that undeniably surged through her, throbbing in the bone, an afflux and a reflux in the blood, the flesh, as if the ghost tides of a long-dead sea pulled at the race memory in her cells, reminding her of life before land.

Earlier in the night, at their house, she had not been aware of this phenomenon at all until Neil had spoken of it. Even after he had drawn her attention to it, she hadn't felt it a fraction as strongly as she did now.

Perhaps these throbbings were akin to magnetic pulses produced by colossal engines of unimaginable size, based on a technology as incomprehensible to her as the internal-combustion engine would be incomprehensible to any tent-dwelling native wandering the cityless plains of America a thousand years before the birth of Christ.

She looked at her wristwatch. The hour hand spun toward next year, while the minute hand whirled perhaps sixty times faster toward last year, as if to rob time of its power and to encourage those with timepieces to consider the moment, and to realize that it is all they ever have.

Throughout the tavern, a palpable anxiety had drawn people to their feet. They, too, consulted their watches if they had them, or looked toward the Coors clock on the back wall.

With the mysterious pulses came the impression of a looming mass in transit through the rain: Neil's mountain descending, Lee Ling's falling moon.

"Coming in from the north," Neil said.

He continued to be more sensitive than Molly to the nuances of this phenomenon.

Others, too, had sensed the point of approach. Several among the drunkards, the peace lovers, the fence-sitters, and the fighters—none of whom had yet left on their various missions of resistance—also faced north, staring at the ceiling at that end of the room.

Conversation had ceased. No glassware clinked.

Most of the dogs gazed up, as well, but still a few sniffed the floor, their instinct for danger blunted by their fascination with the scents of old beer and food stains.

"Bigger than I thought before," Neil whispered. "Bigger than any mountain or three mountains. And low. Very low. Maybe just . . . ten feet above the highest treetops."

"Death," Molly heard herself say, surprised by her own voice, but she sensed, by virtue of a gift more profound than instinct, that the word she spoke was not adequate and that the traveler in the storm was something both more impossible and less mysterious than she had heretofore imagined.

Toward the front of the tavern, a child began to weep. Her sobs were thick and miserable, but so rhythmic that they seemed false, and strange.

26

ALTHOUGH THE UNSEEN ENIGMA, CHARTING ITS course of conquest through the night sea overhead, compelled attention as nothing before in Molly's experience, the crying of the child grew so eerie that her gaze, and others, settled from the ceiling to the source of that misery.

The crying was not that of a child, after all, but arose from the doll that Molly had snatched from the backseat of the abandoned Lincoln Navigator on the ridge road.

It lay facedown on the bar where she had left it. The head was turned toward the room, eyes closed. From its open mouth issued the bawl and boohoo that were among the sounds and words recorded on its voice chip.

Molly was reminded of the music boxes in their bedroom. The waltzing porcelain figurines. The carousel horse turning, turning.

In her mind's eye, she also saw the twitching cadaver that had been Harry Corrigan. Dead Harry quoting Eliot through broken teeth, out of a blasted mouth that no longer had a roof.

She realized that the corpse-as-marionette was just a different category of the same effect that animated the music-box figures and caused the doll to sob. To the unknown masters of this night, the dead were toys, and the living.

As Molly was about to turn her attention to the ceiling once more, one of the dogs growled softly, and then another. They were watching the doll.

That plastic-and-rubber baby was equipped with flexible joints but featured no batteries—yet it moved. Turned onto its side. Lifted its head off the bar.

Everyone present had seen the impossible this night, and more than once. They had been inoculated against easy astonishment, and they at first regarded this development with more curiosity than fear or wonder.

If the two dogs had not continued to growl low in their throats and bare their teeth, some in the tavern might have looked away, less concerned about this strangeness than about the unknown leviathan plying the currents of the night above Black Lake.

Then the doll stopped crying and levered itself into a sitting position, its legs hanging over the edge of the bar, its arms at its sides. The eyes opened. The head turned.

Injection-molded, machine-made, glued and stitched and painted, this minikin in pink pedal pushers and yellow T-shirt was blind, of course, yet its eyes moved left and right and left again, surveying the people gathered in the tavern as though it could see them with perfect clarity.

In a childlike voice, it said, "Hungry. Eat."

Logic wasn't taxed by the argument that those two words would have been included in the vocabulary on the toy's voice chip.

Yet when the doll spoke, those onlookers standing nearest to it backed away.

Molly moved closer to Neil.

"Hungry. Eat," the doll repeated.

The mouth was hinged at the corners. When the doll spoke, its lips moved, revealing a small pink tongue.

Still surveying the tavern, the minikin cycled through some of the contents of its phrase bank: "I love you . . . baby's sleepy . . . nighty-night . . . my tummy hurts . . . diaper wet . . . Mommy, sing for baby . . .

baby likes your song . . . I will be good, Mommy . . . I'm hungry . . . baby needs pudding . . . yum-yum, all gone . . ."

The doll fell silent. Tipping its head back, it gazed at the ceiling, as if it felt the behemoth passing in the rainy night.

Indeed, something in the doll's attitude—the cock of its head, the slight forward lean of its body, the unnerving intensity of its glass eyes— gave rise in Molly to the thought that it was not merely aware of the leviathan above but was also in *communion* with it.

Lowering its head, shifting its gaze to those in the tavern once more, the doll said, "Diaper . . . diaper . . . diaper." Then it dropped the second syllable: "Di . . . di . . . di. . . ."

Someone said, "Shut the damn thing up," and someone else said, "Wait, let's see."

"Sing . . . sing . . . sing," said the doll, then shortened the word to just the suffix, ". . . ing . . . ing . . . ing." A pause. Then the combined form: "Dying . . . dying . . . dying . . ."

Looking around, Molly saw faces as pale as her own must be.

Lee Ling watched, one fist to her mouth, biting on her knuckles, and her husband, Norman, stood with his shotgun cradled across his arm, as if he wished he could do something with it.

The doll declared, "Dying hurts," and although it had no source of power to facilitate such animation, it raised its right hand to its mouth, as if in imitation of Lee Ling.

The articulated shoulder and elbow joints might have allowed the minikin's arm to bend as it did. Its molded rubber hands were not jointed, however, and should not have been able to commit the self-mutilation that followed.

Reaching between its hinged lips, the doll pinched its pink vinyl tongue and tore it out.

"Dying hurts."

Up went the left hand, which clawed at the left socket, pried out the semispherical eye, and dropped it on the bar, where it bounced, blue and blinkless, along the mahogany, and spent its final energy in a short-lived blind spin.

"All your babies," the doll said, in a cracked cadence that resulted from cobbling words together from various phrases on its voice chip, out of context, "all your babies will die."

27

"ALL YOUR BABIES WILL DIE."

On the repetition of that threat, Molly looked toward the children gathered at the far side of the room. All were on their feet, craning their necks. She wished that they could be spared this psychological warfare, if that was in fact the purpose of the puppeteer behind this bizarre performance.

The doll sat one-eyed, working a finger of its right hand in the empty socket in the manner of a swimmer trying to drain a water block in an ear.

If wet gray wormlike forms had burst in frenzied wriggling from the gouged socket, Molly would not have been surprised.

"All your babies will die."

The weight of those five words, seemingly a promise of human extinction, pressed as heavily on her as the maximum density of the hovering mystery above Black Lake that, with the rhythmic throb of its engines or its heart, compressed her lungs, oppressed her spirit.

The doll's right hand rose to the right socket, tore loose the second orb. Always sightless since the day of manufacture, it had now double-blinded itself.

"All your babies, your babies, your babies will die."

His choking rage expressed in a throttled curse, Norman Ling stepped to the bar, raising his shotgun.

"Norman, God's sake, no shooting here!" warned Russell Tewkes, the tavern owner.

As the eye fell from the rubbery hand, the sorcery enlivening the figure seemed to subside in power or even to vacate it entirely. The doll sagged, slumped backward on the bar, and lay still, its eyeless gaze turned toward the ceiling, the night, and the gods of the storm.

Pale with fear, hard-faced with anger, Tewkes used one cupped hand to sweep the torn vinyl tongue and the two glass eyes off the bar into a trash can.

As the taverner next reached for the doll, someone cried out, "Russ, behind you!"

Revealing that his nerves were trigger wires, Tewkes turned with snap-quick torque that belied the apparent ponderousness of his beer-barrel body, fisting his hands as if to defend, in classic barroom style, against any looming threat.

At first Molly didn't see what had inspired the warning.

Then Tewkes declared, "That's not going to be me. Like hell it is."

A mirror ran the length of the long bar. Tewkes stared at his reflection, in which the right side of his face was crushed.

In spite of his declaration, half convinced by the testimony of the mirror, Tewkes raised one hand to his face to reassure himself that a catastrophe had not already befallen him. In the reflection, his hand looked twisted, mangled.

Gasps of recognition and thin cries of horror arose from others in the tavern as they realized that Tewkes was not the only one among them whose reflection purported to be a preview of his mortal fate. In the mirror, they saw their friends, saw their neighbors, sought themselves—and in every instance were presented with a cadaver, each the victim of extreme violence.

The lower jaw had been torn from Tucker Madison's face. The deputy's upper teeth bit air.

In reflection, Vince Hoyt's Roman-emperor head lacked the top of its skull, and the phantom Vince pointed out of the mirror, at the real Vince, with an arm that terminated in bristling bone below the elbow.

Here stood a gnarled burnt mass that had once been a man, still smoking, grinning not with humor or menace, but because his teeth had been revealed in dental-chart explicitness when his lips had been seared away.

Molly knew that she shouldn't look for herself in this gruesome mural. If it was a glimpse of unavoidable destiny, it would foster despondency. If it was a lie, the image of her death-corrupted face and body would nevertheless fester in memory, diminishing her will to action, compromising her survival instinct.

Morbid curiosity may be integral to the human genome: In spite of her better judgment, she looked anyway.

In the premonitory mirror, in that *other* tavern of the standing dead, Molly Sloan did not exist. Where she should have been, there was only vacancy. Behind that vacancy stood the ripped and grisly reflection of the man stationed at her back on *this* side of the looking glass.

Earlier in the night, in her bedroom vanity mirror, where she had glimpsed a future version of that chamber jungled with vines and mold and fungus, she had seen her reflection; she had not appeared therein as a corpse or in any way distorted, but entirely as she looked in reality.

Now, with dread, she sought Neil's reflection. When she found that he also had no place in that back-bar panorama of animated cadavers, she didn't know whether she should be relieved by their lack of representation or should assume that it meant their fate involved something worse than the decapitation, amputation, and mutilation visited upon the others.

She glanced at him beside her, in the flesh. Their eyes met, and she knew that he had recognized the absence of their reflections and, like her, was confused about the meaning of it.

The lights failed. Absolute darkness flourished.

This time, no doubt, the loss of power would be permanent.

Prepared for this eventuality, eight, then ten, then perhaps twenty of the gathered citizens switched on flashlights. Sabers of light slashed the darkness.

Many of the beams found the mirror, perhaps evidence of a collective fear that the grotesque Others on the far side of the silvered glass had in the blackness stepped through to this world. The dazzle made it impossible to see the current reflection.

Someone threw a beer bottle. The long mirror shattered, and the fragments rang to the floor in a cascade of ominous notes.

Although the mirror was his property, and though it broke around his feet in a surf of dangerous shards, Russell Tewkes didn't object.

In the sweep and clash of flashlight beams, in the flares from falling silvered fragments, Molly noticed something that strummed yet another arpeggio of terror from her taut nerves.

The eyeless, tongueless doll had a moment ago been recumbent on the bar. In the brief but total blackness, it had disappeared.

28

IN ANTICIPATION OF THE LOSS OF POWER, GROUPS OF candles had been placed on all the tables as well as at various points along the bar. Matches flared, wicks caught flame, and flashlights were extinguished as warm golden light shimmered across faces pale and dark, leafed the mahogany walls, and throbbed in nimbuses across the ceiling.

With the welcome return of light, a memory flared, and for a moment Molly stood transfixed in consideration of it.

Neil said something to her, but she was more in the recent past than in the present, crouching in the janitorial closet, watching the self-repairing fungus knit shut its surface membrane. And listening to Derek Sawtelle . . .

She surveyed the nervous crowd for the professor.

When Neil put a hand on her shoulder and gently shook her to get her attention, she said, "What the hell's going on? What's the truth here, or is there any truth at all?"

She saw Derek across the room, he was staring at her—and smiling as though he knew what she must be thinking. Then he turned from her and spoke to one of his companions.

"Come on," she said to Neil, and led him toward Derek.

With only a few exceptions, the occupants of the tavern were on their feet, milling around, sharing reactions and reassurances, too shaken to sit down.

More of the dogs were afoot, as well, following their noses on circuitous paths. Perhaps they were still enchanted by the layers of old food and drink stains on the floor, but Molly wondered if they might not be searching for the vanished doll.

When she reached Derek, he was pouring gin from a bottle into a glass of half-melted ice and slices of lime. He turned to her as though he had been monitoring her with a third eye in the back of his head.

"Molly, Neil, dear friends, I assume that bit of Grand Guignol theater has convinced you that Bacchus and Dionysus are the only gods worth worshiping. Let's pray that Russell's stockroom is filled with enough cases to keep us well oiled through the final scene of the final act."

"Cut the bullshit, Derek," she said. "You're not as drunk as you pretend to be. Or if you are, you still have enough of your wits about you to play your role in this."

"My role?" He looked around, feigning bewilderment. "Are there cameras turning?"

"You know what I mean."

"No, I'm afraid I don't. And I doubt very much that you yourself know what you mean."

He had scored a direct hit. She didn't know what was happening here; however, she was confident that it was more complex than she had thought, and she smelled deception.

She said, "In the janitorial closet, when we were watching that damn thing repair its wound . . . I didn't tumble to it at the time, but you quoted Eliot to me."

A shadow passed through his eyes, a shadow and a glimmer, like the rutilant scales of something swimming just below the surface of murky water. This glimpse, whatever it was, whatever it meant, was not something you would see in the eyes of a friend.

"Eliot who?" he asked.

"Don't play games. T. S. Eliot."

"Never cared much for old T. S. I prefer novelists, as you know, particularly the macho type. T. S. is too much of a gentleman for me, not a line of bullying in his whole body of work."

"You said to me, 'All our knowledge brings us nearer to our ignorance.' "

"Did I really?" he asked. If there wasn't mockery in his voice, it brimmed in his eyes.

"It didn't entirely flow out of what you said before it," she remembered, "but I attributed any incoherence to the gin, and didn't immediately recognize the quote."

"I wasn't necessarily quoting, dear lady. Perhaps I am from time to time capable of saying something wise all of my own."

She wouldn't let him slip out of it as easily as that. "The following line in Eliot is 'All our ignorance brings us nearer to death.' "

"Well, that certainly resonates with the situation."

"Harry Corrigan, my father, you—all quoting Eliot. How are you connected with them? What's going on here?"

Derek's smug, sardonic grin was identical to Render's. "Neil, your lovely wife seems to have cast her lot with conspiracy nuts—the black-helicopter crowd."

"You spoke those words," Neil confirmed. "I remember."

"Be careful, Neil. Paranoia can be contagious. You better grab your own bottle of gin and inoculate yourself."

"If you think someone's out to get you, and someone *is* out to get you," Molly said, "it's not paranoia. It's reality."

Pointing at the ceiling, indicating the leviathan that they could sense without seeing, feel without hearing, Derek said "*That* is reality, Molly, hanging over all our heads. All of us dead, a whole world dead, and no escaping it, nothing to be settled except the hour when the ax falls on the last of us."

She saw in Derek Sawtelle no fear, no despair, not even the sweet melancholy that he had touted as the ideal retreat from sharper emotions. Instead, in his suddenly feverish eyes and in the points of his Cheshire-Cat smile, she saw triumph, which made no sense at all, but which was apparent nonetheless and unmistakable.

"Now, dear Molly, stop thrashing about for meaning in silly conspiracy theories, and grab what pleasure can be had. The drinks are on the house."

Frustrated, confused about so much but not about Derek's barely veiled hostility and lies, Molly turned away from him. She pushed a few steps through the milling crowd before she realized that she didn't know where to go or what to do next.

She seemed to have no option but to wait for death and embrace it when it came.

29

NEIL TOOK HER BY THE ARM AND LED HER TO AN empty booth along the north wall of the tavern.

She refused to sit. "We're running out of time."

"I hear the clock."

"We've got to do something, get ready."

"All right. But what? How?"

She said, "Maybe the bank is the best idea. Secure the place. Hunker down. At least go out fighting."

"Then we'll go there now, with the rest of them."

"That's just it. The rest of them. They were all dead . . . in the mirror. Do they die at the bank? Is that where they get . . . torn apart like that?"

She shook her head. She looked around the tavern. She could see the barely checked panic in people who, minutes ago, had been talking strategy, tactics, and the possibility of survival. Now they believed the mirror. They expected to die horribly, and soon.

"I'm scared," she said. "I've been handling this pretty well so far . . . but I'm starting to lose it."

Neil put his arms around her. He always knew when to say nothing.

Molly trembled against him. She listened to his heart. Steady Neil.

When her heart had begun to time itself to his slower beat, he guided her into the booth and sat across from her.

This table had no candles, and she was grateful for the shadows. She didn't want anyone but Neil to see her tears. She prided herself on her toughness, her resilience.

Maybe honest pride didn't matter anymore, but for reasons she couldn't put into words, she thought it mattered more than ever.

Neil said, "Before we can figure out what to do, maybe we've got to ask ourselves what we *know.*"

"Less and less."

With irony, he repeated the Eliot quote: " 'All our knowledge brings us nearer to our ignorance.' "

The booth benches featured open space under the seats. Molly tucked her legs back—and thought of the missing doll.

In the brief darkness between the loss of public power and the lighting of the candles, the doll could have crawled into this booth, under her seat. Eyeless but all-seeing. Tongueless mouth filled with the breathless silence of a stalking predator.

She resisted the urge to scramble out of the booth and search under it with a flashlight. To do so would be to succumb to the most childish of fears, after which she would find it more difficult to summon the courage to face the real and more serious terrors that surely were coming.

It was just a doll. And if she should feel a small hand on her ankle, it would be only the hand of a doll, no matter how demonically animated, just the hand of a doll.

She wiped at her damp cheeks. "Are they really taking our world from us?"

"The evidence says so."

"Or is that just the way we're reading the evidence?"

"I don't see how else to interpret it."

"Neither do I. That thing in the janitor's closet . . ." She shuddered.

She could still feel the airborne titan overhead, and now when she turned her attention to the ceiling, she could sense the vessel's movement, too, as it progressed southward through the storm. She seemed to be increasingly sensitized to it.

"But fast-track terraforming is Derek's theory," she said, "and I don't trust him."

"What is it with Derek?" Neil asked. "Why did he act like that with you?"

"I don't know."

"You said maybe Render wasn't *only* Render."

"And I still don't know what I mean by that."

"Is Derek really Derek but not *only* Derek?"

"For sure, there's *something* wrong with him."

Rubbing the nape of his neck with one hand, he said, "I'm back to the alien-parasite movies."

"Then why haven't they burrowed into all of us? Why aren't we all controlled?"

"Maybe we will be soon."

She shook her head. "Life isn't science fiction."

"Submarines, nuclear weapons, television, computers, satellite communications, organ transplants—it was all the stuff of science fiction before it was reality. And the biggest sci-fi theme of all is alien contact."

"But with the power to change a world—why the psychological warfare? They could just crush us like ants, which they seem to be doing anyway, in the cities if not here."

"You mean the doll, the mirror."

"And Harry Corrigan, and this T. S. Eliot weirdness. If they can replace our entire environment with theirs, scour away human civilization in days or weeks, eradicate it more efficiently than a seven-continent nuclear war, they wouldn't bother to screw with our minds like this."

Remembering the doll as it had stared at the ceiling just before it mutilated itself, Molly glanced up again and wondered if increased sensitivity to the storm-sailing leviathan would open her mind to its influence. Perhaps, eventually robbed of her free will, she would mimic the doll and gouge out her eyes.

"We aren't already dead because they have some sort of use for us," she suddenly realized.

"What use?"

"I can imagine several. . . ."

"So can I," he said.

"None of them good."

"Remember the movie *The Matrix*?"

"Forget movies. That's the way they want us to think, that's how we're being *guided* to think. But this is nothing like any movie ever made."

She watched Vince Hoyt talking animatedly to a man she didn't know. Unwanted, into her mind came an image from the mirror: the coach with the top of his skull gone.

"Maybe they don't have a use for all of us," she said, "but certainly for some of us. We've been targeted, not for death but for manipulation. That stuff with the doll and the bar mirror—everyone saw it, but maybe it was only meant to influence you and me."

"Maybe only you," he said. "Derek came to you. Render came to you. Harry Corrigan came to you. None of them to me."

Molly rebelled at the thought that their individual destinies might differ radically, and that therefore their paths must sooner or later diverge. "I don't know what it means, but it means *something* that we were the only ones not reflected in that mirror."

"Not the only ones," he corrected. "The kids weren't there, either."

The six children now stood together near the booth in which they had previously been seated. If earlier they had exhibited some spirit of adventure, it had given way entirely to fear. They appeared to be ready to bolt at the slightest provocation.

Acting on instinct and with natural purpose, the dogs gravitated where they were needed most. While six canines still roamed the room, three—a golden retriever, a German shepherd, and a black-and-tan mutt with the build of a boxer but with the shaggy face of a Scottish terrier—had gathered around the children to soothe troubled hearts as dogs have always done, and no doubt to defend their young charges against any threat.

Watching the kids and the dogs, Molly again felt enlightenment teasing her from just beyond the open fields of conscious thought, a shapeless shape moving in the shadowy woods of the subconscious, both enticing and disturbing.

"Besides the children," she asked Neil, "who else didn't cast a reflection in the mirror?"

"I don't know. It all happened so fast, there wasn't time for a head count. Maybe a couple others. Or maybe just the eight of us—you, me, the kids."

The soundless throbbing in the bones, the blood, the lymph, pulses sympathetic to the rhythms of the magnetic engines powering the behemoth overhead, began to subside.

She sensed the great weight and the malevolent shadow passing off them as the vast ship moved south, and to avoid despondency, she dared not think about the hordes of inhuman creatures that must be aboard it and the cruel irresistible power it represented.

Throughout the tavern, candle flames swelled brighter, as if their light had been oppressed in much the way that the tides of the seas are managed by the phases of the moon.

Molly's mind seemed to function more quickly and clearly, too. She perceived purpose where before she had seen nothing but mists of confusion.

Working it out step by step, she said to Neil, "What is Render, my father?"

"What do you mean?"

"What one word defines the essence of him?"

"*Psychopath,*" Neil said.

"That's a distraction from the truth."

"*Murderer,*" he said.

"More specifically?"

"Murderer . . . of children."

As Neil spoke, a dog came to their table—the German shepherd that had stood with the group of kids. It stared intently at Molly.

She sat up straighter in the booth as her immediate future, previously all murk and mystery, began to clarify. "Yes—Render's a child murderer. And what am I?"

"To me—everything," he said. "To the world—a writer."

"I love you," she said, "and what we've had together. It doesn't get better. But if this is the last night of the world, if I've no more living left to define myself, then I'm defined forever by the best and worst things I've ever done."

Frowning, Neil followed half a step behind in her series of conclusions. "The best . . . you saved the lives of those school kids."

"He murders children. Once . . . I saved a few."

With an anxious whine, the German shepherd drew her attention.

She had thought that the dog wandered to their booth with no more purpose than to explore that section of the floor and to cadge tidbits from them if they had any food to share.

Its gaze was unusually intense, however, and more than intense: strange, compelling.

She considered how the dogs, en masse, had reacted to her when she had first arrived in the tavern. They had seemed to be watching her surreptitiously ever since.

"Neil, we've been thinking pretty much only about ourselves, how to survive. That leaves us with nothing to do but find a hidey-hole, hunker down, and wait."

He understood: "You've never lived that way—passive, just waiting for what's next."

"Neither have you. There are children tonight, in this chaos, who aren't being given the shelter and protection they need, they deserve." She was relieved to have a purpose, to be suddenly filled with the urgency of meaningful commitment.

"And if we can't save them?" Neil wondered.

Ears pricked, head cocked, the dog turned to Neil.

"Maybe no one can save anyone anymore," Neil continued, "not with the whole world lost."

The dog whined at him as it had whined at Molly.

Intrigued by the shepherd's attitude and behavior, she wondered if something extraordinary might be happening; but then the dog padded away, weaving through the crowd, soon out of sight.

"If we can't save them," she said, "then we'll try to spare them from what pain and terror we can. We've got to put ourselves between them and whatever's coming."

He glanced at the six children.

Molly said, "I don't mean them. Their parents are here, and the group is big enough to protect them about as well as anyone can be protected in these circumstances. But how many kids are out there in town? Not teenagers. I mean, younger kids, small and vulnerable. One hundred? Two hundred?"

"Maybe that many. Maybe even more."

"How many of them have parents who are dealing with this the way Derek and his crowd are dealing with it—getting drunk and worse, leaving their kids afraid and undefended?"

"But we don't know most of the people in town," Neil said. "There are—what?—maybe four hundred or even five hundred houses, and we don't know which families have kids. It'll take hours and hours, maybe a full day, for just the two of us to go door-to-door. We don't have that much time left."

"All right. So maybe we can get a few of these people to help us," Molly said.

Neil looked doubtful. "They've got their own agendas."

Weaving among the tables and the milling residents of Black Lake, the German shepherd returned. In its mouth, the dog held a red rose, which it brought to Molly.

She couldn't imagine where it had found a rose in the tavern. She hadn't noticed any floral arrangements.

The dog seemed to want her to take the flower.

"You've got a suitor," Neil said.

Inevitably, she thought of her father murdering the boy in the rose garden. His voice snaked through her memory in sinuous coils of words: *I buried his little disposable camera at the foot of a rosebush. It was the Cardinal Mindszenty rose, so named because of its glorious robe-red color.*

At first inclined to suspect a connection between Render and the dog, Molly hesitated to accept the rose.

Then she looked into the shepherd's eyes and saw what is to be seen in every dog's eyes if it has not been broken by a cruel master: trust, strength without arrogance, a desire to give and receive affection—and an honesty so pure that deception, if contemplated, cannot be perpetrated.

The shepherd wagged its tail.

Molly pinched the stem of the rose, and the animal unlocked its teeth to surrender the fragrant bloom.

As she took the flower, Molly saw evidence of a thorn prick, a spot of blood on the dog's tongue.

She thought at once of Render—although not as he had appeared this night, rather as he had raged maniacally in that third-grade classroom twenty years previously—and not of Michael Render only or even primarily, but also of one of his victims, a girl named Rebecca Rose, with shaggy blond hair and blue eyes, who died that afternoon in Molly's arms.

Rebecca Rose. A shy girl with a faint lisp. Her last words, whispered in delirium, apparently a meaningless delusion: *Molly . . . there's a dog. So pretty . . . how he shines.*

Now the shepherd watched Molly. In his eyes were mysteries to rival any others in this momentous night of enigmas, puzzles, and perplexities.

On a rose thorn, his blood.

Rose of forgetfulness, brought to her by the dog, became the Rose of memory, cut down so young.

By the cock of his head, the shepherd seemed to question whether Molly Sloan—sensible Molly, she with the strong mainspring wound tight, she who always lived less in the moment than in the future, she who strived toward meticulously planned goals and was prudent in all things except her writing, she who avoided drama in her life but poured it out upon the page—could understand the intentions of a flower-bearing Sphinx, this rebus on four paws, which wanted so urgently to be properly read and understood.

The rose trembled in her hand, and a loose petal fell, like a sanguinary drop, to the tabletop.

And the dog waited. And the dog watched. And the dog smiled.

In a night of dark wonder and extraordinary events, this was a moment no less important but of a different character from all that had come before it.

Her heart raced. Her thoughts quickened, too, perhaps eventually toward a breathtaking revelation, but first through blind alleys of dead-end speculation.

She put down the rose. She reached to the dog. He licked her hand.

"What?" Neil said, for he knew her almost well enough to read her thoughts.

In her mind, she walked the waters of a lucid pool and stepped ashore with an insight nearly clairvoyant in character: "The dog is going to lead us to any children who need help."

Neil regarded the dog, which turned its limpid eyes upon him as though its purpose could be read by anyone as easily as Molly had read it.

"Don't ask me how he knows what we need to do," Molly said. "But he knows, all right. I don't understand how he'll find them, but he will. By scent, by instinct, by some greater gift."

Neil stared at the dog. He stared at Molly.

"I know it sounds crazy," she said.

He looked at the long empty frame from which the bar mirror, peopled by the living dead, had shattered and fallen.

"Then it's the dog," he said. "After all, what do we have to lose?"

30

NAMED VIRGIL, ACCORDING TO THE LICENSE TAG ON his collar, the shepherd was young and trim, bright-eyed, affectionate, and eager to begin the work.

Engraved under the license number were the name and address of his owner: James Weck, on Pine Street.

A few inquiries among those in the tavern quickly established that Weck was not present. Apparently, Virgil had been loose in the night and had found his way here, alone.

Russell Tewkes, swigging deeply from a large mug of beer, having chosen to tie his fate to that of his best customers, the inebriates, mocked those who were getting ready to depart on missions to stock and fortify the bank building. When he realized that Neil and Molly were preparing to leave as well, he said, "Can't you face reality? There's nowhere to hide from this."

"We're not hiding," Molly assured him. Constrained by a sudden rush of paranoia, she decided not to tell him what their intentions were.

"When they get up here in the mountains, the aliens—they'll gut you like fish and leave you flopping in the street," Tewkes said.

Disturbed less by the tavernkeeper's prediction than by his demeanor, neither Molly nor Neil replied.

Tewkes had not couched his words as a warning but had spoken in an ugly, taunting tone of voice. He almost seemed to hope that this horrendous fate would befall them, that the idea of Neil and Molly disemboweled and writhing in agony perversely pleased him.

His merry-monk face had lost its humor, and *monk* could be used to describe it now only in reference to an angry ape, for it had a primitive cast, sly and stupidly calculating. His features were blotchy and red with barely throttled emotion. The Friar Tuck fringe of hair bristled in chaotic spikes, as if in a rage he had tried and failed to pull it out.

As they began to turn away from Tewkes, he lurched one step closer, slopping beer from his mug, and said, "You go out there, you better be careful of your tender parts. The red-eyed scavengers are creeping."

More Eliot from this most unlikely quoter of verse: *The red-eyed scavengers are creeping. . . .*

"Again," Neil said, for though he didn't share Molly's extensive knowledge of the poet, he recognized the incongruity of those words spoken by this individual.

When Molly turned to Tewkes again, she saw in his wrenched red face and in his feverish eyes—far hotter than reflected candlelight could explain—mockery, contempt, and hatred. The arteries in his temples swelled and throbbed. His nostrils flared. His clenched jaws worked back and forth as though in his rage he were grinding his teeth into powder.

She couldn't understand how such bitter emotion could have been seeded and made to flourish in the previously pleasant tavern owner *from one hour to the next.* More to the point, why should this enmity be focused with such intensity on her, when she hardly knew Russell Tewkes and had never done a thing to anger or indeed even annoy him?

Raising his mug, Tewkes swilled a mouthful of beer, held it briefly in his bloated cheeks, then spat it on the floor at her feet.

Neil started to move toward Tewkes, but Molly restrained him with a touch. Virgil growled, and she silenced him merely by the whispering of his name.

If Russell Tewkes was still to any degree the man he had once been, then beyond doubt, he was something else as well. Parasite or spotted fungus, or some other corruption, had found its way into his mind and heart.

The atmosphere inside the tavern had turned. She could not smell the change or taste it as she would have tasted airborne soot, could not see it, either, but she could feel it: an insistent abrasiveness. A darkness settled through the room, as well, not one related to the power failure, not one that any number of candles could relieve, but one akin to the dark matter of the universe, which physicists are unable to see but which they know exists by virtue of its ominous gravity.

She wanted to get out of here. Quickly.

Five of the children were with Deputy Tucker Madison's group, the fighters who intended to make a fortress of the bank. They would be leaving in moments.

The sixth, a girl of nine, had joined her parents among the fence-sitters. She nervously twisted her glossy blond hair between thumb and forefinger, and her lovely sapphire eyes were haunted by all the mangled ghosts that she had seen in the mirror.

She said her name was Cassie. She tried to smile when Molly complimented her on her hair, but the smile faltered.

Cassie's parents, especially her mother, reacted angrily to Molly's suggestion that the tavern was not safe and that they should accompany the others to the bank.

"What the hell do you know?" the mother demanded. "You don't know any more than we do. We're staying here until we know more, until we learn more. It's dry here, we've got candles. We've been safe here. Until the situation clarifies, there's no reason to move, it's *crazy* to move."

"Clarify the situation for yourself," Molly advised. "Go to the men's rest room. Inside the janitorial closet. Take a look at what's growing there."

"What're you talking about?" In spite of her question, the woman had no desire to listen. Clearly, Cassie's mother was frightened by the possibility that Molly might in fact have information that would force her to make a reasoned choice. "I'm not going in the men's room. What's wrong with you? Get away from us!"

Molly wanted to grab Cassie, take her with them by force, but that would lead to violence and delay, and would further terrify the girl.

As Russell Tewkes blustered toward them to take up the argument, Neil said, "Molly, let's get out of here."

Of the eight dogs in addition to Virgil, five were about to leave with the fighters. The other three gathered around Cassie. Two mutts and a golden retriever.

Molly read each of those three solemn gazes, and felt an uncanny connection with the animals, experienced a communication beyond any that could have been fashioned from words. She knew that they would guard the girl, would if necessary die to protect her.

Just as Render seemed to be Render but also someone else, just as Derek and Tewkes looked like themselves but acted like someone new, so the dogs at a glance appeared to be merely dogs but were something more. Unlike the murderer, the professor, and the tavern owner, however, the dogs were not agents of despair; quite the opposite.

With growing wonder that rivaled fear for possession of her heart, Molly touched each of the animals, smoothing the fur on their heads, and each in turn nuzzled her hand.

"Gentle hearts," she told them, "and courageous."

"What's going on here?" Russell Tewkes inquired, arriving in a reek of beer breath and sweat.

"We're leaving," Molly said, and turned away from him.

She and Neil had almost reached the front door when the rain stopped as abruptly as if a spigot had been shut off.

31

SPENT CATARACTS OF WATER DRAINED OFF STREETS
and out of gutters. New cataracts, of the blinding type, frustrated the eye
and deceived the mind.

The town had nearly vanished in fog. Thick curdled masses of mist
slid down from the higher ridges in a soft avalanche and also rose off the
swollen lake below.

For a moment, Molly held her breath for fear these clouds would
prove poisonous. But then she breathed, and lived.

Along the street, houses and other structures formed a geometry more
suggested than seen. The calligraphy of trees, deciduous and evergreen,
full of cursives and flourishes, was continuously erased only to be half revealed again by the lazily roiling mist.

To Molly, the sudden silence, following the long roar of the rain, had
all the drama of a roof-rattling thunderclap. Stepping out of the tavern
with Virgil, closely followed by Neil, she seemed to have gone deaf, a perception abetted by the muffling effect of the dense fog.

More than the cessation of the rain, more than the murk or the silence,
the arrival of dawn surprised her. A glance at her watch—which func-
tioned when out from under the oppressive influence of the mysterious
·leviathan—confirmed that daybreak should have arrived.

The descending light was deep purple, less like a brightening sunrise than like a fading dusk. This glow imparted to the fog a purplish tint with ribbony veins of gold.

In ordinary times, these royal colors would have been a majestic beginning to the day. In the current circumstances, however, the weird light and the cloaking mist augured chaos and violence.

The mist had no scent. The rain had left no smell behind.

One phase of the taking of the earth had ended.

A new and surely more terrifying phase had begun.

In every end is a beginning—and perhaps in this beginning, for her and Neil, would be the end of all things mortal. The last twist of the knife.

Visibility proved inconstant. Even when she stood still, one moment she could see only five feet, the next moment ten; never more than twenty; sometimes only as far as from eye to hand.

People poured out of the tavern, though many remained behind with their lubricants and illusions. Each took only a few steps before he became a ghostly form with the muffled voice of a mummy in its windings.

In this slowly churning, ever shifting purple opacity, a flashlight seemed useful. When Neil probed with his, however, the beam refracted strangely through the murk, revealing nothing and further confusing the eye.

Switching off the flash and pocketing it, he said, "Better to have both hands for the shotgun, anyway."

Molly had drawn her pistol as she'd come out of the tavern door. She felt no better armed than a blowgun primitive cast by some fluke of time onto a modern battlefield contested by armies with tanks and laser-guided missiles.

A ragtag group of the resistance fighters set off for the bank, on foot and closely marshaled. Their footsteps and then their voices quickly faded.

Another group, in a Chevy Suburban and a Ford pickup, drove away, into the lower reaches of town, toward Norman Ling's food market. Although they proceeded at a creep, they soon vanished into the throat of the fog; and a swallow later, their headlights dimmed, damped.

The roar of engines swiftly softened and, with distance, changed into a throaty grumble, as if beasts from the Jurassic period prowled swamps in the purple dimness far below.

She worried that the dog would race ahead of them, vanish in the earthbound clouds, but she hoped that he would obey her when she called him back. The fog might complicate their search, but no more than the pounding rain would have done.

"All right, Virgil," she said, "let's do the work."

The dog seemed to know what she meant, and he started forward at a pace they could match.

They walked the center of the street, their hoods thrown back, but still wearing their raincoats in case the storm returned.

They had not gone far when a forlorn voice called out of the mist: "Help me. Someone help me."

The dog stopped, ears pricked forward.

Molly scanned the gloom, seeking the source of the cry.

"Where?" Neil asked.

"I don't know."

Then the pleading came again, this time with a thin note of anguish: "Please. Someone please. Oh, God, please help me."

She recognized the voice. Ken Halleck: the postal clerk with the muttonchops and the wide smile.

With rifle and pitchfork, Ken and his seventeen-year-old son, Bobby, had been guarding the front door of the tavern.

On leaving that establishment, Molly had not realized that Ken and Bobby were missing. The end of the rain, the arrival of dawn, and the purple mist had fully commanded her attention.

"I hear someone," Halleck said, his voice shuddering with pain, with fear. "Please, don't leave me here alone, suffering like this. I'm so afraid."

Virgil deduced Halleck's location and advanced a few steps in that direction before halting. His head lowered and his hackles rose. He growled softly, more to warn his companions than to challenge whatever menace he detected in the dismalness ahead.

Molly hesitated, but when Halleck cried out again, this time in a racked voice even more pitiable than before, she could not turn away from him, even if he might be—as the dog's reaction seemed to suggest— bait in a trap.

"Careful," Neil whispered, moving with her, at her side, into the livid mist, leaving the wary dog behind them.

Foreboding, forbidding, the odorless miasma closed around them, cloyed, so thick it seemed to muffle even the beat of her heart in her own ears. But in a few steps it began to draw away, like layer upon layer of opening curtains.

Through lifting veils, Molly saw an object in the street, dark against the darker blacktop. In another step she realized that it was the severed head of Ken Halleck.

In the bodiless head, the eyes opened, filled with impossible life, and with unspeakable misery.

The lips moved, the mouth cracked, and words came forth: "Do you know where Bobby is, my Bobby, my son?"

32

THE HUMAN IMAGINATION MAY BE THE MOST ELAS-
tic thing in the universe, stretching to encompass the millions of hopes
and dreams that in centuries of relentless struggle built modern civilization, to entertain the endless doubts that hamper every human enter-
prise, and to conceive the vast menagerie of boogeymen that trouble
every human heart.

Yet there had been discoveries and sights in these momentous hours
that Molly could not have imagined and with which her reason wrestled
and lost. Not the least was this severed and yet apparently living head, although it had been foreshadowed by the brainless walking corpse of
Harry Corrigan and by the self-mutilating doll.

For a moment, Ken Halleck's eyes transfixed her. Pathetic. Patho-
formic. Demonic.

The aliens had introduced on Earth some malevolent energy that did
not differentiate between vegetable and animal, between organic and in-
organic, between the animate and the inanimate. It thrived equally in the
living and in the dead, and in what had never lived at all.

In Ken's voice now, a tremor of anguish, of grief: "Where is my
Bobby? What have they done to him? I want to see my boy."

The mind not only reeled but rebelled, and not only rebelled but retreated to denial, desperate to refute this abomination no matter how vividly the senses confirmed it.

You might imagine surviving in an environment transformed to match that of a world on the far end of the galaxy, dressed with strange malignant plants, populated by a Sabbat broth of repulsive and vicious animals. You might hope for a hospitable corner in some extreme latitude, where you could live out your days in mousehole secrecy, with simple food and the pleasures of the timid.

But Molly couldn't imagine *wanting* to survive in a madhouse world where the dead walked, severed heads conversed, dolls made threats, and every horror of the elastic human imagination might be encountered—and worse. Such a place could offer no moment of peace, no chance of happiness.

Here, now, she might have given up the hope of survival, except that she would be left with two options: wait until some nightmare creature found her and tore her to pieces—or kill herself. Either course counted as self-destruction, however, and suicide was not permissible in her philosophy or her faith.

Besides, the children had to be found. What might happen after she had gathered them together under her inadequate protection was something she chose not to dwell upon.

"I love my boy, my Bobby," said Halleck's head, "where is my Bobby?"

Neil raised the shotgun, but Molly stayed him with a touch.

"It isn't Ken," she said. "There's no need to put him out of his misery. Ken's dead and gone."

"I just want to stop the damn thing," he said angrily. "Just shut it up."

"You won't. It'll take the blast and keep on talking. And that'll be even worse."

Besides, she believed they should conserve their ammunition. Although a few rounds from a 12-gauge had not deterred whatever had come after Harry Corrigan in his house, there might be adversaries in the hours ahead that would be vulnerable to a well-placed punch of buck-shot.

Retreating, they couldn't at once find Virgil in the murk. He barked softly, sought them out, and led them again on the right path.

Before they had gone a dozen steps, a metallic rattle-and-clank challenged the muffling mastery of the mist. They approached the racket cautiously.

This time the parting fog revealed a man in the street, near the curb, on his knees, in the lurid light of this strange dawn. He knelt at an opening to a storm drain, his back to them, hunched forward, attempting to pry the heavy steel grate out of its niche in the pavement.

Although the rain had stopped, runoff still fed the gutters. Dirty water, thickened by a jetsam of leaves and litter, surged over his hands.

A low growl from Virgil counseled caution again.

Molly and Neil stopped, said nothing, waited for the man to sense their presence.

His gibbous posture, the intensity of his focus, the curious nature of the task to which he was committed—these things brought to Molly's mind disturbing fairy tales of hateful trolls indulging unholy hungers.

With the hard scrape of metal on blacktop, the grate came loose. The troll slid it aside.

He raised his head, but had no head. He looked over his shoulder at Molly and Neil, but even if he knew they were behind him, he could not see them, because he was Ichabod Crane's nemesis, minus a horse.

The knock-knock-knock of Molly's heart might also have been the fist of madness rapping on the door of her mind.

In this unearthly purplescent morning and sky-shrouding fog, where the laws of nature seemed to have dissolved entirely in some instances and to have been remade in others, Molly half expected that day would not follow dawn. Sunset might swiftly succeed sunrise, without the intervening hope of light, and the next night would then be endless, moonless, starless, and filled with the furtive sounds of a thousand creeping deaths.

The urge to shoot the headless atrocity proved difficult for both Molly and Neil to resist, but if the guillotining blade had not convinced the thing that it was dead, a 9-mm round through the heart wouldn't persuade it to lie down and expire.

The decapitated body of Ken Halleck—manipulated by a parasite puppeteer or by some extraterrestrial power that, based on effect, might as well have been sheer sorcery—lowered itself through the open hole into the storm drain. It dropped out of sight, landing with a splash below.

For an instant the night was still except for the gurgle from the gutters and the drip-drip-drip of sodden trees.

Then Molly heard the sloshing and the hollow thumping of the headless wonder as it slogged through deep water, under the streets of Black Lake, with unimaginable intent. Perhaps it would find a ledge in the storm drain, lie down above the rushing torrents, and offer its flesh as the spore bed for a colony of fungi or another life form of more sinister purpose.

PART FIVE

"We are born with the dead:
See, they return and bring us with them."

T.S. Eliot, *Little Gidding*

33

WAGLESS, ALL BUSINESS, AND AS QUICK AS THE FOG allowed, Virgil led them to a residence on La Cresta Avenue, which was neither near the crest of the mountain nor an avenue, but halfway between the lake and the ridge line, a two-lane street not appreciably different from all the others in town.

The single-story house, in the Craftsman style, looked cozy and welcoming, in spite of the fact that the fierce rain had stripped all the leaves from the trumpet vines that climbed its trellises and had battered beds of cyclamens into red- and purple-petaled ruin.

As they approached the front porch along handsome flagstones, Neil suddenly stepped off the walkway, squished three steps across the soggy lawn, and said, "Look at this."

The object of his interest was a stone pine, and not the tree itself so much as what clustered on its fissured bark. Squinting in the bruised light, Molly saw patches of a blackish thallus, flecked with green, growing on the trunk in crustlike forms.

She'd seen lichen similar to this, although no earthly lichen featured luminous elements to equal these. Every emerald-green fleck was softly radiant; the glow pulsed in what she suspected might be a sympathetic rhythm that matched the long, slow throbs of the engines powering the airborne leviathan that had only recently passed over them.

Along the perimeter of every thallus, the aggressive lichen grew at a visible rate, outward in all directions, as if she were watching time-lapse photography. During the minute that she and Neil studied it, the crust advanced almost half an inch.

At this rate, the trunk and every branch would be covered in this scaly scab in only a few hours.

Lichen were themselves complex symbiotic organisms composed of a fungus in union with an alga. They frequently thrived without damage to the host tree.

In this instance, Molly suspected that the stone pine would not survive the encrustation. Either it would perish and fall, hollowed out by a species of rot as alien as the organism colonizing its bark, or it would be invaded, mutated, and remade into the genetic image of a plant from another world.

The radiant emerald pulse that stippled the blackish thallus had a jewel-bright gleam. In different circumstances, the tree might have appeared to be inlaid with a wealth of precious gems, glittering and magical.

No aura of fairyland wonder surrounded the pine, however. Quite the opposite: In spite of its bejeweled aspect, and though the lichen infestation had only recently begun, the tree appeared cancer-ridden, mottled with malignancies.

Virgil had not approached the pine, but had remained on the flagstone walkway, watchful and tense.

Molly shared the dog's wariness. She didn't touch the lichen, fearing that it might transfer to her fingertip and prove able to colonize human skin as readily as it did tree bark.

On the other side of the walkway stood a matching pine, and from a distance, even in this half-light, she could see the luminous lichen thriving on that specimen.

Virgil led them up the porch steps to the front door.

No candles, oil lamps, or other emergency lighting shone inside. The windows were dark except for dim reflections of the purple glow that suffused the lazily stirring mist.

If they entered without knocking, they were inviting gunfire.

On the other hand, if children inside were already in any kind of danger—from Michael Render or from something even less human—Molly and Neil might raise the level of jeopardy by announcing themselves.

Their dilemma was resolved, in part, when the front-door lock clicked and disengaged.

Reflexively, they stepped back and to the side, making less obvious targets of themselves.

Virgil stood his ground.

The door opened in a swift, inward sweep. Although only the influx of fog-filtered morning sunshine illuminated the small foyer, visibility was sufficient for Molly to discern that the space was deserted, as though they were being welcomed by a ghost.

The hallway beyond the foyer remained as dark as a snake hole.

To leave both of Neil's hands free for the shotgun, Molly produced her flashlight.

Stout-hearted, Virgil boldly entered in advance of the light.

From the porch, with the flash, Molly probed past the foyer. A narrow hall table, two vases atop it. A door at the far end. She saw no immediate threat.

Although all of the dogs had exhibited extraordinary behavior this night, though Virgil in particular had astonished with the rose and with his apparent understanding of Molly's mission, entering a stranger's house, uninvited and unannounced, required nerve and full trust in the animal's reliability. For a moment, she couldn't summon either, and Neil hesitated, too.

In response to their reluctance, Virgil turned his head and regarded them with a golden gaze. To Molly, this seemed not to be the usual eyeshine of animals in the dark, but a phenomenon unique to this night, not simple light refraction, not bioluminescence, but something of a wondrous character: nimbuses pooled in sockets, signifying sanctification.

Almost as if enchanted, spell-struck and spell-caught, by the dog's golden stare, Molly shed her reservations. Her mouth was dry with doubt, but she worked up spit, and spat. She stepped across the threshold, entered the house.

Neil followed her, and when they both stood in the foyer, the front door closed behind them with a softness more disturbing than a slam. No draft had pulled it shut.

Fear abided with Molly, and fed on itself, and grew, but she did not turn back to wrench open the door. She knew that it wanted her to flee— whatever *it* might be. If she retreated, *she* would choose the moment of retreat and would not allow it to be chosen for her.

Virgil sniffed at closed doors and open archways to the left and right of the central hall.

The dog had no suspicion of the foyer closet. Molly opened that door anyway, and Neil probed the hanging coats with the barrel of the shotgun.

Although Virgil showed no interest in the study, where the drapes were drawn and the blackness was absolute, Molly scanned that chamber with the flashlight. Shadows stretched and flexed, but they were merely the shadows of furniture, granted movement by the moving beam.

At the living-room archway, the shepherd made a thin sound of canine anxiety.

Amethystine light, from the dusky morning, pressed against the mullioned windows, revealing nothing, but Molly knew what troubled the dog, for she heard it, too: a whispery sound, a rustle and susurration.

The flashlight winked and flared off the glass in picture frames. Off ceramic lamps. Off a vase, a cut-crystal bowl, a mirror above the fireplace. Off a dead TV screen.

With the 12-gauge, Neil followed the beam, but he found nothing to shoot.

The rustling grew louder and seemed to come from all sides.

Ears pricked, tail lowered, the dog turned in a circle.

"The walls," Neil said, and with the flashlight, Molly found him with one ear to the plaster.

She and Neil flanked the archway, and she moved to the wall on her side of that opening. She leaned close, closer.

To a more analytic ear, the sound was not a rustle, exactly, but a fluttering, thrumming, as if a flock of birds or a horde of flying insects were frenziedly beating wings against the back side of the lath and plaster.

34

NOW IN THE WALLS OF THE HALLWAY AND, ON FUR-
ther exploration, in the walls of the dining room, and perhaps in the ceiling as well, the numberless wings, whether feathered or membranous,
beat against confinement and against one another.

Molly angled the flashlight at grille-covered heating vents high in the
walls, but nothing fluttered at the slots between the louvers, trying to get
out. The unknown horde had not yet migrated from the walls into the
ductwork of the heating system.

This was not a house anymore, but an incubator, a nidus for something more repellent and certainly more dangerous than spiders or cockroaches. She did not want to be in this house when the agitated legions
found a way out of their wood-and-plaster prison.

Stalwart Virgil, spooked by the denizens of the walls but not inclined
to bolt, led Molly and Neil to the end of the hall. A closed door opened,
as had the one at the front of the house, under the influence of an invisible hand.

A kitchen lay beyond, barely brightened by the purple morning. With
pistol and flashlight, Molly followed the dog through the doorway, even
more cautious than she had been when entering the house—but then
rushed forward, with Neil close at her heels, when she heard the fearful
cries of children.

A boy of nine or ten stood by the kitchen table. Virgil had startled him, and he held a broom as if he were at home plate, ready to take a swing. He had only this pathetic weapon to do battle with what might swarm from the walls—beetles or bats, or beasts from the far end of the galaxy.

On the table sat a girl of about six, her legs drawn under her, as though she were afraid that jittering multitudes would suddenly surge out of cracks in the baseboard and across the floor. Thirty inches of altitude amounted to the only safety that she could find.

"Who're you?" the boy demanded, trying to sound strong, but unable to keep his voice from cracking.

"I'm Molly. This is Neil. We—"

"*What* are you?" he demanded, for he knew all the movies, too, and suspected body snatchers, parasites.

"We're just what we seem to be," Neil said. "We live north of town, off the ridge road."

"We knew you were in trouble," Molly said. "We've come to help you."

"How?" the boy asked suspiciously. "How could you know?"

"The dog," she said. "He led us here."

"We knew there would be kids alone, in trouble. Virgil is finding them for us," Neil explained. "We don't know why. We don't know how."

Perhaps the directness of their answers helped reassure the boy. Or maybe he was convinced solely by Virgil's new demeanor: the friendly cock of the shepherd's furry head, his panting tongue, his swishing tail.

As the boy lowered the broom, taking a less defensive posture, Molly asked him, "What's your name?"

"Johnny. This is Abby. She's my sister. I'm not going to let anything bad happen to her."

"Nothing bad's going to happen to either of you," Molly assured him, and wished she felt confident that she and Neil would be able to fulfill this guarantee.

Abby's eyes were a dazzling blue like Johnny's, and every bit as haunted as her brother's.

To counter what her own eyes might reveal, Molly forced a smile, realized that it must look ghastly, and let it fade.

"Where are your parents?" Neil asked.

"The old man was wasted," Johnny said with a grimace of disgust. "Tequila and pills, like usual. Before the TV went out, he pissed himself watching the news and didn't even know it. He was talking crazy about making a fortress, went into the garage to get tools, nails, I don't know what."

"We heard what happened to him," Abby said softly. "We heard him scream." She anxiously surveyed the room, the ceiling. "The things in the walls got him."

As if the teeming hosts behind the plaster understood the girl's words, they thrashed with greater fury. Entomologic. Polymorphic. Pandemoniac.

"No," Johnny disagreed. "Something else must've got hold of him, something bigger than whatever's in the walls."

"He screamed and screamed." Abby's eyes widened at the memory, and she crossed her arms on her chest as if those frail limbs might serve as armor.

"Whatever got him," the boy said, "screeched and snarled like a cougar, but it wasn't any cougar. We could hear it real good. The door was open between here and the garage."

That door was currently closed.

"Then it shrieked like nothing I ever heard," Johnny continued, "and it made this sound . . . something like a laugh . . . and there were . . . eating noises."

The boy shuddered at the memory, and the girl said, "They're gonna eat us alive."

Resting the flashlight on a counter, still holding the pistol, Molly went to Abby, drew her to the edge of the table, and put an arm around her. "We're taking you out of here, sweetheart."

"Where's your mother?" Neil asked.

"Left us two years ago," the boy explained.

His voice broke more raggedly than before, as though abandonment by his mother still shook him more deeply, two years after the fact, than did any extraterrestrial horrors that they had encountered here in the past few hours.

Johnny bit hard on his lower lip to repress this emotion, then turned to Molly: "Me and Abby, we tried to leave a couple times. The doors won't open."

"They opened for us," Neil assured him.

Shaking his head, the boy said, "Maybe coming in. But going out?"

He snatched a small pot from the cooktop and flung it hard at one of the kitchen windows. It struck the glass with a solid crack and a reverberant clang, but bounced off, leaving the pane intact.

"Something weird's happening to the house," the boy said. "It's changing. It's like . . . almost alive."

35

OUT OF THE KITCHEN, ALONG THE HALL, TO THE foyer, they were accompanied by a rising chorus of frenzied fluttering within the walls, a rustle, a bustle, an urgent quickening, as if the horde sensed that its tender prey were escaping.

"They talk," Abby confided to Molly as they hurried out of the kitchen, behind Virgil.

"Who, sweetheart?"

"The walls. Don't they, Johnny? Don't they talk?"

"Sometimes you can hear voices," the boy confirmed as they arrived at the foyer closet.

In the event that the storm resumed, the nearest thing to rain gear that the kids had were nylon jackets with warm lining.

As Abby and her brother shrugged into their coats, Molly said, "You don't mean—voices in English."

"Sometimes English," Johnny confirmed. "But sometimes another language. I don't know what it is."

Throughout the house arose a subtle creaking from floorboards, wall studs, ceiling joists. The structure sounded like a ship at sea, riding out the steep swells of a storm fringe.

Virgil, thus far not given to barking, barked. Just once. As if to say, *Let's go!*

The creaking house abruptly creaked louder and with a greater number of complaints from floors, ceilings, doorjambs, window frames, walls. The bone-rattle of plumbing. The wheeze and whistle of hot breath in torquing ducts. Suddenly the place groaned like a tired old behemoth waking from the sleep of ages.

When Neil tried the front door, it seemed to be locked.

"I *knew*," the boy said, and the girl clung desperately to Molly.

Neil worked the deadbolt, wrenched at the door with all his strength, but it resisted him.

Surrounded by groans and creaks and cracks and pops, Molly half believed that the house might close around them like a pair of jaws, grinding their bodies between the splintery teeth of its broken beams, tasting them upon its tongue of floors, pressing them against its palate of ceilings, finally swallowing their masticated remains into a basement, where the rustling legions would swarm over them, reducing flesh to fluid and bones to powder.

Neil stepped away from the door. "Move, get back," he ordered, and raised his shotgun, intending to blast loose the recalcitrant lock.

Virgil padded into the line of fire and pawed at the door—which swung inward.

Molly didn't pause to puzzle over whether Neil, always as steady as a ship at anchor, had lost his cool for a moment and had turned the knob in the wrong direction, fighting with an unlocked door, or whether instead the dog possessed major mojo beyond anything they had heretofore witnessed. Holding Abby against her side, she followed Virgil and Johnny out of the house, onto the porch, down the front steps, onto the flagstone walk.

When she turned, she was relieved to see that Neil hurried close behind her and that he had not been imprisoned by animate architecture.

The house looked no different from the way it had been when they'd first seen it. Craftsman style, no Cthulhu.

In the hush of the purple mist, Molly expected to hear the structure creaking, groaning, midway in a performance to match that of Poe's self-consuming House of Usher, but her expectations went unfulfilled—not for the first time in this bizarre night—because the residence stood as silent, as deceptively serene, as inspiring of convoluted syntax as the stately manor in a ghost story by Henry James.

The front door slowly drifted shut, as though it had been hung with an inward-swinging bias on well-oiled hinges. She suspected, however, that a less mechanical force—one capable of conscious and cruel intent—was at work.

The crusty lichen on the stone pines, flecked with emerald-green radiance, though cancerous in appearance and rapidly metastasizing up the limbs, now seemed to be a benign and almost charmingly festive bit of extraterrestrial vegetation compared to whatever hellish things had been breeding or growing in the walls of the house.

Assuming that the rising sun had not faltered in its ascent, the mist must have thickened overhead even as it had dissipated somewhat here at street level, for the amethystine light had darkened to plum-purple. The promise of morning had already given way to a threatening shadow-land more suitable to a Balkan twilight than to a California dawn.

"Where do we go now?" Johnny asked.

Molly looked at Virgil, who regarded her expectantly. "Wherever the dog leads us."

At once, the shepherd turned away from her and trotted along the flag-stone path to the street.

The four of them followed Virgil into a mist that had thinned and lifted until visibility, even in this false dusk, extended about two blocks.

Molly's initial sense that the overhead fog had grown markedly more dense, even as the lower blear somewhat clarified, proved correct on calmer observation.

In fact, the stratification between the ground-level haze and the higher pea soup was so abrupt that a ceiling seemed to have been constructed over Black Lake at a height of fifteen feet. Everything above that line—

part of the upper floors and the roofs of two-story houses, the higher limbs of trees—vanished entirely from sight in the livid murk.

She felt oppressed by the impenetrability of the overcast and by its proximity to the ground. The sluggish, clotted fog allowed penetration by only a narrow band of the light spectrum, resulting in this plummy gloom, piling a weight of claustrophobia atop the onerous mood.

Something else about the lowering sky disturbed her, but she could not at once identify the reason for her concern.

They had followed Virgil only half a block, however, before that cause presented itself: Things could move half seen or even unseen in that dismalness.

Out of the west came a light in the overcast. The fog diffused it, obscured the source, but the brightness approached across the besieged town.

The nearer it drew, the more evident its shape became: a disc or perhaps a sphere. At the heart of the surrounding corona burned the more intense light of the object itself, which approximately defined it. She guessed it might be the size of an SUV, although she couldn't accurately discern proportions without knowing at what altitude the vehicle cruised.

She had no doubt that it would prove to be a vehicle. The movies had prepared her for this sight, too, as had decades of news stories about UFOs.

The object traveled silently. No purr of engines. No whoosh of displaced air. From it emanated none of the pulsations that had radiated from the larger ship and that had throbbed in blood and bone.

If the southbound leviathan that had recently passed over was the mother ship—or one of many mother ships—then the approaching UFO had most likely been dispatched from that larger vessel. This might be an observation craft, a bomber or the equivalent, or maybe a troop transport.

Or none of the above. This war bore little or no resemblance to any of the many conflicts of human history, and the usual lexicon of battle had no application to these events.

As the UFO drew near, it slowed, appearing to glide with the gravity-defying ease of a hot-air balloon.

It came to a full stop directly above their little group, where they stood in the street, and there it hovered soundlessly.

Molly's heart swelled with a rush of dread.

Teach us to care and not to care. Teach us to sit still: quoting Eliot to herself now, seeking consolation in the cadence, reassurance in the rhythm.

When Abby cringed against her, Molly dropped to one knee, to be at the girl's level, to pull her close and to help her find the courage to face whatever might come.

36

BENEATH THE FLOATING MYSTERY, IN ITS GOLDEN yet baleful light, under its malevolent influence, the four of them gazed up, afraid but unable to look away.

At first sight of the approaching light, Molly had considered fleeing with the children, hiding, but she had realized that if the pilot of the craft wished to find them, they would be found. Surely these ETs could track ground targets by infrared surveillance, by body-heat profiling, by sound-spoor detection, and by other means beyond the capabilities of human science and technology.

She felt watched, and more than watched: intimately scrutinized, physically and mentally analyzed, her fullest measure taken in ways un-knowable and profound. As she became more sensitive to the depth of this analysis, her fear grew more intense and, to her surprise, she was also overcome by shame—her face burned with it—as if she stood naked before strangers.

When she heard herself murmuring the Act of Contrition, she realized that instinctively she expected to die here in the street, in this minute or the next.

Neither the hovering transport's powerful light nor the effect of its silent propulsion system to any degree burned off the fog beneath it. If anything, the mist thickened, conspiring to keep hidden the contours and every detail of the machine.

She expected to be incinerated, reduced to burning tallow in a boiling pool of blacktop, or to be atomized.

Alternately, the prospect of the craft descending to the street, of being taken aboard, of coming face-to-face with their inhuman masters and subjected to God knew what experiments and humiliations made atomization almost appealing.

Instead and unexpectedly, the luminous object moved away from them, receding rapidly. In seconds, every glimmer of its golden glow had been extinguished by the overcast.

The thick mist was empurpled again, and the street cast into false twilight, as before.

After hugging Abby almost too fiercely, Molly rose shakily to her feet. Neil stood with one reassuring hand on Johnny's shoulder. His eyes met hers, and did not blink.

Their mutual sense of relief was palpable, but none of them had a word to say about the event that had just transpired, as though to speak of the craft would be to invite its immediate return.

During the encounter, she had not been aware of the dog. If he had been frightened, he had recovered as quickly as the vessel had vanished in the fog. He stood, alert and apparently undaunted, ready to lead the search for other children.

Molly was eager to follow him—and grateful to have a purpose important enough and difficult enough to prevent her from brooding too intently on the hostile new world they would have to face in the days ahead.

Nonetheless, as Virgil led them farther north along the street, Molly noticed that the radiant lichen crusted a significant number of trees: stone pines, sugar pines, sycamores dressed with the yellow foliage of autumn. The transformation of the earth continued apace.

She saw other sycamores and cottonwoods with beards of gray moss like nothing that previously had grown in Black Lake. Some of this mossy bunting hung in swags as wispy as the mist, but other drapings were dense, conveying an impression of rot and disease.

Two massive trees had toppled, but their fate appeared to have nothing to do with aggressive alien plant forms. They had stood in soil so saturated by the rains that their weight was greater than the power of the sodden earth to hold them erect. One tree had fallen into the street, entirely blocking it, and the other had crashed onto a house, doing serious damage.

Never wandering, never pausing to sniff the ground or the air, Virgil proceeded one block farther north, then turned east and trotted uphill to Chestnut Lane.

Molly expected to be led to another residence, in which the walls would be infested. Perhaps this time the fluttering multitudes would escape their hive and seek whatever sustenance they needed.

The shepherd took them instead toward St. Perpetua's, the church at the corner of Chestnut Lane and Hill Street, the steeple and the roof of which thrust up and vanished into the overcast.

This structure had been built of stone quarried from these mountains. The two oak front doors stood under handsome limestone tympanums that together cradled a stained-glass rose window, all surrounded by a cinquefoil arch.

The north and south walls of the church also featured stained-glass windows. Through two of these, toward the altar-end of the nave, came a constant but slightly quivering light, not nearly strong enough to transform the mosaics of somber glass into bright scenes of grace and miracles, but sufficient to reveal that someone had taken refuge in the building.

Earlier, when Molly and Neil had quickly toured the town in search of neighbors gathered in mutual defense, before finding the crowd at the tavern, they'd cruised past St. Perpetua's. It had appeared to be deserted.

Virgil did not proceed to the front doors of the church. He went to the open gate in the wrought-iron fence that surrounded the adjacent cemetery.

There, the dog exhibited his first moment of trepidation: ears forward, breath held, tail tucked. From rump to stifles to hocks, his back legs trembled.

Yet after only a brief hesitation, the shepherd went through the gate and among the tombstones. Molly, Neil, and the children reluctantly followed.

Two ancient live oaks, growing at maximum altitude and unlikely to have survived higher on the mountain, shadowed the farther reaches of the cemetery. Their massive crowns were for the most part cloaked in the fog, and the aisles of graves under their limbs were obscured by filigrees of blackest shadows worked across a field of purple light.

In those open areas closer to the gate, however, the enduring and anachronistic twilight brightened the yard enough to reveal that some gravestones had been targeted by busy vandals. Simple rectangles of granite, carved angels, two Latin crosses, one cross of Calvary, one Celtic cross, molines and botonées and patriarchals had been toppled and broken.

Graves had been opened. Not most. Perhaps a dozen, fifteen, out of hundreds.

Young Abby sought Molly's hand and squeezed it tightly.

Masses of mud, excavated earth, covered some areas of grass. Scattered across the mud were coffin lids of all varieties: shattered wood, twisted and mangled metal.

The open graves were nearly full of muddy water. In them floated tangled lengths of satin lining from the caskets. A stained and lace-trimmed pillow on which had once rested the head of a cadaver. One black shoe.

Scraps of rotting garments. A few small bones, clean and white, mostly phalanges and metatarsals. . . .

The dog had brought them here to see this.

Molly had no idea why.

Or perhaps she knew the meaning of this outrage, but lacked the nerve to follow logic where it would take her.

37

THE NARTHEX OF THE CHURCH HAD A SINGLE WIN-
dow: the stained-glass, multifoliate rose above the front doors. When
filtered through red-and-gold glass, the plum light lost all ability to illuminate.

This was a dark place, paneled in mahogany. The air smelled sweet
with incense and rank with mold.

The dog sneezed twice, and snorted to clear his nose.

Molly's flashlight found a colony of fungi in a corner, not black and
yellow but pure white.

The specimen consisted of two forms growing in an apparently random mix. Round bladderlike structures clustered in many sizes, swollen
as if with a barely contained quantity of fluid, glistening with an exuded
milky mucus. What appeared to be soft fabric sacs, not quite fully in-
flated, slowly swelled and subsided and swelled again as though they
were lungs.

The colony measured approximately four feet wide, three feet deep,
and six feet high. Massive. Malignant. *Aware.*

How Molly knew it was aware, she could not say, and perhaps she
reached this conclusion largely by imagination rather than by reason or
even intuition. Yet she remained certain that the interiors of the white
bladders, if not the pale lungs, teemed with malevolent and sentient life.

She wished that Abby and Johnny could have waited outside. The kids couldn't be left alone, however, and neither she nor Neil was ready to compromise their commitment to stay together at all times.

Virgil pawed at the door between the narthex and the nave, pawed with such insistence that he seemed to suggest they had little time to do what must be done.

When Molly pushed the door open, she glimpsed a white marble holy-water font immediately to the right, but was more drawn to the sight of scores of candles clustered at the front of the church, toward the extreme right side of the chancel railing.

By habit, she dipped two fingers in that small marble reservoir. Instead of cool water and the usual sense of peace, she felt a damp, spongy, foul something.

Snatching her fingers back, aiming the flashlight more directly at the font, she discovered a severed human hand lying in the water. Palm up. Digits bristling like the legs of a dead crab.

A cry caught in her throat, then issued as half whimper and half wheeze.

A thing as familiar as a hand, in such unexpected and offensive context, seemed alien in the extreme, less grisly than shocking, but grisly enough.

To spare the children from this sight, Molly at once turned the flashlight away from the font, toward the main aisle of the shadowy nave. Twitching on the wooden floor, the beam revealed her state of mind.

"Stay away from the font, don't even look at it," she warned them, and hoped that the poor light would spare them the sight now etched in her memory.

Although fresh, Molly's recollection of the hand was imperfect. She suspected that something about that severed member had been revelatory, premonitory, but the crucial detail eluded her.

She did not turn back to take a second look. The nave ahead of her compelled attention, for three children and two men were gathered in the light of the many candles in the southwest corner, just outside the sanctuary.

From a distance, the posture of that group of five appeared defensive, fearful. Judging by their tense but passive attitude, they had no guns, and they seemed to expect not a group rather like themselves but storm troopers from another world.

Molly suddenly realized that from the perspective of the five among the candles, she and Neil, and their two charges, were embraced by darkness, their true nature indiscernible. Consequently, as she proceeded along the center aisle, she called out a friendly greeting, identifying herself and her husband.

The five remained silent and still, and stiff with tension. Perhaps their experiences of the night just past had led them to expect deception; their response would depend on the evidence of their own eyes.

The candles, though numerous, did nothing to relieve the gloom in the congregational section of the nave. Likewise, the dim purple daylight at the stained-glass windows failed to unravel a single thread of the tightly woven shadows.

As she followed Virgil along the aisle, Molly heard a low voice murmuring what might have been an Our Father, and a second voice even more softly reciting what sounded like the Hail-Mary rhythms of the Rosary.

She realized that others had taken refuge in St. Perpetua's, turning to God in this crisis as she had once expected more of the townspeople might have done. These faithful sat singly and in pairs, sat quietly here and there among the pews, humble shapes in the darkness.

She didn't disturb their prayers and meditations by picking them out with her flashlight, but respected the privacy of their worship and their penance.

As she reached the crossing, that open area between the front row of pews and the chancel railing, a tremor passed underfoot, accompanied by the creak and pop of tongue stressing against groove in the oak planks.

She swept the well-waxed floor around her with the light. A couple of buckled boards, lifting slightly from the subflooring, suggested pressure from below.

Virgil sniffed at them only in passing, making a wide berth around the deformed planks.

The church had a basement. Down there among the supplies and the stored-away holiday decorations, between the furnace and the water heater, perhaps some beast with no Christian purpose had taken up residence.

Every candle in the red glasses on the votive rack was alight. Others, from a box of spares, had been set on the chancel railing and around the base of a life-size statue of the Holy Mother just inside the sanctuary.

In the ruby, gold, and fluctuant radiance, Molly saw that the three children shared freckles, green eyes, and a certain cast of features that identified them as siblings.

The face of the youngest—an auburn-haired girl of perhaps five—glistened with steady, quiet tears. Abby at once took her hand and stood with her, perhaps because they knew each other, or just because she realized that she could lend some courage to the younger girl.

The other children were boys, a pair of identical twins, eight or nine years old. Instead of their sister's auburn locks, they had dark hair, almost black. While they looked scared, they also appeared to be both tense and restless with that healthy rebellious energy that from time to time animates the best of boys. They wanted to *do something*, take action, even as they recognized that the resolution of their current hated situation was beyond their power.

Neither of the men with the children appeared to be related to them.

The first, tall and thin, had a prominent Adam's apple, and a sharp nose. While he chewed on his lower lip almost vigorously enough to draw blood, his hopping-hen eyes pecked nervously at Molly, then at Neil, then at the kids, then at the worshipers in the pews, then toward the dark altar.

The other was shorter, heavy, literally wringing his pudgy hands with anxiety, and earnestly apologetic. "I'm sorry. I'm so sorry, but there was no other way."

"Sorry about what?" Neil asked.

"We don't have guns," the heavy man said. "We hoped you would—and you do. But now I'm wondering—how could guns make a difference?"

"I'm not good at riddles," Neil said.

"We could have warned you off, but then what would happen to us? So we let you walk into a trap. I'm so sorry."

Another tremor passed through the floor. The ruby-glass candle holders clinked against the metal votive rack. The flames quivered on the wicks, licked higher, bright tongues in silent screams.

38

WHATEVER RESTLESS PRESENCE STIRRED IN THE church basement, the heavyset man, like his tall companion, appeared to be less interested in the threat under their feet than in the dark chancel behind them and the worshipers in the pews before them. His nervous stare roved from one knot of shadows to another.

"Can you get us out of here?" the tall man asked, as though he had forgotten the location of the doors.

Behind her, Molly heard movement from various points in the church, as if those in the pews had risen in unison, in response to an invitation to Communion.

Turning, she recalled the hand in the holy-water font. Because of the shock of that repulsive contact, she had blanked on a crucial detail, which no longer eluded her. The severed grotesquery had not been that of a man dismembered in the current conflict, for it had been bloated, discolored, pocked with corruption.

The hand had belonged to a man dead and buried for some time. Preserved by the embalmer's art, it had only gradually succumbed to the process of decay, but it had not weathered the grave unblemished.

One by one, her flashlight picked out ten figures standing among the pews: these sham worshipers, these soulless worm-riddled hulks, in their rotting funeral suits and dresses. Blind behind their sewn-shut eyelids.

Deaf to truth, incapable of hope. Resurrected in only a physical sense—
and perhaps in a spirit of mockery. Mockery. Travesty. Desecration, prof-
anation.

Here again was that unearthly power that did not differentiate between the living and the dead, or even between the organic and the inor-
ganic. It seemed that Earth was being taken and remade not by ETs from
another spiral arm of the Milky Way or from another galaxy, but by beings from another *universe*, where all the laws of nature were radically
different from those in this one.

Humanity's reality, which operated on Einsteinian laws, and the utterly different reality of humanity's dispossessors had collided, meshed.
At this Einstein intersection, all things seemed possible now in this worst
of all possible new worlds.

In rising to their feet, the dead stirred within themselves the gases of
decomposition. What had seemed to be the reek of the white fungus
grew more pungent and could be identified more accurately.

With a sense of smell at least ten thousand times more acute and more
sophisticated than that of any human being, Virgil must have known
what had been sitting in those shadowed pews, but he'd sounded no
alarm as he had led her past them. He stood now among the five children. His dedication to their rescue exceeded even the most extraordinary
canine behavior that Molly had ever seen before, and she was reminded
that in some way she couldn't understand, the dog was more than he
seemed to be.

The mortician's stitches had not in every case held, and one among
these nightmare parishioners had both eyes open. The beam of the flashlight did not reveal cataracted or corrupted eyes; instead, the contents of
the skull bulged from the sockets—a familiar black fungus spotted with
yellow.

As effectively as a leech taking blood, fear suckled on Molly's hope. As
her heart raced once more, however, she took courage, if not comfort,

from the fact that these expatriates of the grave frightened her less than the encounter with Render at the tavern.

Another cadaver, short on flesh and long on bone, caged a mass of the black-and-yellow fungus in its open ribs. Another colony wound its right arm, from shoulder to wrist, like an entwining serpent.

The floor of the church shuddered again, planks creaked, planks cracked, as if something below had awakened in hunger, preparing for its hour to devour.

Three candles fell off the communion railing. One extinguished itself, and Neil stamped out the other two.

The dead began to move. They didn't shamble, didn't snarl or hiss, didn't thrash with rage, made none of the standard movie moves. They headed toward the aisles—north, south, central—blocking all the public routes out of the church, stepping slowly but with a strange stately dignity.

To return to the narthex and escape by the front doors, Molly would have to confront at least three of these mock Lazaruses, which she would not—could not—do, especially not when she had the kids to think about, perhaps not even if she'd been alone, not with a pistol, not with a flamethrower.

In sync with his wife's thoughts, Neil suggested an alternative: "There's another way. Through the sacristy, out the back door into the rectory yard."

"That's no good," the tall man said in a voice thick with dour certainty.

As if in confirmation, a clatter came out of the sanctuary beyond the communion railing, from the chanceled darkness past the reach of candle glow.

Although she was loath to turn her flashlight away from the ten cadavers in the nave, Molly swung the beam toward the sound. A priest stood at the high altar.

No. Not a priest. The remains of one.

Father Dan Sullivan, who had served this parish for almost three decades, had died in August of the previous year. Now he had returned to the altar, as if the daily rituals of his life were encoded in the cells of his embalmed body, still compelling him to his work.

From this angle, Molly had a view only of his profile, but she knew who he must be. He wore the black suit and Roman collar in which he had been buried thirteen months ago. His white hair—once red—was tangled with filth, his clerical suit streaked with mud.

A moment after the light found him, the dead priest gripped fistfuls of the antependium, the embroidered cloth that draped the front of the altar, and jerked violently on it. The tabernacle crashed to the floor and burst open, scattering pyx, paten, and chalice.

They would have to pass by this specter to get to the sacristy. One such adversary, however, was less daunting than ten of them.

More tremors in the floor, more violent than before, shook the columns, climbed to the ceiling, made the extinguished chandeliers arc through darkness on the ends of chains that creaked and clinked, link to link.

The remaining candles on the railing fell off, rolled under pews, flames licking floor wax and brightening as they turned.

Neil switched on his flashlight and handed it to the heavyset man. "I'll lead the way, you follow close on my right and keep the light ahead of me."

Virgil bounded over the low chancel railing, and the five kids scrambled after him.

In the nave, the macabre parishioners approached unhurriedly, as if they could see the future and knew that their malicious intentions would be fulfilled whether they made haste or not.

39

PAST THE RACK OF VOTIVE CANDLES IN RUBY GLASSES, over the low communion railing, into the sanctuary, Molly followed the tall man, who followed the children and the dog, who themselves followed the flashlight-wielding fat man and Neil.

The first light swept left to right, right to left, ceaselessly scanning the way ahead, as Neil had instructed.

Molly used her beam to lever stubborn shadows out of suspicious corners, expecting to pry loose an atrocity of one kind or another, sooner or later.

Between them and the altar stood the choir enclosure. Stepped rows of chairs had been knocked askew by the tremors that had shaken the building.

On the inclined ambulatory, they passed beside and then above the choir box and the silent organ. The door to the sacristy lay to the south of the altar, ten feet beyond the top of the ramp, where the floor leveled off.

As they ascended with wariness but also in something of a rush, the abomination that had been Father Dan moved to intercept them.

Molly's light revealed the dead priest's face. Bloated. Livid. Split like the skin of an overripe plum at the corners of the mouth. Left eye sewn shut; right open, torn threads dangling from the upper lid. The blinkless milky eye reflected light with a silver sheen.

Because this, too, was an agent of despair, the sight of which seemed intended to drain hope and dilute courage, Molly wished to look away but could not. Dread and morbid fascination held her—and a sense of pending insight similar to what she had felt in the tavern, shortly after the encounter with Render. Here was death undone and life that was not alive. Here was the insane new world order imposed by princes from some distant star, miracles of darkest design that offended, fascinated, sickened, spellbound.

Abruptly the priest's face blossomed, as though his features and the facial bones they overlaid were a fragile facade—less than a facade, an illusion. What nested within burst out, and the exterior at the same time folded to the sides and inward, so that under the shock of tangled white hair was revealed a mass of crimson tentacular forms stippled with what appeared to be six- and eight-inch thorns, or stingers, the whole of it simultaneously writhing and bristling, a thing suitably demonic to police the tenth circle of Hell if Dante had found more than nine levels.

Quarreling echoes of the shotgun blast chased one another around the groin-vaulted ceiling, vibrated saints and angels in the stained-glass windows.

Chest-slammed, the infested cadaver blew backward, crashed to the floor. It kicked the fallen chalice into a noisy roll and tangled in the rumpled antependium.

Evidently the thing that had taken residence in the corpse would not be dissuaded by buckshot. It thrashed, trying to cast off the altar cloth and regain its feet.

The cold congruence of Molly's cupped hand and the butt of the pistol provided less comfort by the minute. Even an entire magazine of hollow-point 9-mm rounds, well placed at close range, might not stop this hag-ridden cadaver when the hag was perhaps a resilient life form more plant than animal.

The group kept moving in flashlight flares and swoops of shadow.

They had taken only two steps, however, when the floor shook as never before: shook, splintered, cracked open.

Molly stumbled, almost fell.

Between Neil, in the lead, and the man behind him, shattered planks erupted in a jagged bouquet of oak.

A stench breathed out of the basement, and with that reeking exhalation rose a thing less than half glimpsed in the jittering flashlight beams.

Molly thought, *Bug.*

Quick impressions in bad light. Insectile. Enormous. Polished carapace. Beetle horns. Wickedly serrated mandibles. Armored abdomen. Pedipalpi. Numerous compound eyes, inexpressibly strange and vaguely luminous. Suddenly a yawning maw and a razored gullet to rival that of any shark.

Screaming, the heavyset man was plucked off the sanctuary floor and dragged into the basement.

In an instant the apparition had appeared, and in the next instant had vanished.

By the bucking of the floor, by the fat man's kicking legs, by their own panic, the five children had been knocked together, three thrown to the floor, and one—the freckled girl with the auburn hair—had fallen into the hole. Having grabbed the jagged end of a plank, she hung by both hands, legs dangling in the basement.

From the darkness below the girl, the lost man's tortured cries begged for death and pleaded mercy, for he was not at once broken and sucked dry, but suffered instead an attenuated death that didn't bear contemplation.

40

THE MYSTERY OF EVIL IS TOO DEEP TO BE ILLUMI-
nated by the light of reason, and likewise the basement of the church,
while no more than twelve feet in depth, presented to Molly a blackness
as perfect as that you might find gazing outward to the starless void beyond the farthest edge of the universe.

The heavyset man had dropped his flashlight before being dragged
into the chamber below. It had rolled against the ambulatory wall; and
now it shone toward the sacristy, revealing little.

Molly dared not direct her light into the hole, for fear of exciting the
creature that had risen from it—or a host of others. Instead, she thrust the
flashlight at the tall man, instructing him to sweep the chancel and pin-
point, for Neil, any looming threats that might be checked even tem-
porarily by a shotgun blast.

She dropped to her knees at the broken-oak rim of the pit and seized
the dangling girl by her arms.

The ghastly screams rising from below did not motivate the girl to give
herself to rescue, but froze her. She would not relinquish her grip on the
shattered plank.

"Let go, I'll lift you out, I'll lift you up," Molly promised.

Containing three greens in striation—apple-green, jade-green, cela-
don—the girl's eyes were beseeching. She wanted help but had no trust.

Seeking some connection to break the ice that froze the child's nerve, Molly said, "Honey, what's your name?"

From below came shuddering, stuttering miseries of sound out of the lost man, a thrashing, a wet sucking noise—and underlying all the rest, a cold whispering as of a thousand voices expressing eager appetites.

The girl began to sob with terror.

Her twin brothers bent to the hole, and Molly warned them to get back, but one of them urged his sister to relent: "Bethany, she wants to help you. Let her help."

Evidently the thing that wore the mortal coil of the dead priest had gotten to its feet again, for the shotgun boomed.

Through the layered reverberations bouncing back from groin vaults and stained-glass windows, Neil called out to Molly, *"Hurry!"*

"Bethany," she implored, "let go of the plank."

Another crash of shotgun, so soon, suggested that the cleric's cadaver was not the only immediate threat.

Molly had the girl's eyes now, and she did not look away from them to see what danger loomed, but said with all the passion that her voice could carry, "Bethany, trust me. I'll die for you. If you fall, I'll come in there after you. *Trust me.*"

A yellow radiance flared behind Molly, the shimmering brightness of thriving flames. The rolling candles must have found combustible material.

"Trust me!"

The girl's gaze slid away toward something to the right of Molly, and her sobbing subsided.

The dog. Good Virgil had come boldly to the splintery edge of the hole.

Below, the fat man's last cry spiraled into a groan and then into silence.

Holding fast to Bethany, looking past her, Molly saw nothing more than shades of blackness moving in the basement, different intensities and textures of restless darkness. The many whispering voices might have been angry urgent speech or only sound without substance.

For a moment Bethany seemed to be in communion with the dog. Then she said to Molly, "Help me," whereupon the cloud of panic clarified in her green eyes.

Gripping the girl's upper arms, Molly lifted, as though curling weights. The girl let go of the plank and, kicking as if something were plucking at her feet, came out of the hole, onto the floor of the ambulatory.

Reflections of flames now capered on the walls, whipped bright tails in salamander flourishes across the windows, added luster to wooden surfaces. Molly smelled smoke and saw it curling in greasy coils around her legs.

Urging Bethany and her brothers to move past the shattered floor to safer territory, Molly glanced back and saw real flames, not the reflection of them, in the nave, unfurling and billowing like the flags of a war-mad nation.

Opening the gate in the communion railing, a corpse in fiery clothes came forward, its hair ablaze, but resolute.

Molly turned from that walking tallow and followed the tall man, who followed Bethany and her brothers, around the broken planks, toward Neil and Abby and Johnny, toward the sacristy.

This time the tremors had the power of a seismic event. The floor leaped, fell back, rocked.

The tall man staggered, almost fell into the hole, windmilled his arms, kept his balance, but—

—that cousin to earwigs, brother to centipedes, sister to wasps, that beast which might have been the god of all insects *thrummed* out of the basement, skewered the man's abdomen with a stinger as long as a knight's lance, and took him screaming down into the pit.

Molly felt sudden blistering heat at her back. In her mind's eye, she saw the fiery hand of the blazing corpse reaching for her hair. She ran.

41

TALL MAN SCREAMING IN THE DARK BELOW, CRACKLE of combusting wood, hissing of undetermined origin, excited cries of frightened children, and Neil shouting words broken into meaningless fragments of sound by the pounding hammer of Molly's heart . . .

He stepped forward, leveling his shotgun at her. She tucked and rolled into the low smoke, and he fired over her.

Although she held her breath, she tasted the greasy vapors and scrambled to her feet, gagging, spitting.

Out of church rows instead of corn rows, across this field where only souls were cultivated, the dead parishioners in their ragged grave clothes approached like scarecrows set walking by sorcery, some on fire and spreading flames as they moved.

The floor quaked, the walls shook, a stained-glass window cracked along a line of leading.

Virgil barked as if to say, *Time to go.*

Molly agreed.

The shotgun roared.

Johnny had retrieved the flashlight dropped by the fat man. He gave it to Molly.

All energy and instinct, flashlight in her left hand and pistol in her right, she disdained the knob and kicked open the sacristy door.

Although flapping a dazzle of bright wings behind her, firelight feathered into darkness just past the threshold.

She shouldered through the rebounding door, thrusting recklessly into the room, chasing shadows with the beam, ready to shoot anything that light alone could not banish.

The church rocked, cabinet doors flew open, and she fired two rounds into cassocks and chasubles just to be sure that they were only vestments hanging from a closet rod.

Virgil padded past her, unfazed by the gunfire, quick to the outer door.

Hollow haunting groans and semi-electronic yowls, reminiscent of the voices of whales, rose from the very bones of the church, as if out of a hundred fathoms. This time the floor both trembled and *sagged*.

Turning, shouting for the kids, Molly discovered that all five had already followed her.

Beyond them, Neil stood in the doorway, facing the sanctuary, prepared to defend their retreat.

The floor had turned spongy, quivering like a membrane with each step she took. She threw open the outer door, and the dog dashed from the church.

Alert for hostile forces—known, unknown, and unimaginable—she led the children into the rectory yard, where the purple light had grown no brighter with the progress of the morning. The ceiling of fog still hung low, so dense that the position of the sun could not be discerned.

Except for their little group, there were no signs of life, Earthborn or otherwise. Black Lake lay bound in stillness, wrapped in muffling mist, as ready for eternity as a pharaoh embalmed for the tomb.

As Neil backed out of the sacristy into the yard, a storm seemed to break inside the church. A hard clap of thunder shuddered the building, as violent as any lightning-chasing crash that ever shook the heavens.

Crumblings of loose mortar rattled out of the stone walls. Dust and paper debris plumed from the open sacristy door.

Surely the floor had collapsed into the basement. The roiling fire damped suddenly, briefly, then flared higher and brighter than before, flamboyantly illuminating the sacred geometries of the colorful windows.

Even this roar brought no citizens into the street. They were huddled in their homes with baseball bats and handguns, or gone to other redoubts—or dead. Or worse than dead: living farms for alien fungus, living egg cases for the entomological wonders of another world.

42

THE DRAMA OF THE BURNING CHURCH PLAYED
bright upon the gloom, but Molly was surfeited with spectacle. Trusting
that the collapsed floor and the storm of fire would eradicate the pestilence in the basement and reduce the hag-ridden cadavers to ashes and
knobs of charred bones, she turned away and urged the children across
the yard, toward the street.

Looking shaken but grimly determined, Neil joined them. "Where
now?"

"If Virgil has more places to lead us," she said, "we'll follow him, but
not until we've gone back to the tavern."

"Why there?"

Molly remembered Cassie, the nine-year-old girl with sapphire eyes,
daughter of fence-sitters, left behind.

She recalled, as well, how the nine dogs had roamed the tavern end to
end, assiduously sniffing the well-worn floor. She had assumed they were
savoring the fragrant stains of dropped food and spilled drinks.

Her assumptions had changed.

"If the tavern has a basement, there's something in it, sure as hell.
We've got to get those people out of there before it's too late."

They were just twenty feet from the street when a refugee out of an
LSD-inspired hallucination moved in the purple half-light, approaching

from their right across the rectory lawn. They halted but didn't at once re-treat.

A colony of white fungi, smaller than but otherwise identical to the one they had seen in the narthex of St. Perpetua's, was on the move: round bladderlike structures in various sizes, glistering with a milky ooze, and soft veiny sacs that continuously swelled and partially deflated and swelled again, as though the creature had been turned inside out, re-vealing clusters of internal organs. It progressed on eight short legs that reminded Molly of those on a Jerusalem cricket—insectile but thick and tough.

The children crowded close to Molly. She discovered that their trust gave her courage in return for whatever strength her presence imparted to them.

Neil fished shells out of his coat pockets, pumped one into the cham-ber of the shotgun, and loaded three more in the tubular magazine.

Asymmetrical, about twice the size of Virgil, low to the ground, the thing proceeded at a measured pace. Although it didn't seem to be built for speed and had no apparent visual apparatus to guide it, Molly didn't discount the possibility that it could move much faster when necessary, guided by some sense other than—but as reliable as—eyesight.

Well fed and content, crocodiles also appeared to be slow and un-gainly. When hungry or irritated, however, they could outrun most dogs or any human.

If this too-solid apparition was a mere fungus or another more sophis-ticated phylum of plant, it wasn't likely to be a dangerous predator in the tradition of the potted carnivore in *Little Shop of Horrors*. On the other hand, innocuous plant life didn't sprout legs and travel.

Behind them, church windows burst from the heat. Showers of bright glass rained down and puddled into darker mosaics on the wet lawn.

Like cloud-fluttered moonglow in a dream rich with psychosis, orange firelight rippled across the rain-soaked lawn, over the loathsome bulbous fungus that now seemed obscene in its slimy tumescence.

She remembered her certainty, at first sight of the larger specimen in the narthex, that it was malignant, if not malevolent. And *aware*.

Drunk or not, Derek Sawtelle had gotten to the heart of the matter when he had said that on the world from which these invaders came, perhaps the differences between plant and animal life were not as clearly defined as on Earth. Consequently, predators might not be easily recognized in all instances.

The creature didn't deviate from its original line of direction, didn't start toward them, but marched steadily southward. It crossed their path and kept going.

As it began to move away, a sound so unexpected and disturbing issued from it that Molly felt her reason wobble like a spinning coin losing momentum. This thing, this pale atrocity, let out a sound that was too much like a grief-stricken woman weeping quietly, quietly but in the most poignant misery.

For an instant she tried to deny the source of the lamentations, and scanned the nearby night for a human figure to match the voice. She could see no one.

The eight-legged abomination was indeed the mourner, although the quality of its cry was most likely natural to it and not mimicry, a similarity explained sheerly by chance.

To hear it as grief or misery was no doubt to misunderstand it. The cry of a loon pealing across the stillness of a lake on a summer night will sound lonely to the human ear even if loneliness is not the state of mind that the loon intends to express.

Nevertheless, to hear such pitiable human sounds issuing from a creature so alien and repulsive in every regard was profoundly disquieting, chilling.

The thing fell silent—but a moment later, from between or behind the houses across the street, came a faint answering pule.

Another of its kind was out there in the purple morning, and the monstrous crier halted, as if listening to this response.

A second reply rose from a different direction, also faint—but this one was of a deeper timbre and sounded less like a weeping woman than like a weeping man.

When those other voices fell silent, the abomination moved once more, continuing on its original course.

Surreal. Unreal. Too real.

"Look," Neil said, pointing north.

Another luminosity, like the one that had hovered over them on La Cresta Avenue, appeared in the dense fog layer, traveling soundlessly across the town from the northeast to the southwest.

"And there."

A second glowing craft brightened out of the west and proceeded eastward on a serpentine course.

Behind the secreting overcast, the masters of the morning sky were attending to the business of conquest.

PART SIX

"*But at my back in a cold blast I hear*
The rattle of the bones, and chuckle spread from ear to ear."

T.S. Eliot, *The Waste Land*

43

EN ROUTE FROM ST. PERPETUA'S TO THE TAIL OF THE
Wolf Tavern, Johnny and Abby stayed close to Neil, while Virgil trotted
behind them, alert to the possibility of attack from the rear or from either
flank. The dog seemed to understand that for the moment his primary
duty was to guard rather than to lead.

At the front of their small column, traveling with the twins and their
sister, Molly learned that the boys were Eric and Elric Crudup, born on
New Year's Day ten years ago this coming January. They had been named
after Viking heroes, although neither of their parents could claim a single
Scandinavian ancestor.

"Our mom and dad like aquavit and Elephant beer," said Eric. "They
chase one with the other."

"Aquavit and Elephant beer are made in Scandinavia," Elric explained.

Their sister—more Scandinavian-looking with her lighter locks than
her brothers were with their dark hair—went by her middle name,
Bethany, because her first name was Grendel.

Her mother and father had named her Grendel because they knew it
to be Scandinavian. The girl was almost four years old before her parents
discovered that Grendel was the name of the monster slain by Beowulf.
Their knowledge of Scandinavian myth and English literature had not

been as complete as their appreciation for Scandinavia's finest alcoholic beverages.

Neither of the two men who perished in the church had been related to the Crudup siblings. The heavyset man, whom they'd known—but not well—as Mr. Fosburke, had taught sixth grade at their elementary school. The tall man had been a stranger to them.

Eric, Elric, and Bethany believed their parents were alive, although they—and the maternal grandmother who lived with them—had "gone through the ceiling," during the night, leaving the children to defend themselves.

Later, when the power went off, the three kids had become too frightened to remain at home. They had fled two blocks through the rain to the protection of the church. Where evil found them.

. . . *gone through the ceiling* . . .

Under the sea of purple fog, in this dim mortuary light of the drowned sun, with the trolls and menaces of another world set loose in unknowable numbers and forms, Molly had to remain alert to every shadow, which might be simply a shadow or instead a mortal threat. On the move and in a hurry, she couldn't concentrate on conversation intently enough to finesse from Eric, Elric, and Bethany a coherent explanation of exactly what they meant by "gone through the ceiling."

The children hurried with her, eager to share what they had witnessed.

"Just floated up out of the family room," said six-year-old Bethany, who seemed to have rebounded with remarkable resilience from the trauma of having dangled, baitlike, above the basement lair of the insectile horror.

Elric said, "Floated like astronauts with no gravity."

"We ran upstairs," Eric said.

"And we found them in our folks' bedroom, but they kept going up," said Elric.

Bethany said, "I was scared."

"We all were," said the twins simultaneously.

"Not Grandma. She wasn't scared."

"She went crazy," Eric declared.

Bethany took offense. "She did not."

"Fully, totally nut-ball," Eric insisted. "Laughing. I heard her laughing."

From a nearby backyard or alleyway came the weeping of a woman, which might have arisen in fact from a grieving mother or a desolate widow, but Molly wouldn't have bet on either.

In normal times, she would have gone at once to investigate these lamentations, to offer assistance, consolation. Now she dared spend her compassion only on the children. These cries of anguish and woe were a lure, and her pity would be repaid with a hook, a gaff, a gutting.

She walked faster, thinking of Cassie at the tavern, in the care of the drunk and the self-deluded, and the Crudup children matched her pace.

"Anyway, whether Grandma went crazy or not, that was later," said Elric. "First we ran upstairs and saw how they came through the floor from the family room."

Eric said, "And then they floated right up through the bedroom ceiling, too."

"They grabbed at us," said Bethany, "like maybe we could weigh them down, but we were scared, and anyway they couldn't hold us."

"They could never hold on to us or anything." Eric sounded angry about offenses committed long before the taking of the earth had begun.

"When it happened again later," Elric remembered, "I tried to hold Grandma by the foot."

Bethany said, "And I held Elric 'cause I was afraid he'd go right up with her."

Bewildered by this tale, which on any other night would have sounded like a report of a nightmare or a hallucination and might have been easily dismissed, Molly said, "What do you mean *through* the ceiling?"

"Through," said Eric. "Like the ceiling wasn't solid at all, just a *dream* of a ceiling."

Elric said, "Like when a magician puts his assistant in a box and saws her in half, and the blade goes right through her legs but she isn't hurt and the blade isn't bent."

"We thought we would float up, too, since they did," Bethany recalled, "but we didn't."

Eric said, "We climbed the pull-down ladder into the attic, and they were screaming up there."

"Not Grandma," Bethany reminded him.

"No. She was getting ready to go crazy later."

"Not true."

"Is true."

"Anyway," Elric continued, "they were screaming and trying to hold on to things, like the attic rafters."

Eric said, "Screaming at me and Elric, 'You little bastards, *do* something.' "

"They used lots of words, all worse than 'bastards,' " Bethany said. "But we agreed *months* ago never to talk like they do."

"We would've done something," Eric said, "but there wasn't anything we *could* do, and they couldn't hold, so they went right through the roof."

They turned the corner into a street where half the trees were festooned with gray moss, like a scene from the swamps of Louisiana or from the mind of Poe on opium. The gnarled trunks were embossed with luminous lichen and deformed by growths that Molly had not seen before, ringworm forms the size of ashcan lids, fat and festering under the bark.

"We couldn't get onto the roof," Elric told Molly, "we couldn't see what happened after that."

"But we could hear them out there," Bethany said solemnly.

"Screaming," Eric said, "out there in the rain above the house."

"We were scared."

"Real scared."

"So pretty quick their voices faded in the rain," Eric said.

"They were beamed up," Bethany explained.

"To the mother ship," the twins said in unison, shaped by the enduring age of techno-fantasy that their parents and grandparents had bequeathed them.

"Mother ship. That's what we think," their sister agreed. "So they'll be back. People who get beamed up sooner or later get beamed down again, but sometimes in other places."

Even in the middle of the street, they had to pass under the spreading boughs of the infected trees. Molly almost turned back, but they were on the last leg of the shortest route to the tavern.

In the windless stillness, Molly thought she heard furtive noises overhead. Squinting up into the fretwork of branches, which at fifteen feet vanished in the purple fog, she could not see much, for where the limbs were not leafed or hung with moss, they were leafed *and* hung with moss.

The kids, creeped out as well, resorted to more chatter to talk themselves through this haunted woods.

"When we went up into the attic, after Grandma," Elric told Molly, "this thing was there, though we didn't see it at first."

"We smelled it though, right away," said Eric.

Bethany said, "It smelled like rotten eggs and burnt matches."

"It smelled like shit," Elric said bluntly.

"Poop," Bethany corrected, clearly disapproving of his use of the vulgarity. "Rotten eggs, burnt matches, and poop."

Through the piercings in the woody fretwork above them, against the purple backglow of the luminous overcast, Molly saw quick and fluid movement. She glimpsed too little to judge the form or size of whatever tracked them from branch to branch.

"We didn't see the thing until Grandma was gone through the roof," said Elric.

"And then we didn't exactly see it," Bethany recalled.

"The power hadn't gone off yet," Eric said, "so there was a light in the attic."

Elric remembered: "But when you looked at the thing straight on, you couldn't see any details, only this shape."

"And it kept *changing* shape," said Bethany.

"You could see it clearest like from the corner of your eye," said Eric. "It was between us and the attic trapdoor, and it was coming toward us."

"Then we were *way* scared," said Bethany.

"Shitless," said Elric, but he at once apologized to his sister, although perhaps not with complete sincerity. "Sorry, Grendel."

"Dork," said the girl.

"Geek."

"Walking fart," she countered.

The longer they proceeded beneath the canopy of branches, the more movement that Molly detected above them, although it remained stealthy. She suspected that they were accompanied by many arboreal presences, not just a single creature.

When she glanced back at Neil, Abby, Johnny, and Virgil, she saw that they, too, were aware of the secretive travelers in the trees.

Neil held the shotgun in both hands, in a semi-relaxed grip, the muzzle pointed upward as he walked, ready to swivel left or right and fire into the branches at the first provocation. This lovely man had passed thirty-two years in gentle pursuits—scholar, shepherd, cabinetmaker—but this night he'd proved to be a courageous protector in a pinch.

"The thing in the attic," Elric said, "might've got us if she hadn't made it back off."

"Would've gotten us *for sure*," said Bethany.

"She just sort of shimmered out of thin air. She was like that guy in that old movie, that *Star Wars* guy," Eric said, "but she wasn't a guy, and she didn't have a light sword—or any sword."

Immediately ahead of Molly, though not stirred by a breeze, leaves spoke to leaves, moss trembled at this conversation, and a hand of one of their stalkers appeared, only the hand, gripping a branch for perch, for balance.

"Obi-Wan Kenobi," Elric said.

"That's the guy," Bethany agreed. "An old guy."

The revealed hand was approximately the size of one of Molly's, perhaps with an extra digit, fiercely strong by the look of it, deep scarlet, scaly, reptilian.

"She wasn't old though," said Eric.

"Pretty old," Bethany disagreed.

"Not as old as the *Star Wars* guy."

"No, not that old."

Four knuckles per finger, endowed with black claws as pointed as rose thorns, the scarlet hand released the limb and vanished into foliage as the nimble creature proceeded ahead of them.

Speaking of the menacing presence encountered in their attic, Elric said, "I don't know how she made it stay away from us."

"She spelled it away," Bethany replied.

Molly wondered how something her size could move so swiftly from tree to tree, yet in near silence and with so little disturbance of the leaves and moss. And she wondered how many of them were swarming through the branches both below and above the dense fog.

"She didn't spell it away," Eric said impatiently.

"Magic words," Bethany insisted. " 'The force be with you.' "

Molly counseled herself to keep moving. Intuition told her that any hesitation would be interpreted as weakness and that any sign of weakness would invite attack.

"That's stupid," Eric said. "She didn't say 'the force be with you' or anything like that."

"Yeah, so what did she say?"

They were just fifty feet from the next intersection. Ahead lay Main Street, with three generous lanes of pavement instead of two narrow ones; trees did not overhang the entire width of it, as they did here.

"I don't remember what she said," Eric admitted.

"Me neither," his brother said.

"She said *something,*" Bethany declared.

Just three steps ahead of them, the scarlet hand or one like it appeared on another bareness of branch.

Molly considered firing her pistol into the tree. Even if she hit the creature and killed it, however, this might be reckless. Instinct—which, with intuition, was all she had to go on—told her that firing a shot might invite instant vicious assault by others in the wooden highways overhead.

Simultaneous with the appearance of the hand, an appendage, at least four feet long, red mottled with green, more than an inch in diameter at the shank but dwindling to a tasseled and barbed whip at the end, perhaps a tail, slid out of the leaves, drooped down before them in a lazy arc—then snapped up, shearing moss, and out of sight.

Bethany and her brothers had seen this sinuous display. They had been meant to see it. The exposed tail was intended to be a challenge and a prod to panic.

The kids halted, clutching at one another for reassurance.

"Keep moving," Molly whispered, "but don't run. Walk. Just like you were doing."

Fear made the children cautious, but a slow pace was better than a sprint, which might, as with a tiger, invite pursuit. They would not win a chase.

They were thirty feet from the end of the canopy.

As if all these terrors were a mad composition, systemized in meter, orchestrated, out of the bleak morning came again the weeping of a woman, answered by the more distant but nonetheless miserable weeping of a man, and also ahead of Molly and to her right, an iron manhole cover rattled in the blacktop, knocked upon from below by some restless entity, perhaps by the headless body of Ken Halleck.

44

HUMAN WEEPING OF INHUMAN SOURCE, RED REP-
tiles as big as cougars in the trees, a headless dead man or something
worse knocking on the manhole cover, knocking to be released from the
storm drain: Mere anarchy had been set loose upon the world, a blood-
dimmed tide that threatened to wash sanity up by the roots, tangle it like
weeds, and sweep it away.

Molly kept moving, although she doubted they would escape the
canopy of trees. To her surprise, they reached the intersection with Main
Street, where the only architecture overhead was the ceaselessly changing, frescoed purple vaults of fog on fog.

Before she could indulge in even a timid hope, one of those silent luminous craft appeared again in the overcast, racing toward them out of
the west, one second glimpsed, six fast heartbeats later hovering overhead. Shape without form. Light that did not reveal its source. Its awesome power was suggested by the absolute stillness of its levitation.

As before, Molly felt physically scrutinized to a cellular level, every fil-
ament mapped in the rich braid of her emotions, every turning of her
mind from its brightest to its darkest places explored in an instant and
understood in finest detail. By analytic rays, by probing currents, by telepathic scans, by science and technology beyond the conception of the human mind, she was pored through, and *known*.

In the previous encounter, she had felt naked, terrified, and ashamed. She felt all those things now, and in no less measure than before.

The children appeared to be bedazzled, as might be expected, and afraid, as they should be, but she did not believe that any of them felt violated as profoundly as she did.

Glancing at Neil, in whose face and slightest gestures she could always read volumes, Molly saw more than raw fear; she recognized terror in all its subtleties from anguish and anxiety to incipient panic, but also what might have been piercing sorrow. Struggling with his sorrow was anger at this intrusive examination, to which no name could accurately be given except perhaps "psychological rape."

Her heart flooded with anger, too, in a volume to rival blood, for it seemed to her that if their world was to be taken and if all of them were to be slaughtered sooner or later, then they were owed the minimal mercy of a swift and easy death. Instead she felt as if she were a living toy on a leash held by a vicious master: savagely teased, tormented, tortured.

She couldn't explain to herself how an extraterrestrial species, a thousand years more advanced than humanity, with the wisdom to beat the limitations of the speed of light and cross galaxies in a clock tick, could be so barbarous, so pitiless. A civilization sufficiently sophisticated to construct ships larger than mountains and machines capable of transforming entire worlds in mere hours ought also to be a civilization exquisitely sensitive to suffering and injustice.

A species capable of the merciless destruction committed in the night just past, however, must be without conscience, without remorse, incurably sociopathic.

Evil.

Surely, a civilization built by individuals motivated by pure self-interest, incapable of empathy, without pity for others, would attain no grand heights. Evil would turn upon itself, as it always did, and such a species would reduce itself to dust long before it could reach for the stars.

Unless . . .

Unless perhaps it was a *hive*, in which every individual lacked a conscience, lacked even the concept of pity, reveled in cruelty, and had no personal identity different from those of all the other billions of its kind. Then each might direct its evil urges outward from the hive, bend its intellect to the creation of dark technologies, in the interest of furthering the evil of all. Their need to destroy, their implacable fury, would be brought to bear upon anything not of the hive or not of use to the hive. They would raze, ruin, and extirpate everything in their path.

If for a decade or a century they colonized Earth, they would eventually move on to some other world. They would leave behind a lifeless sphere, as barren as Mars, all sand and rock and ice and mournful wind.

The as yet unseen destroyers of worlds *delighted* in the havoc they unleashed, in the terror and the blood. Their driving need was the destruction of all that was Other to them, and their sole bliss was the suffering they administered. This truth could be confirmed by ample evidence everywhere in Black Lake.

These thoughts raced through Molly's mind even as she kept the children moving along Main Street under the silently hovering craft. Luminous reflections of the fog-veiled vessel played on the pavement as it tracked them step by step to the tavern.

No guards were posted at the door.

As before, the neon beer-company logos in the windows, now all dark, were backdropped by lowered shades. Nothing of the interior could be seen.

The pact Molly had made with Neil—that henceforth they would go everywhere together, would die side by side if death found them, and would never leave each other to die alone—must be amended.

If the two of them went inside to persuade those in the tavern that one form of death or another was breeding in the basement beneath them, the five children would be left outside alone. Easy pickings.

On the other hand, if they took the children inside, they would be exposing them to perhaps the very horror from which they had saved them in the church—or to something worse, considering that something worse, hour after hour, was the specialty of the enemy.

In this instance and in other situations to come, she and Neil would have to split up. If they didn't have the courage to act alone when necessary, they might as well go directly to the bank right now, with the five kids for whom they had made themselves responsible, and forget about the other children who might need them.

Like Cassie. In the tavern.

Neil wanted to go inside, but they agreed that whoever stayed with the kids ought to have the shotgun.

Indicating the luminous craft hovering in the shrouding fog, Molly said, "Shotgun won't bring that down, but the spread pattern of buckshot ought to stop more big bugs and nasty animals than all the rounds in my pistol."

Neil tried to give her the 12-gauge, but she wouldn't take it. She had never fired a shotgun before. She suspected that the hard recoil would compromise her effectiveness at least until she learned how to compensate for it.

Only a fool or a suicidal depressive would choose to learn the proper handling of a new weapon while in the heat of battle.

Neil would stay in the street, guarding the kids.

Armed with the 9-mm pistol, Molly would go into the tavern, argue the wisdom of evacuation to those inside, and one way or another get Cassie out of there.

Along Main Street, nothing moved in the moody half-light except the thin violet mist, which eddied lazily in the breathless morning.

The silence of a fly in amber, of a fossil hidden in the heart of a stone, lay upon Black Lake.

Then in the distance a man wept in misery. A weeping woman answered him. And then another.

All three sounded as if they were torn with emotion, convincing, until you realized that the cadences of their grief were identical, one to another.

The morning had grown warmer. Molly took off her raincoat.

The red dragons of the trees might be watching from a distance. Maybe they only hunted in their arbors. Or maybe they came down to kill in the street; it didn't really matter, she supposed, because if not them, something else would.

Fifteen feet overhead, the thick velvet fog was a curtain drawn between dying humanity—which was both the tragic protagonist and the audience—and the last act of Armageddon. Stagehands were moving into place the final scenery of doom.

The luminous craft hovered, attentive. Molly had not grown accustomed to the all-penetrating scrutiny of those aboard it. She felt humbled, curiously ashamed, frightened, and angry.

She nurtured the anger. Like hope, it staved off despair.

Virgil nuzzled her left hand, then returned to his watchful patrol between the children and the dead town.

Molly didn't need to tell Neil that she loved him. He knew. And she knew what she meant to him. They said it as well as it could be said with just a meeting of the eyes, a touch of hands.

With the pistol and a flashlight, she went into the tavern.

45

FLAMES WORRIED WICKS IN SCORES OF AMBER GLASS globes, as before. The walls and ceiling of Russell Tewkes's tavern appeared to tremble like painted curtains in the lambent candlelight.

The air itself seemed luminous, similar to the atmosphere in a dream of angels, and for a moment Molly was relieved to think that those who had been here when she'd left had later left themselves. No one sat in the booths or at the tables. No one stood at the bar, nor was Tewkes stationed behind it.

Derek and the drunks were gone. As were the peace lovers. And the fence-sitters, with Cassie.

Had she not studied the scene one second longer, had she turned and walked out, she might have thought that the lot of them had gone to the bank, after all, to assist in preparations for its defense. Lingering, however, she realized that her preferred scenario was not the one that had played out here.

First, the guns. Rifles, shotguns, and handguns had been left behind.

Neither the drunks nor the peace lovers had been armed, but many of the fence-sitters had been prepared to defend themselves if ultimately they made up their minds that self-defense was necessary or desirable. Not *all* of them would have gone out into this changed and changing world without weapons.

Second, the clothes. Coats and jackets had been left behind on chairs. Then she saw sweaters and shirts draped over some of the coats, and a pair of jeans.

Venturing farther from the front door, deeper into the tavern, she found drifts of discarded clothing on the floor. Slacks, khakis, more jeans, more shirts, blouses, socks, men's and women's underwear. Shoes and boots and belts and rain hats.

Implications of violence: All colors and styles of loose buttons littered the floor. Clothes had been torn off in such rage or frenzy that the buttons had popped loose. Numerous garments were ripped along the seams.

Yet apparently no guns had been fired.

Silence pooled fathoms deep. She held her breath, listened, but her ears might as well have been stoppled by a mile of ocean.

She kicked gently at some buttons. They rattled away from her shoe, across the floor planks, proving that she had not been struck deaf.

Wristwatches had been cast away. Sparkling on tables and across the floor were the warmth of gold, the chill of silver: necklaces, lockets, bracelets, rings.

Mystified as to what had happened, Molly could only suppose that the thirty to forty missing people had been forced to strip against their will. Because she had known several of them and because those she'd known had been people of common modesty, she couldn't conceive of any situation in which they would have disrobed willingly.

Yet no guns had been fired.

So . . . perhaps a shared madness had seized them, resulting from the unwitting intake of a psychosis-inducing toxin.

Certain rarely encountered exotic molds, including one that made its home in corn, could cause visual and auditory hallucinations, and an entire community could be swept up in the resultant mass hysteria. Some believe this—and not merely religious fanaticism—to be the root cause of the Salem witch trials, for they occurred in the season of the mold.

Molds were a class of fungi, and fungi appeared to constitute a more significant phylum of the invading extraterrestrial ecology than they did in Earth's natural order.

Toxins produced by alien fungi might induce delusions, shared hallucinations, and mass hysteria of a kind and an intensity new to human experience. Temporary psychosis. Enduring madness. Perhaps even homicidal frenzy.

On the tables and on the floor were broken beer bottles. Corona. Heineken. Dos Equis.

Some appeared to have been broken not by accident but with the intent to create weapons. The long neck of a Corona made a serviceable hilt, while the broken body of the bottle provided multiple jagged blades.

On one of these lacerating weapons, Molly found blood. Then on another. And a third. Still wet.

Arterial spatters stained a few articles of discarded clothing, though the modest volume didn't indicate wholesale slaughter or even much of a battle.

As many as forty people were missing. Evidently naked. But . . . alive? Dead? Where?

Once more Molly held her breath, willed herself to listen *through* the adamant knocking of her heart, but again she heard nothing.

At the back of the large public room, past all the tables, lay the hallway to the men's and women's lavatories. To the right of the hallway, in the back wall of this main chamber, waited a door marked EMPLOYEES ONLY.

The candlelight in this forward area of the tavern, where the townspeople had been gathered, did not much relieve the shadows at the back of the big room. Yet because of flickering light beyond it, she could see that the door, which had previously been closed, stood a quarter open.

She didn't relish further exploration alone, accompanied by only a host of horrific expectations.

Considering that the rest of her days were likely to be lived in a tangle of enigmas and unfathomables, she could live without knowing the answer to this one mystery. Although she was an inquiring person by nature, it seemed clear that the price of curiosity in this case would be the same for her as for the fabled cat.

One thing kept her from retreating. Cassie.

If the girl still lived, she was somewhere in peril and great distress. She could not be abandoned.

Perhaps coincidence accounted for the fact that Cassie's hair was blond, as had been Rebecca Rose's hair, that her eyes were blue, as had been Rebecca Rose's eyes.

All of her life, however, Molly had believed that there were no coincidences. She was not going to start believing in them now.

In all things, she saw design, though often the meaning of it was difficult to discern. Sometimes it was damn near impossible. As here, as now.

During the writing of a novel, when she came to trust in the reality of her characters, they began to act of their own volition, doing things that charmed, intrigued, and appalled her. Allowing them free will, she rejoiced in their wise choices and in their triumphs, was saddened by their stupidities, meannesses, and often grieved when they suffered or died. In the interest of their self-determination, she chronicled rather than created the events of their lives, seldom pulled their strings, and generally offered them only gentle guidance through signs and portents that they either understood and acted upon or, to their misfortune, refused to recognize.

Here, alone under the roof of the Tail of the Wolf, she hoped for gentle guidance, and if she failed to recognize it when it was given to her, or misinterpreted it, she hoped for some vigorous pulling of strings on her behalf.

The issue was not whether she should retreat or go forward. She could not retreat. She knew her role. She rescued children; she did not abandon them.

If Cassie had been a brunette, with no resemblance to Rebecca Rose, Molly still could not have walked away from her. The question wasn't whether or not to rescue the girl but how best to find her and extract her from this place.

At the back of the public area, the EMPLOYEES ONLY door stood ajar. In the room beyond, flickering light seemed to beckon her.

Maybe this was guidance. Maybe it was a trap.

46

BROODING ABOUT THE DOOR, KEEPING A WATCH ON it, Molly walked to the end of the bar. She opened the gate and peered into the narrow service area where Russell Tewkes had worked the taps and mixed the cocktails.

She probed with her flashlight. No one crouched there among the brittle, bristling ruins of the shattered back-bar mirror.

A sludge of darkness filled the hall that led to the lavatories. Her beam washed it away, revealing no one.

She considered investigating the rest rooms. The prospect didn't thrill her.

She worried about what size the black fungus had achieved. What capabilities might it possess?

In the women's room, she had never closed the window following Render's departure. Anything might have crept in from this goblin night. In that tight space, the three closed stall doors would offer the challenge of three spring-loaded lids on jack-in-the-boxes packed with surprises designed in Hell.

Besides, the two lavatories together could not have accommodated forty people. She didn't expect to find them in small groups, whether dead or alive, but in one place.

Here again she felt the truth of being at the still point of the turning world, with past and future gathered in the moment.

Although she had resisted this knowledge all her life, had lived determinedly in the future, focused there by ambition, she understood at last that *this* was the real condition of humanity: The dance of life occurred not yesterday or tomorrow, but only here at the still point that was the present. This truth is simple, self-evident, but difficult to accept, for we sentimentalize the past and wallow in it, while we endure the moment and in every waking hour dream of the future.

What Molly had done thus far in her life was the history of her soul, unalterable, ineradicable. What she hoped to do in the future was of no meaning if she failed to do the wise thing, the good thing, moment by moment by moment, here at the still point, here in the dance of life.

Cassie. Finding Cassie. Moment by moment by moment, finding Cassie, the past would be made, and the future.

With pistol, with flashlight, with trepidation, she cautiously approached the door.

Through the open wedge, she saw six or eight candles in glass globes, deposited on the floor. Salamanders of apricot light crawled the walls.

She nudged the door with one foot, and it swung smoothly inward on well-oiled hinges.

Candlelight revealed no occupants. Neither did the flashlight when, from the threshold, she swept the space with it.

Beyond lay what appeared to be a receiving room measuring approximately twelve by fifteen feet. Windowless. Gray tile floor with a drain in the center. Bare concrete walls.

A wide steel door directly opposite the one in which she stood would open to the alleyway behind the tavern. Cases of beer, liquor, wine, and other supplies had been delivered through it.

In the wall to her right, reflections of candle flames purled in the brushed stainless-steel doors of an elevator.

The tavern didn't have a second floor. The elevator transported supplies down to the basement.

In the wall to her left stood another door, ajar. Logic insisted that she would find basement stairs beyond it.

Between the doorway in which she stood and the basement door, the flashlight beam detailed a trail of wet blood on gray concrete: not a river of gore, just patterns of droplets intact and droplets smeared.

With no electrical service, they had not taken the elevator down to whatever madness waited to be discovered below. Whether under duress or of their own accord, though in either case surely in the grip of unimaginable terror, they had descended the narrow passage in single file, naked and bleeding.

A chill walked the stairs of Molly's spine as she considered that strange procession and wondered what ceremony or savagery had occupied those people in the cellar.

She glanced back into the deserted tavern. Nothing had changed.

Trying to avoid as much of the blood as possible, she stepped off the threshold and followed the beam of her flashlight along the trail that her neighbors had so recently marked with sanguinary clarity.

The brass doorknob, once shiny, was patinaed with blood from uncounted trembling hands. She toed the door open toward her, into the receiving room.

Beyond this threshold lay a small landing, pale wood stippled with crimson. She hesitated to set foot upon it, leaned through the doorway instead.

A cold draft rose past her, redolent of a scent that she had never before encountered and that she would have been hard-pressed to describe. It was not a foul smell, in fact not even unpleasant, and yet disturbing.

A cramped flight of steep wooden steps descended to a lower landing, from which a second and shorter flight turned left into the cellar.

Apparently, they had taken no candles beyond the receiving room. Only the flashlight brightened the stairs.

The thought of her neighbors' blind descent struck such pity in Molly that her knees weakened.

O dark dark dark. They all go into the dark.

She could not see the last few treads of the lower flight. The cellar lay entirely beyond her view, and she could not angle the beam in any way to illuminate that space.

Though I walk through the valley of the shadow of death, I will fear no evil.

Easier said than done. Fear half throttled Molly, and she had not yet entered the walled and stepped valley before her.

To learn the fate of those who had marked this route with their blood, to discover if Cassie was alive—and the whereabouts of her three guardian dogs—Molly would have to go down at least as far as the lower landing. Once there, she could stoop to the best vantage and with her flashlight pierce the darkness in the lower chamber.

She couldn't decide whether this was a test of her courage or of her wisdom. Under the circumstances, prudence might be the good thing, the right thing; but how difficult it was, in the quick, to tell the difference between prudence and cowardice.

Not the faintest murmur rose with the curiously scented draft. Not a sigh. Not a cough. Not a whimper. Not a word of whispered prayer.

With forty people pressed into a cold storeroom, a sound or two of discomfort might be expected, an agitated movement motivated by distress.

Although the thunder of forty fearful hearts might be entirely contained in forty breasts, surely the frightened breathing of so many would raise a betraying susurration. Not all of them would be holding their breath simultaneously, waiting for Molly to stop holding hers.

Yet, coiled in a stillness deeper than mere silence, the tavern cellar waited in a hush.

Her mouth seemed too dry for speech, but she worked up a simple question: "Cassie?"

The cellar took in the name and gave nothing back.

Sweat as cold as ice water trickled along her right temple and curled around her ear.

She raised her voice because she had previously spoken in little more than a whisper: "Cassie?"

A response came not from the girl, not from the realm below, but from the receiving room behind Molly: "I can bite, but I can't cut."

47

CROUCH, PIVOT, POINT, SQUEEZE, ALL IN ONE FLUID action: Molly did the first three, checked herself halfway through the trigger squeeze, and did not shoot the woman.

Clarinetist, lover of swing music, waitress at Benson's Good Eats, twentysomething, dark-haired, gray-eyed, Angie Boteen stood in the receiving room, naked, holding a broken Corona bottle by the neck.

"Always been squeamish, especially about knives, razor blades . . . broken glass," Angie said.

She sounded like herself, yet didn't. She looked like herself, yet wasn't. Anxiety in her voice made it real, but at the same time she seemed to be dreaming on her feet, detached.

"I need to be cut, I want to be cut, I want to obey, I really do, but I've always been afraid of sharpness more than anything."

Relying on the candles, Molly shoved her flashlight under her waistband, in the small of her back, freeing both hands for the gun.

"Angie, what the hell happened here?"

Ignoring the question, as if she didn't hear it, Angie Boteen appeared to have stepped out of the dance of life, out of the still point, and stood in the past:

"When I was six, Uncle Carl, he cut Aunt Veda 'cause she cheated on him, slit her throat. I was there, saw it."

"Angie—"

"She lived, croaked when she talked, scar on her throat. He went to prison, and when he got out, she took him back."

Molly felt as naked as Angie, exposed, standing in this doorway with the basement stairs at her back.

"After prison, people treated Uncle Carl different. Not worse. More careful, more respectful."

Reluctant to look away from Angie Boteen, Molly nevertheless glanced back, to her left, and down. No one on the stairs.

Refocusing on Angie and on the jagged bottle, she discovered that during this moment of distraction, the woman had taken a step toward her.

"No closer," Molly warned, thrusting the pistol at arm's length, in a two-hand grip.

In the globes on the floor, inconstant candle flames leaped, languished, and leaped, fattened and thinned, so upward across the woman's face flowed light, flowed shadow, continuously distorting, making it difficult for Molly to read her expression.

"So then what happened," Angie said, "is I hook up with Billy Marek, he's been in trouble with knives, cut some people, done time."

Under the appearance of a trance, repressed emotions tore at the woman and could be detected in her voice. Anguish. Anxiety. Wild terror on a choke chain. But what other sensibilities did the fluctuant candle flames disguise? Psychotic needs? Anger? Homicidal rage? Hard to tell.

"I know he'll never cut me 'cause I'll never cheat, but people respect him, so they respect me."

Although Molly had a moment ago checked the stairs, already she imagined an ascending presence. Maybe it wasn't imagined. Maybe it would be real this time.

"He cut someone for me once," said Angie. "I wanted it done, and Billy did it. I felt bad later. I was sorry later. But he did it. And he would've done it again if I asked, and that made me feel safe."

Molly eased out of the doorway, to the left, her back against the wall, putting distance between herself and the naked woman but also between herself and the stairs.

"If he was here," Angie said, "I'd ask him, and he'd cut me, Billy would, he'd cut me just right, not too deep, so I wouldn't have to do it myself."

Molly could almost believe madness was in the air: contagious, carried on dust mites, easily inhaled, following a path of infection straight from lungs to heart to brain.

Reminding herself of her purpose, trying to get control of the situation, she said, "Listen, there was a little girl here earlier. Her name was Cassie."

"I want to obey, I really do, I want to obey and satisfy like the others. Will you cut me?"

"Obey *who*? Angie, I want to help you, but I don't understand what's going on here."

"The cuts are an invitation. They cluster at the cuts. They come in through the blood by invitation."

Fungus, Molly thought. *Spores.*

"Thousands of them," Angie said, "coming through the blood. They want to be in the flesh, in the live flesh for a little while, before I'm dead."

Even if the bolero of shadows and candlelight had not flung distortions across Angie's features, the woman's dementia would have prevented Molly from reading her emotions and inferring her intentions.

"Angie, honey, you've got to put down the bottle and let me help you." Molly didn't have to fake compassion. In spite of her fear, she was shaken by sympathy for this distraught and confused woman. "Let me take you out of here."

This offer was met with agitation, anxiety. "Don't bullshit me, you bitch. That's not possible, you know it's not. There's nowhere for me to go, nowhere to hide, nowhere, ever. Or you, either. You'll be told what to do, you'll be told, and you'll do it or suffer."

The cold concrete wall against Molly's back pressed its chill through her clothes and into her flesh, her bones, brought winter to her spirit. She was shivering and couldn't stop.

"I've got to obey." A long harrowing groan came from her, and she struck her breasts with one fist. "Obey or suffer."

With growing desperation, Molly tried again: "Cassie. A nine-year-old girl. Blond hair. Blue eyes. *Where is she?*"

Angie glanced toward the basement stairs. Her voice was sharp, urgent: "They're all below, they made the invitation, they cut, they cut, they opened their blood."

"What's happening down there?" Molly demanded. "Where will I find the girl if I go down there?"

Holding out her left hand, palm up, Angie said, "I bit. I bit so hard, and there's blood."

Even in the shimmering deceptions of candlelight, the teeth marks were clearly visible in the meaty part of the woman's hand, and thick clotted blood.

"I can bite, but I can't cut. I can bite, and there's blood, but that's not acceptable, because I was told to *cut.*"

Stepping between the candle globes, she moved toward Molly, and Molly backed off, circled away.

Offering the broken bottle, the jagged end still first, Angie said insistently, angrily, *"Take this and cut me."*

"No. Put the bottle down."

Sorrow welled in those mad eyes. A warm salty tide brimmed, spilled. Anger instantly became despair and self-pity. "I'm running out of time. He's going to come up those stairs, he's going to come back for me."

"Who?"

"He rules."

"Who?"

Her eyes burned red in scalding tears. "Him. It. The thing."

"What thing?" Molly asked.

Hot tears washed years off Angie Boteen's face, and rendered it the countenance of a terrified child. "The thing. The thing with faces in its hands."

48

THE HOSPITAL OF ST. MARY OF BETHLEHEM, WHICH opened its doors in London in the fifteenth century, served as an asylum for the insane, was known as Bedlam, and closed its doors to that purpose in an age distant to this one, but now Bedlam existed again, and it was the entire world, pole to pole.

Maybe a creature with faces in its hands stalked the tavern cellar, something that Goya might have imagined and painted in his darkest hours, or maybe this menace existed only in Angie Boteen's mind. Whether real or not, it was real to her.

"Afraid of sharpness. I'm weak," she said. "Always been weak. I want to obey, they expect obedience, but I can't cut myself. I can bite, but I can't cut."

Molly retreated, circled, stepping cautiously among the candles, like a conjurer trying to stay within her protective pentagram.

Circling, advancing, holding out the broken bottle, Angie said, "Take this. Do me, slash me. Before he comes back." A glance at the stairs. Then at Molly. "Slash me, before he comes back angry."

Molly shook her head. "No. Put it down."

Simultaneously imploring and furious, Angie advanced: "Whatever you hate, see that in me. Whoever you envy, everything you fear, see all that in me—then cut, *cut me, CUT ME!*"

Tough as she was, tough as she always had been, boiled in terror at a young age, Molly nonetheless felt something cracking in herself, a barrier that must hold if she was ever to find Cassie, if she was to be the rescuer of children that so many children needed her to be.

Incipient tears welled in her eyes. She blinked them back, fearful that they would blur her vision. In the blur, she would be vulnerable to Angie, to whatever had driven the forty people into the basement, to the thing with faces in its hands if it existed.

"Angie . . ." Molly's voice broke, speaking to the wounded child at the heart of this woman. "What've they done to you?"

Even in her madness, Angie Boteen recognized the tenderness that wrung tears from Molly. Understanding the finality of those words, she threw the bottle aside. It shattered on the elevator doors.

"Wish I was dead already." Angie began to shake as though she'd only now become aware of being naked in a cold room. "Wish I was."

Lowering the pistol, Molly said, "Let me take you out of here."

Angie stared with dread toward the cellar stairs. "It's coming."

Edging closer to the door to the tavern, Molly also aligned herself with the cellar door and raised the pistol once more.

The woman cared nothing for Cassie, only for her own plight, but Molly persisted: "A nine-year-old girl. You must have seen her. She was the only child left here."

Angie Boteen began to sink into the floor as if she were standing in quicksand.

49

*AN EXTRATERRESTRIAL SPECIES, HUNDREDS OR THOU-
sands of years more advanced than us, would possess technology that
would appear to us to be not the result of applied science but entirely supernatural, pure magic.*

That was what Neil had said, quoting some science-fiction writer after
the events at the Corrigan house.

In the hours since, Molly had seen ample evidence of the truth in that
contention, not least of all the transit of Angie Boteen through the
receiving-room floor.

Concrete is what *concrete* means. Real. Actual. Solid—as in "an artifi-
cial stonelike material made by mixing cement with various aggregates."

Yet this slab of steel-reinforced, poured-in-place concrete, the stuff of
bomb shelters and ammunition bunkers, seemed to adjust its billions of
atoms to precisely fit the interstices between the atoms of the woman's
body. The floor did not appear to soften. It did not part like the jaws of a
shark eager to swallow. It did not blossom outward in concentric circles
as does water that has accommodated a dropped stone. What it *did* do
was accept Angie Boteen as if she were a spirit—less than ectoplasmic
vapor, the merest apparition—and pass her through in smooth descent
from the receiving room to the cellar.

Angie was not a ghost. Her flesh was as solid and as vulnerable as

Molly's. She had thrown the Corona bottle, which had shattered on the elevator doors. Her bare feet had left prints in the blood trail leading to the basement stairs. Her tears had dripped from her jaw line, leaving tiny dark spots of moisture on the concrete, each more of a mark on the floor than she had made by passing through it.

She didn't vanish as instantly as a message cylinder sucked down a pneumatic tube; neither did she offer any resistance nor meet with any. Perhaps she took six seconds to precipitate from ground floor to the lower realm, beginning with the soles of her feet and concluding with a final wisp of trailing hair.

Considering how frightened she had been of the thing with faces in its hands, and assuming that this entity must have had something to do with drawing her through the cement and various aggregates, Angie made surprisingly little noise during her departure. She didn't scream. She didn't cry out to God for help or to well-respected Billy Marek with his knives.

She said softly, "Oh," not in surprise but in recognition—of what, Molly could not guess—and looked down at her legs vanishing through concrete. Her eyes widened, but she appeared less afraid than at any moment since she had stepped into the receiving room.

When Molly held out a hand, Angie reached for it, saying, *"Sauvez-moi, sauvez-moi"*—which was what the astronaut Emily Lapeer had cried out aboard the International Space Station when coming face to face with the uninvited visitors. "Save me, save me," Angie repeated in French, in the very voice of Emily Lapeer, and something in her eyes was different than before, hostile and mocking.

She wasn't afraid, because she wasn't Angie anymore. Angie was a powerless prisoner under the rule of whatever had entered into her and now used her body.

Snatching her hand back, Molly watched the naked woman sink to chin, to nose, to brow, as though drowning in hardened concrete. Gone.

If Molly had taken the hand, maybe she would have been dragged along with Angie, slipping through concrete and rebar as easily as mist through moonlight.

This possibility briefly paralyzed her. She hesitated to move a foot, for fear that the surface tension of the floor might prove to be as fragile as that of a summer pond.

Then she remembered a salient detail from the radio report about the space station. Inboard of the airlock, before Arturo had started screaming, Lapeer had said that something was entering through the *closed* hatch: "—just phasing *through* it, materializing *right out of the steel.*"

The risk of being taken down into the cellar through the floor might be exceeded by the danger of some menace rising out of there and into this receiving room.

Floors, walls, and bank-vault doors offered no protection. No fortress could stand against this enemy. No place on this new Earth could provide security, peace, or even privacy.

Reality isn't what it used to be.

That had been a favorite aphorism of the dopers who tended to gravitate to the liberal-arts programs and literature courses when Molly had been a student at Berkeley. They were the ones in the writing program who rejected the traditional values of literature in favor of "intellectual freedom through emotional and linguistic anarchy," whatever that meant.

Reality wasn't what it used to be. This afternoon it might not be what it was this morning.

Lewis Carroll meet H. P. Lovecraft.

The inmates of Bedlam, so misunderstood and unable to cope in their own time, might find these new circumstances more in line with their experience and their view of life.

Molly, on the other hand, felt as though her sanity was in the precarious position of a runaway train rollicking down a mountain on loose tracks.

If the ET with faces in its hands was master of a technology that allowed it to rise through the floor as easily as Angie had been taken below, if there were no barriers to its movements, then descending the basement stairs now, in search of Cassie, would be no more dangerous than standing here or being out in the street with Neil. Caution had no merit, and prudence no reward. Fortune would favor the bold, even the reckless.

Again, by candlelight, she followed the blood trail to the cellar door. She was almost to that threshold when movement, glimpsed peripherally, made her halt, turn.

A dog. The golden retriever—one of the three dogs that stayed behind with Cassie—stood in the doorway to the tavern. Posture tense. Eyes solemn. Then a wag of the tail.

50

THE TWITCH OF THE DOG'S TAIL CONVINCED MOLLY
to follow it by flashlight out of the receiving room, to the women's lavatory. No dog would wag if he had lost a child entrusted to his care, and
especially not one of these dogs, in which seemed to be vested an un-
common intelligence plus a loyalty even greater than their four-footed
kind usually exhibited.

Cassie stood in the rest room, her back pressed in a corner, guarded by
the two mixed breeds. Just for a moment, these mutts presented bared
teeth to Molly, surely not because they mistook her for a threat but perhaps because they wanted her to see—and to be reassured by—their diligence.

Someone had closed the window through which Render had escaped.
The floor at that end of the room was still puddled with rain, but nothing
grew in it.

Distraught, Cassie came at once into Molly's arms, buried her face
against Molly's throat, and trembled uncontrollably.

Molly comforted the girl, stroked her hair, and determined that she
had not been harmed.

Under the logic of the old reality, getting out of the tavern would have
been a priority. Flee first, counsel the child later.

In the new reality, the world outside would be as dangerous as any room in the tavern, including the cellar.

Any outdoor place was in fact *more* dangerous than the tavern. In spite of the resident of the janitorial closet and regardless of what spores might be fruiting in the self-mutilated congregation in the cellar, the grotesque and hostile life forms of another planet roamed open places in increasing numbers.

The masters of this magical-seeming alien technology were able to extract their prey from any sanctuary, through walls or floors or ceilings, and surely they themselves could pass through solid matter in the same fashion. The lower life forms, however—the equivalent of Earth's mammals, reptiles, insects—had no such ability; walls were barriers to them.

The frenzied fluttering horde in Johnny and Abby's house had been struggling to find a way out of their nest behind the lath and plaster. The insectile behemoth in the church basement would not have torn violently out of the oak floor if it had been able to phase through that planking with ease.

Consequently, although the tavern provided no safe haven against the powerful lords of this invasion, it offered some protection from the venomous creatures of their ecology.

"They're all dead, aren't they?" Cassie asked.

Because the girl's mother and father were among the missing, Molly said, "Maybe not, honey. Maybe they—"

"No." The girl didn't want to be coddled. "Better dead . . . than with one of those things inside you."

This seemed to be a reference to something other than spores entering the body through lacerations. Most likely, Cassie had never seen what grew in the janitorial closet or the white colonies that now crawled the half-light of the purple morning.

"What things?" Molly asked.

"The things with faces in their hands."

Angie had mentioned one such being. The girl spoke of *things,* plural.

The three dogs stirred and made thin anxious sounds and growled softly, as though they remembered the entities of whom she spoke.

"What does that mean, Cassie—faces in their hands?"

The girl's voice fell to a whisper. "They can take your face and keep it in their hands, and show it to you, and other faces, and crush them in their fists, and make them scream."

This explanation failed to dispel Molly's confusion. The answers to a few more questions gave her a somewhat better idea of what had happened to Cassie's parents and to others in the tavern, but left her with an inadequate image of the things with faces in their hands.

Three of them had risen through the tavern floor, into the midst of the people gathered there. They were humanoid in form—between six and seven feet tall, with two legs, two arms—but far from human in appearance.

The extreme alien aspect of these creatures caused even the peace lovers to panic. Some had tried to flee, but the ETs had halted them simply by pointing, not with a weapon or instrument but with a hand. Likewise, a mere pointing at once silenced those who screamed and caused those with weapons to drop them without firing a shot.

To Molly, this suggested telepathic control—another reason to wonder if the taking of the world could be resisted to any significant extent.

The three ETs had then moved among the people, "taking their faces." What this meant, Molly could not adequately ascertain.

At first, according to Cassie, there was just "smooth" where each person's face had been, and the face that had been removed was "alive in the thing's hand."

Subsequently, for a moment, an alien face—like those of the three who had risen through the floor—formed out of the smoothness where the stolen countenance had been. Then it faded, and the original face, the human face, returned.

This had suggested to Cassie that alien masters had been installed inside these people, but that was definitely movie thinking and might not be the correct explanation.

The girl had not witnessed all of those in the tavern being subjected to this process, because in fear she'd fled to the women's lav, with the dogs accompanying her. She hadn't been willing to risk leaving by the front door, because to get there, she would have been forced to pass too close to the ETs.

Here in the lavatory, Cassie had waited, expecting one of the things to seek her out and to take her face.

Molly wasn't able to sift any useful hard facts from the girl's bizarre account, but she inferred from it that Cassie had been spared neither by accident nor by oversight. The ETs intentionally allowed her to escape. When she'd run, they could have halted her as they had halted any adults who tried to flee.

Abby and Johnny, trapped in a house that was "changing . . . almost alive," had not been attacked either by the beast that slaughtered their drunken father in the garage or by the agitated multitudes whispering in the walls.

Eric, Elric, and Bethany had not been "floated" through the ceiling and into the storm with their parents and grandmother. And in the attic, they'd been rescued from the amorphous predator visible only in peripheral vision, the thing that smelled of "burnt matches, rotten eggs, and poop."

In the church, although Bethany had a close call, all five of the children had been saved from certain death—and perhaps not entirely because of actions that Molly and Neil had taken.

The inference that Cassie had intentionally been spared led to the further inference that at this point in the taking of the world, the war plan called for the ruthless extermination of most human beings above a certain age—but specified the preservation of the children.

At first this seemed baffling if not inexplicable, but then in the mare's-nest of surreal events, among the tangle of dark wonders and impossibilities that defined the past twelve hours, Molly found and followed a thread of logic leading inexorably to a suspicion that chilled her.

One by one, she met the eyes of each of the three dogs. Mutt, mutt, retriever: They regarded her forthrightly, expectantly, tails wagging tentatively.

She scanned the floor, walls, ceiling.

If her thoughts had been read, her suspicion known, she expected that something would enter the lavatory through one solid surface or another, take her face, and then her life.

Here at the still point of the turning world, she waited to die—and didn't.

"Come on, sweetie," she said to Cassie, "let's get out of here."

51

THE OVERCAST REMAINED LOW, DENSE, PURPLE. THE livid half-light might henceforth be a permanent condition of the daytime, from dawn to dusk.

Elsewhere in the dying town, the weeping of a woman was answered by the weeping of a man, which was answered by the weeping of *another* woman, each of the three expressing her or his misery in precisely the same series of wretched sobs and wails. The crawling white fungi seemed to be ceaselessly exploring or perhaps seeding new colonies where they found ideal conditions.

Outside the tavern, after turning Cassie over to Neil's care and giving him a hug, Molly took the three Crudup kids aside to revisit the story they had told her during the journey from St. Perpetua's to the Tail of the Wolf. Fresh from her experience with Angie in the tavern receiving room, and with Cassie's account to consider, she should be able to make more sense of Eric, Elric, and Bethany's tale.

Their mother and father had floated up from the family-room floor as if suddenly exempted from gravity. The couple had passed through the ceiling, then through the ceiling of the second-floor bedroom above, and finally through the roof, out of the house. As astonished and amazed as they were terrified, the kids had dashed up the stairs and then scrambled up the attic ladder, following their parents from level to level.

This had occurred during one of the leviathan's transits over the town, when its hovering weight oppressed and when the silent throbbing of its engines could be felt in the bones. Therefore, the kids had reached the conclusion that their parents had been beamed aboard the mother ship.

Their grandmother, of whom the children spoke with an affection that didn't characterize any mention of their parents, reacted with horror to the extraordinary ascent of her daughter and son-in-law. She had not been comforted by her grandchildren's assurances—based on movies and TV shows—that those who were beamed aboard an alien ship were always beamed down again, even if after rude examinations and sometimes painful experiments.

Less than an hour later, when the grandmother abruptly floated off the floor toward the family-room ceiling, she had not let out a scream, as might have been expected, but only a small cry of surprise as her feet left the carpet. Looking down on her grandchildren, she astonished them by smiling, and she waved before she passed through the ceiling.

By the time the kids caught up with her on the second floor, she was laughing. And in the attic, before she vanished through the roof, she said, "Don't worry about Gramma, darlings. I don't feel the arthritis at all."

Now Eric continued to insist that their grandmother had gone "nuttier than a can of Planters," a contention that angered Bethany no less than it had earlier. Elric remained neutral on the issue.

Because of Molly's troubling suspicion, formed while she had listened to Cassie in the tavern, she was especially interested in the post-grandmother part of this story, when the Crudup children had been alone in the house.

The sickening odor of the hostile presence had made them gag when they had clambered into the attic for the second time. Bethany cupped her hands over her nose and mouth, trying to filter out the worst of the stench, but the twins, being named for Scandinavian heroes, breathed through their mouths and endured.

They hadn't identified the source of the stink until their grandmother had passed through the roof, whereupon they spotted a creature that was more easily seen from the corner of the eye than when you looked directly at it, that was more shape than detail, that kept changing shape, that stood between them and the only exit from the attic.

"It wanted us," said Bethany.

Of that, none of the three children had the slightest doubt.

It would have gotten them, too, they agreed, if not for the woman who looked like Obi-Wan Kenobi.

What they meant was not that the woman physically resembled Sir Alec Guinness (in fact, she was pretty), not that she might have been as ancient as Obi-Wan (old, they agreed, but perhaps only a few years older than Molly), not that she had been dressed in a hooded robe of extragalactic style (they couldn't remember what she wore), but that she'd been a little bit translucent as they remembered Obi-Wan having been when, after his death, he sometimes visited Luke Skywalker to offer guidance.

The kids were not able to agree by what means the woman had made the beast retreat—words of enchantment, a magic ring, elaborate hand mojo that *gestured* it into submission, the sheer force of her personality—but they did agree that she banished it to a far end of the attic, away from the trapdoor, which had been the only exit. They fled that high chamber and never looked back either at the reeking thing of many shapes or at the apparition that had saved them.

"She kinda looked like you," Bethany told Molly.

"No, she didn't," said Eric.

"Well," Elric said, "I sorta think she did."

"Kinda like you," Bethany insisted.

Eric studied Molly's face. "Yeah, maybe she did."

Molly had no idea what to make of this development, whether to make anything at all of it.

More important, in walking these children through their story again, she had found support for the terrible suspicion that had overcome her in the tavern.

She surveyed the surrounding town. In the west, one of those luminous craft, disc or sphere, streaked north to south through the fog layer, and at ground level its passing light made the shadows of houses and trees appear to quicken after it like a horde of malevolent spirits drawn by a Piper playing a tune beyond human hearing.

The ETs, these new masters of a remade Earth, were indifferent to suffering and were capable of cruelties that exceeded in every instance the wickedest acts of humanity, which was frequently a cruel species in its own right. Yet they were allowing—perhaps ensuring—the survival of most if not all of the children.

These destroyers of civilizations were without mercy. If most or all of the children were intentionally being spared, surely their reprieve would be temporary. The ETs must have some special use for them.

52

"WHAT SPECIAL USE?" NEIL ASKED.

"Don't know, can't even guess," Molly said.

They stood in the middle of the street, apart from the six children and the four dogs, speaking softly, looking not at each other but at the surrounding buildings and trees.

For the immediate future and probably for the rest of their lives, which might be one and the same, they would be on sentry duty no matter what other tasks they were engaged upon. When they grew weary, they would have to take turns sleeping.

Maybe the ETs wanted the kids to survive for the time being, and maybe Molly and Neil, as guardians of the children, were not on the extermination list, at least for the moment, but they couldn't trust that she had made the correct inferences from recent events. Their best hope was diligence, if they had any hope at all.

A grim analogy occurred to her. "We're harvestmen."

"We're what?" Neil asked.

"The children are the crop. We've been sent into the fields to harvest them."

She could see that this idea was a spider that crawled his nerves, perhaps because it rang as true as penitential bells.

"We are who we are, doing what we want to do," he said by way of weak denial.

"Which makes us useful to the bastards," she suggested. "But whatever fate the kids are being harvested for, we damn sure aren't going to deliver them to it."

Considering the imbalance of power between them and the aliens, this oath sounded like bravado and felt like ashes in her mouth, but she meant to die, if necessary, in the fulfillment of it.

"Don't trust the dogs," she warned him.

Neil studied the four canines that, alert for danger, slowly circled the children. "They're devoted to the kids."

"Loyal, courageous," she agreed, "as dogs nearly always are. But these aren't ordinary animals."

"We know that much from their behavior," he agreed.

"They're dogs but something more than dogs. At first it seemed magical, with Virgil and the rose and all. But it's the 'something more' we can't trust."

He met her eyes. "You all right?"

She nodded. "It was ugly in the tavern."

"All dead?"

"Or worse."

He said, "If it comes to that . . ."

Trying to help him, she said, "Death, you mean."

"If it comes to that, you want me to give you extreme unction?"

"Can you?"

"I don't hold the office anymore, but I still know the words, and believe them." He smiled. "I think I'll be cut some slack."

"All right," she said. "Yes. I'd like it if you would. If it comes to that."

"Have you prepared yourself?"

"Yeah. The first time one of those bright craft hovered over us, pretty much your classic flying saucer, you and me with Johnny and Abby in the street. I expected death rays like something from *The War of the Worlds.*"

"In the movie," he said, "both Gene Barry and Ann Robinson survived."

"Earth's bacteria killed off all the mighty Martians," Molly recalled.

She didn't expect a Hollywood ending this time.

Remembering how Neil, a film buff, had stood in front of the TV watching moments of favorite old movies for the last time, before they had left home, she knew that he would enjoy a question to test his knowledge.

"Whatever happened to Gene Barry, anyway?" she asked. "Did he make any other movies?"

"Several, including a really great one. *Thunder Road* with Robert Mitchum."

Leaving the kids to the care of the other three dogs, Virgil had come to Molly's side. He chuffed with impatience.

Stooping before the shepherd, scratching gently behind his ears, giving no indication that her trust of him was no longer complete, Molly said, "All right, boy. I know. Time to do the work."

At this, Virgil turned from her and padded away, hurrying south on Main Street.

They set out again: Molly following Virgil, the six kids and the other three dogs close behind her, Neil guarding the back of the column.

The wine-dark day, clammy between the sodden earth and the low overcast, said *funeral,* said *cemetery.*

Black-and-gray bunting, shadows and moss, swagged the trees, and along the curb, parked vehicles seemed to be waiting to form a ceremonial procession as soon as the hearse appeared and led the way.

The shops and houses rose like blank-walled mausoleums, lacking names and epitaphs, as if the dead had been forever forgotten as soon as they had been interred.

The breathless day lay in throttled silence again. The mimicry of weeping women and sobbing men had ceased.

No feathered omens of death—no ravens, owls, crows—dared the ominous sky. None sang or hooted in the trees, either, or hopped the wet yards in search of fat earthworms, or gathered to sit shivah on fences or on porch railings.

Despite a lack of winged portents, Molly sensed that most of the people in Black Lake were dead. Not long ago, she had thought they might be found huddled in their fortress houses, armed with guns and knives and baseball bats, prepared to defend their families, but she knew better now.

Those who had not been slaughtered had instead been taken and imprisoned to serve as subjects of experimentation or as objects of cruel play. Nothing lived in most of these houses anymore—unless otherworldly vermin crawled the damp rooms, unless unearthly plants rooted in cellars, in rich beds of decaying cadavers, spreading pale leaves and black blooms.

Molly glanced back at the children and winced when she saw that they regarded her so hopefully, with such evident conviction that she could be relied upon. A few smiled thinly, and their pathetic confidence moved her. She looked forward again to prevent them from seeing the tears that she blinked away.

Although she was prepared to die for them, she didn't deserve their trust. In this worldwide holocaust, during which entire armies had perished before one soldier could fire one shot, she was acutely aware that she and Neil were inadequate to the task before them.

A failed writer with a pistol, a failed priest with a shotgun. In their lives they had succeeded—truly and unequivocally succeeded—at only one thing: love. In their enduring and always growing love for each other, they had found redemption, peace.

Their enemy, however, was impervious to the power of love. Judging by all available evidence, these invaders lacked even the capacity to grasp the concept.

Virgil turned right at the corner, onto Marine Avenue, and when Molly followed him, she thought for an instant that the humid air and the peculiar light had conspired to play a trick, the equivalent of a mirage or Fata Morgana. It seemed that an enormous mirror filled the intersection a block to the west, reflecting Virgil and the procession that followed him.

Then she realized that the dog leading the other procession was not Virgil, but an Irish setter. Two armed women, not one, were at the head of the column, and one armed man—shorter and older than Neil—brought up the end. In the middle were a dozen children and half a dozen dogs.

The other group was proceeding north on the cross street. They paused, staring uphill at Molly. She couldn't clearly see their faces in this poor light and at the distance of a block, but they must be astonished.

She waved, and they returned the greeting.

Their lead dog, the Irish setter, kept moving. After a brief hesitation, they decided to continue following it rather than turn onto Marine Avenue and come uphill to satisfy their curiosity. Their work was not finished.

Besides, they recognized the task on which Molly and Neil were embarked, as she recognized theirs. The population of children in Black Lake was too large to be rescued by a single team. And if there were two teams, most likely there were three or more.

This might have lifted Molly's spirits if she had not come to suspect that they were not rescuers but harvesters.

The other group moved out of sight on the cross street.

Virgil led Molly toward a nearby Victorian house that was elegant in its dormers, gables, and gingerbread.

She glanced at her wristwatch. Almost noon. Ten hours had passed since she'd first seen the luminous rain, the coyotes on the porch. She sensed that they were running out of time and that the final blow of this war, whatever it might be, would be struck soon.

PART SEVEN

"In my end is my beginning."

T.S. Eliot, *East Coker*

53

DORMERS DECORATED WITH CARVED FLORAL-THEME pediments, a wealth of millwork applied with exuberance, primrose gardens surrounded by palisades of wrought iron, fluted porch columns with Italianate capitals, a paneled and intricately painted entry door with stained-glass window: This house was the epitome of architectural order, evidence of humanity's long struggle against chaos and of its search for meaning.

During Molly's lifetime, architects had largely championed sterility, which is order bled of purpose, and celebrated power, which is meaning stripped of grace. By rejecting the fundamentals of the very civilization that made possible its rise, modernism and its philosophical stepchildren offered flash in place of genuine beauty, sensation in place of hope.

All her life, she had watched civilization grow uglier, meaner; now as she followed Virgil up these porch steps, she was overcome by a devastating sense of loss. This beautiful house, on which so much love had been expended in the design and construction, was a symbol of all that would be scoured out of existence by the new ecology and by the brutal new masters of the earth. The destruction that had been wrought in incremental steps by a century of modernism had been exceeded a thousandfold in less than one day; and soon all the works of modernism itself would be obliterated by cold-blooded creatures that embodied the future for which modernism yearned.

All of humanity's follies seemed worth embracing if that were the price to preserve everything beautiful in human civilization. Although the human heart is selfish and arrogant, so many struggle against their selfishness and learn humility; because of them, as long as there is life, there is hope that beauty lost can be rediscovered, that what has been reviled can be redeemed.

Life of the human variety, however, might soon be eradicated as thoroughly as if it had never existed.

With Virgil at the door, Molly looked back at Neil in the street with their six hostages to fortune. Seven years of marriage had gone by so swiftly; seventy would not have been enough.

The kids looked excruciatingly vulnerable. Evil seemed always drawn to children, especially to children. To those through whom flow the strongest currents of evil, the corruption and destruction of the innocent is the greatest bliss.

Virgil made a gruff sound.

As at the residence where they had found Johnny and Abby, the door opened, perhaps because the dog had the power to command it or because a malign force in the house wished to induce Molly to enter, in the spirit of the spider extending an invitation to the fly.

The dog crossed the threshold. Molly hesitated.

If these were the last hours of her life, she wanted to spend them in the service of children, whether or not she could save them in the long run. She was weary, however, and her eyes were sore from lack of sleep. Too many terrible sights had emotionally drained her. Consequently, between the good intention and the act lay a chasm of self-doubt.

She stiffened her resolve with a line of Eliot's verse: *Life you may evade, but Death you shall not.*

Grim courage could be taken from such hard truths.

She entered the house.

Although no one had touched it, the door closed behind her and Virgil.

As in that other house on another street, she heard a rustling in the walls—the teeming of many-legged multitudes or the beating of uncounted wings.

This time she did not have the moral support of Neil, only the guidance of the German shepherd, which might be in the service of some evil. To trust her intuition and her faith, which had never failed her, she must also trust the dog.

Face to windowpanes, the purple day peered in but brightened nothing. She switched on the flashlight and tried not to think about how much—or little—juice might be left in the batteries.

Virgil went to the stairs and climbed.

Ascending behind him, Molly heard the whirling wash of noise in the walls suddenly organize into a rhythmic tide. This repetitive ebb and flow brought her to a halt at the landing.

In the metered susurrations of this thousand-voiced sigh, she detected intention, meaning, and something like desperation. Listening more closely, she twitched with surprise when the soft cadenced rustling resolved into words: *"Time to murder . . . time to murder . . . time to murder . . . time to murder. . . ."*

Although the voices of this malicious choir were many, each registered hardly louder than a breath. The cumulative effect was a whisper of such insidious subtlety that it almost seemed to arise within her head, less like a real sound than like an auditory hallucination.

Abby had insisted that sometimes the walls talked. The girl had not revealed what they said.

". . . time to murder . . . time to murder . . ."

Molly could not determine whether this was a threat or a command meant to mesmerize by repetition—or something else entirely.

She told herself that she should ignore this compelling dark chorus. Instead, curiosity drew her nearer to the wall of the landing.

Under the cultivating beam of the flashlight, roses bloomed in the wallpaper, mostly yellow, some pink, thornless, leafy.

She slid one hand across the paper roses, not sure what she expected to feel. Maybe a swelling in the plaster. Evidence of structural deformities.

The wall was flat, dry, and solid. A faint vibration tingled across her palm, nothing more.

"*. . . time to murder . . . time to murder . . .*"

Among the voices in English, she thought that she detected others speaking a different language.

She leaned her head against the wall, one ear to the yellow roses.

A faint but disturbing smell came from that printed rosarium—perhaps chemicals in the paper or in the paste beneath.

When she focused her attention on the voices in foreign tongues, they clarified as though aware that she had a particular interest in them. She heard the same three-word phrase in French and Spanish. Insistent voices chanted in what might have been Russian, Japanese, Chinese, German, Swedish, and others in languages that she could not hope to identify.

Then the rhythm broke. The metered waves of sound collapsed into a wordless rush of thousands upon thousands of crisp little noises, the pita-patation and swish, the tick and buzz, of a busy nest.

Trying to divine by sound alone what kind of pestilence swarmed behind the plaster, she kept one ear to the wall a moment longer—until a lone voice whispered out of that soft tumult of flutter and squirm: "*Molly.*"

Startled, she pushed away from the wall.

Tread by tread, the flashlight beam played down the stairs, then riser by riser upward to where the dog waited above, and found no one who could have said her name.

Planetary apocalypse suddenly had become unnervingly personal. Something of unearthly origin, crawling inside the walls to unknown purpose, had spoken her name with a creepy intimacy, filling her with revulsion.

And again, in a needful, yearning tone: *"Molly."*

54

EYES RADIANT AND FAMILIAR IN SHADOW, FLARING and strange in the flashlight, Virgil greeted Molly at the head of the stairs, not with a wag of his tail but with an urgent whine, and led her directly to the only one of five doors that was closed.

In that room, a child cried faintly, perhaps a boy, sobbing not as though in immediate jeopardy but as though he had been worn down by long endurance of terror.

She tried the door with the same hand that held the flashlight. The knob would not turn.

For a moment, she waited for the door to open at the command of the dog or whatever presence had let them in downstairs, but it remained closed.

Reluctant to pocket the pistol, she put the flashlight on the floor instead, and tried the door again with her free hand. Locked.

She called out to the weeping child, "Honey, we're here to help you. You're not alone anymore. We'll get you out of there."

As if her words had been an incantation, the door abruptly swung inward, revealing darkness complete, the blackness of a hungry maw.

Out of the walls and ceiling came her name, whispered with a ravenous eagerness: *"Molly, Molly, Molly, Molly . . ."*

She spooked backward a step.

Undaunted, Virgil dashed past her and into the room.

The door crashed shut.

She tried the knob, knowing that it wouldn't turn, and it didn't.

Stooping, she retrieved the flashlight from the floor. Rising, she detected movement in the hall, something closing fast from her right side.

He body-slammed her: a man not as big as Neil, but big enough. Hit hard, she fumbled the flashlight, dropped the gun, and went down.

Falling atop her, driving the breath out of her, he said, "You ain't gettin' them. They're my sacrifices."

The flashlight lay mere inches to their left, revealing him. Close-cropped red hair. A sensuous face—heavily lidded turquoise eyes, full lips. A cord of keloidal scar tissue tied his left ear to the corner of his mouth, souvenir of a long-ago knife fight.

"The little lambs are mine," he said, his breath a stench—the sourness of beer, the sharpness of garlic, the wretched pungency of rotted teeth.

He cocked a fist the size of a three-pound canned ham and drove it at her face.

She turned her head. His punch mostly missed her, his thumb knuckle cracked the cartilage in her left ear, and he struck the carpeted floor.

They both cried out with pain, and she knew that she wouldn't be able to dodge another blow. He would smash her nose, her cheekbones, and batter her to death.

He was half again her size, and she could not push him off, so before he could strike again, she raised her head off the floor and bit his face. Would have gone for his throat. Couldn't thrust her head in at the right angle, had to go higher. Lower teeth under his jawbone, upper teeth sunk in his unscarred cheek.

He howled and reared back from her, and she held on as if she were a terrier. He flailed on her shoulders, on the sides of her head, glancing blows, thrown in panic, and Molly wouldn't relent.

He reared up farther, just far enough, and she unlocked her bite, spat him out, shoved him off, levered him aside, thrashed away from him.

The savage, shocked by savagery when it was committed against him, rolled onto his side, and clasped both hands to his torn face, assessing the damage with whimpered disbelief.

Spitting out his blood, gagging on the taste, spitting again, and then again before she would allow herself to gasp for breath, Molly seized the flashlight, scrambled to her feet.

She had seconds, three or four. His shock would be brief, his rage swift, his vengeance brutal.

Lambs, he had said. *The little lambs are mine.* Must be more than one child in the room where Virgil had gone. *Sacrifices,* he had said.

Phantom bells rang in her damaged ear, and the half-crushed cartilage prickled like glass.

Somewhere the pistol. She had to find it. Her only hope.

Carpet, spatters of blood, carpet, dirty footprint, coins that had perhaps spilled from his pockets, all in the questing beam of light, but no pistol.

Cursing her in a slurred voice, air whistling through his torn cheek with each word, he was on his hands and knees, coming up.

Hoping to buy time to find the handgun, she kicked at his head, missed. He snared her foot, almost toppled her, lost his grip.

Carpet, carpet, blot of blood, more coins, carpet, a hand-rolled cigarette—weed, twisted at both ends—carpet, no gun, no gun. He might have fallen on the pistol.

No more time. She ran to the nearest room, fencing shadows with the flashlight, threw the door shut behind her, fumbled for the lock, hoping there would be one, and there was, just a privacy latch, no deadbolt.

The latch clicked, and he hit the door hard, shook it by the knob. He would kick it next. The latch was flimsy. It wouldn't hold.

55

MANDOLIN AND FLUTE AND TAMBOURINE AND French horn on a bed of holly, encircled with ribbons, formed the motif on the seat of the straight-backed needlepoint chair to the left of the door.

In the hall, the bitten man kicked the door. The latch twanged but didn't spring, though one more kick would pop it.

Molly tipped the chair onto its back legs and quickly wedged the headrail under the doorknob.

A second kick shattered the latch mechanism, but the bracing chair held the door and resisted a third kick as well, exquisite needlepoint proving a match for savagery, as ought to be the case in a properly ordered world.

He cursed her, pounded on the door with a fist. "I'll be back at you," he promised. "I'll be back when I'm done with my lambs."

Then maybe he went away.

Whether he was waiting for her or not, he was just a man, not something from another world. He hadn't been able to phase *through* the barricaded door.

Numerous encounters with threats unearthly and unthinkable had left her unharmed, yet an ordinary man had wounded her. In this fact was a significance that she could sense but not grasp, and once more she felt herself to be on the doorstep of a revelation of enormous importance.

She had no time to connect the puzzle pieces to which intuition had called her attention. Contemplation required peace and time, and she had none of either.

The beast she'd bitten had said the lambs, the children, were his *sacrifices*. To what, to whom, on what altar, for what purpose did not matter, only his intention—and stopping him.

Her crushed and bleeding ear ached, but it no longer rang. She could hear well enough.

The only sound was the ceaseless movement inside the walls, the rustle and slither. No voices rose from the whispery throng.

Through her rolled waves of nausea. Saliva flooded her mouth. She could still taste blood, so she spat instead of swallowing, and spat again.

Turning from the door, probing with the flashlight, the first thing she saw was a hatchet embedded in the side of a tall wooden cabinet. Blood on the blade, on the handle.

Sickened, she didn't want to look further, but she had to, and did.

She was in a home office, unrevealed by two windows looking out on moss-strangled trees in the purple noon. A door stood open to an adjacent bathroom.

She shared the room with two chopped bodies—a man on the floor, a woman tumbled in an armchair. She had become inured to horror, yet she didn't look at them too closely or too long.

Family photos on the wall behind the desk revealed that these were the parents of the children locked in the room near the head of the stairs. The kids in the pictures were a dimpled boy and an older sister with black hair and Cleopatra bangs.

Appearing in none of the photos, the scarred man must be an intruder. She had known that Michael Render would not be the only sociopath to embrace the chaos of a crumbling civilization.

Sacrifices.

Hurriedly, she searched the desk drawers, seeking a weapon. She hoped to find a handgun. The best she could come up with was a pair of scissors.

Behind her, the scarred man said, "Drop them," and pressed the muzzle of a gun, probably her own 9-mm pistol, against the nape of her neck.

56

THE NEEDLEPOINT CHAIR REMAINED BRACED UNDER
the knob; but the killer had not phased through that barrier or any other.

The adjacent bath was shared between this study and a bedroom. He
had been in the house long enough to know it well, and he had come into
the study by way of the bath and the neighboring room.

Molly didn't at once drop the scissors, as commanded. Her vivid imagination painted a tableau of rape and torture that made it worth the risk
of twisting around on him, trying to put the scissors in his guts, hoping to
dodge the shot.

But she didn't know the future and could not act on a fear of what it
might be. The past and future are equally unredeemable, and the only
time of consequence is this moment, *now*, where life occurs, where
choices are made for reasons practical and philosophical.

Dropped, the scissors clattered on the desk top.

He shifted the muzzle of the pistol to her throat, encircled her with
one arm, pawed her breasts through her sweater, motivated not by lust
but by the desire to hurt her, which he did, squeezing hard.

"You like to bite, huh?" His voice was strangely affected by his punctured cheek, his breath reeking as before but now also redolent of blood.
"You eat lamb?"

If she screamed, Neil would come, but he would leave the six children in the street, protected only by the dogs, which were now under suspicion.

"You eat lamb?" he repeated, squeezing her with such cruelty that she almost gave him the satisfaction of crying out in pain.

"No. I don't like it."

"You're gonna acquire a taste for it," he said. "I'm gonna take you down the hall, see my two lambs, gonna watch while you bite those tender babies."

In the walls, in the ceiling, the unknown presences churned with greater frenzy.

"The harder you bite them, the more fun places you think to bite them, the better your chances I'll let you live."

Vamping for time, expecting his answer to be one kind of crazy or another with no enlightening content, Molly said, "Sacrifices, you called them. To what, why?"

"They want the kids, kids more than anything, but they can't touch them."

"Who?"

"Them that rule the world now."

"Why can't they touch the kids?"

"Don't you know nothing? Kids ain't for sifting," he said. "But ain't no rules apply to *me*. If I do the kids, them with the power will be good to me."

Molly felt like a blind woman reading lines of Braille in which random dots had been omitted. Some vital understanding loomed just beyond the limits of her vision.

He withdrew his arm from around her, but he dug the muzzle of the pistol harder against her throat, just under the hinge of the jawbone. "You pick up the flashlight on the desk and move slow and easy with me. Don't try nothin' or I'll blow your pretty head off."

The bleak afternoon brightened beyond the windows. Cold white radiance streamed down, rinsing the purple out of the air.

She recognized the quality of light. One of the silent, glowing craft must be hovering over the house.

As before, she felt closely observed, examined, but more than merely examined: She felt *known* in heart and mind and body, known in terrifying completeness.

Her assailant apparently felt the same thing, because his body stiffened and he shrank a step back from the windows, pulling her with him. "What's this shit?"

Fear distracted him, and when the pressure of the muzzle eased at Molly's throat, she *knew* this was the time to act, for she was in the moment as seldom before, clear-eyed and quick of mind, all the experience of her past and all the hopes of her future focused here at the still point that was *now*.

From the desk she snatched the scissors. Simultaneously she pulled away from him and heard the double click of the trigger but not the boom of a shot.

She swung toward him. The pistol a foot from her face. Muzzle so huge, so dark. He pulled the trigger again. The gun didn't fire.

As ruthless as any Fate snipping a lifeline, she slashed at his gun hand with the scissors. He cried out and dropped the weapon.

She threw the scissors at him, stooped, and snatched the pistol off the floor.

Rising to full height, she saw him reach for her. She squeezed the trigger, and the gun bucked in her hand.

He served as the sacrifice that he had intended to make of the children. The bullet found his heart with such accuracy that he was dead before he could look surprised, a cooling corpse before he hit the floor.

His two misfires followed by her point-blank shot were not a series of coincidences, and the gun was not defective. Some power was at work on her behalf, some agency uncanny.

Behind the plaster, the teeming hive had fallen silent.

57

THE BRILLIANCE OF THE HOVERING UFO, POURING through the windows, brought too much revealing light to this body-strewn abattoir. Molly retrieved her flashlight from the desk and departed by way of the bath that connected this study to another room.

A high window in the shower stall admitted light, which revealed her moving figure in the mirror—and the figure of another who was not present. She saw the other in a glance, halted in shock to look again, but only she herself was now reflected.

She didn't know if her mother, Thalia, glimpsed in the mirror, had actually been there or whether this vision had been merely the ephemeral expression of her fondest wish, hallucination, even perhaps a flicker of madness.

She wanted to linger, studying the mirror, but the lambs, having been spared from sacrifice, needed her. Through the next room, into the hall, her way was lighted by the vessel above, by virtue of windows and skylights.

When she reached the door near the head of the stairs, it swung open wide in front of her.

This was a girl's bedroom. Stuffed animals reclined against the headboard of a bed skirted in flounces. Satiny drapes trimmed with rickrack.

Posters of teen idols on the walls, polished boys with an androgynous quality. Frills and thrills.

Two chairs stood back to back. The girl with the Cleopatra bangs, perhaps ten or eleven, and her dimpled brother sat in them, secured at wrists and ankles by duct tape.

Virgil guarded the children, and he had something formidable to guard against.

A colony of fungi—white spheres, pale lung sacs—crouched in a corner. A second colony, having sprouted those thick yet insectile legs, hung from the ceiling over the bed. Except for the inflating and deflating sacs, they were motionless, although busy life might be asquirm within them.

On the bed were the depleted roll of duct tape and the knife that the killer had used to cut it.

Hoping that the bright vessel would continue to hover over the house, shedding light through the windows, and that she would not be forced to work by flashlight in the company of the ambulatory fungi, Molly plucked the knife off the bed and sawed at the binding tape.

Their names were Bradley and Allison, and Molly did her best to soothe their fears as she also explained how directly and quickly they must leave the house. She lied about the fate of their parents when they asked anxiously after them.

Saving all these children's lives might be easier than helping them to accept a future founded on the shaky ground of personal tragedy and catastrophic destruction.

Resolutely, she turned her mind from that consideration. To do this work, she must live in the moment, and to give the children hope and counsel them out of the despair that came with dwelling on things forever lost, she must eventually teach them to live in the moment, too.

She realized only now that since stepping across the threshold at the front door of this house, she had at some point acquired the conviction that they would have a future, when previously she could not find reason to foresee long-term survival. She knew some of the reasons for this change of heart, but not all of them; evidently her subconscious had perceived other causes for optimism that it was not yet ready to share with her.

Because Bradley was young and more frightened than his sister, Molly freed him first and told him to stay close to Virgil, in whom most of her trust had been restored by recent events.

As she finished freeing Allison, Molly heard a wet, decidedly organic sound and looked up as the skin on a round, cantaloupe-size fungus in the overhead colony peeled back like the lids of an eyeball. Under those membranes lay a human face.

Of all the impossible and grotesque things that she had seen since the coyotes on the porch, this rated as the most bizarre, the least comprehensible, the most disturbing. Repulsed, she nevertheless could not avert her eyes.

A longer look revealed that the face in the fungus wasn't molded dimensionally. The surface of the sphere under the peeled-back lids was smooth and curved and transparent, and the human face appeared to float within it like an object in one of those Christmas snow globes.

This particular face was that of a man with blue eyes and blond mustache. His gaze turned to Molly, and he seemed to *see* her. His expression was anguished and imploring, and he appeared to be crying out to her, though he produced no sound.

White membranes peeled back from a second fungus in the colony, revealing another face held in another sphere: a woman screaming and in a state of abject torment. Her screams were silent.

These were not real faces, but watching them in a paralytic state of awe, of dread, Molly suspected—and quickly came to believe—that each represented a human consciousness, the mind and memory of someone who had actually lived. They had been stripped out of their physical bodies at death and somehow captured in these hideous structures.

Each colony of white fungi was some kind of organic penitentiary in which were imprisoned the consciousnesses of those people who died at the hands of the new masters of Earth. More accurately, perhaps, the colonies might be data-storage systems in which were accumulated human minds complete in every aspect, including memory, cognitive functions, and personality.

Molly's pounding heart seemed to tighten and shrink within her breast, as if withered by these considerations.

More lids peeled back, revealing additional faces, not only on the colony that crawled the ceiling but also on the one that crouched in the corner, and Molly suddenly *knew,* from the way they focused on her and on the children, and from their expressions, that they were *aware* in their prisons. Aware, alert, and desperate, some of them had been driven mad by their condition and raged insanely, silently.

Wisely, Virgil split for the upstairs hall.

Anxious to spare Bradley and Allison from further exposure to this abomination, Molly hustled the kids after the dog.

At the doorway, she glanced back and saw another lid peel away from another sphere, revealing the face of the scarred man whom she had shot no more than two or three minutes ago. His gaze found her, and his features twisted with hate.

Abruptly the faces were allowed voices, and from them arose a shrill cacophony of weeping, wailing, screaming, pleas for help, shrieks of rage, cursing, and ululations of mad laughter.

As Molly fled behind the children, down the stairs, the bright craft hovering above the house moved on, leaving the windows muddy purple once more and casting the interior into darkness.

58

NEIL WANTED TO EXAMINE HER MANGLED AND blood-caked ear, but Molly insisted they must get on with the work. Virgil was already on the move, padding east along the street, back the way they had come.

This time the children—eight of them now—proceeded at the head of the column, behind the dog. Molly and Neil followed them, watchful but not any longer in the grip of hair-trigger paranoia.

"The only thing we have to protect the kids from is people," Molly said. "Ordinary, born-of-man-and-woman *people*. The bad ones, the sick ones. But the ETs and everything that's come with them from their world . . . they'll leave the children untouched."

"How can you know that?" he asked.

She quoted the scarred man. " 'Kids ain't for sifting.' "

"What?"

"Things happened in that house, gave me a different perspective. I'll tell you later. The main thing is, the kids are untouchable."

"Why?"

"I'm not sure, but I'm working on a theory. Another thing is . . . I think those of us searching for them are untouchable, too."

"Something sure touched your ear."

"Not one of *them,* nothing . . . alien. There was this guy, this psycho, he killed their parents, was going to kill Bradley and Allison."

"I thought I heard a shot. But it was muffled, and I couldn't be sure. I almost came in."

"It was over by then."

He regarded her with something more than amazement, perhaps wonder. "You used to just write books."

"Did I? Maybe a long time ago."

The shepherd led them into Black Lake's small downtown center.

Swags of blackish moss draped all the trees and suffocated some of them. Moss had begun to clothe the buildings, as well: fringes along the rain gutters, the windowsills.

"So," he asked, "are we rescuing or harvesting them?"

"Rescuing, I think. And I feel better about the dogs."

Quick dark figures capered across the roofs and porch roofs, in and out of the low fog layer, leaping from building to building. They were the size of monkeys, with the agility of macaques and capuchins, but without the playful spirit of monkeys. Their heads were too large for their bodies, which were covered in scales rather than fur, and from a distance their asymmetric faces appeared to have been half melted in a fire. With hands that featured as many fingers as—but a greater complement of knuckles than—the hands of man or monkey, they sometimes tore at themselves as if they were in torment, though the only sounds they made were choking noises that in some instances resembled a wicked chuckling.

Fungi grew everywhere: across lawns and parks, in flower beds and flower boxes. They sprouted from cracks in sidewalks, on the walls of clapboard and wood-shingled buildings. They were not all pale white or black with yellow spots, but came in a great variety of shapes and colors that suggested not a fairyland panorama but a phantasmagoric wasteland of continuously mutating forms in the sweat-drenched dream journeys of a comatose junkie on the edge of overdose.

"What I'm wondering," Molly said, "is if maybe we've been wrong to think the ETs are a monolithic force, a hive dedicated to a single mission, driven by a single desire."

"It sure looks that way."

"Yeah. But it's like bad data processing: garbage in, garbage out. Misperceptions in, misconceptions out. There could be factions among them just like there are among human beings. And maybe one of those factions doesn't believe in completely obliterating a species and its civilization."

"If so, they're in the minority, and judging by what's happened so far, they don't have a hell of a lot of clout."

"Except maybe they've won a concession that forbids targeting children."

"But they're still taking our world from us," he said, "and how is anyone, especially a child, supposed to survive in this madhouse ecology?"

She frowned. "They can't. Not with any happiness or hope. But we've got something about this wrong, and I'm trying to straighten it out in my head."

Virgil led them to the bank. During the previous night, in a discussion with the live-free-or-die group at the tavern, Neil had recommended this building as the best place to fortify and defend, assuming there was any hope of meaningful defense or any point in making a last stand.

At first, Molly thought they'd reached the end of their rescue mission. She expected to settle in here with those who chose to fight and to prepare to face the end, if it came, with what dignity and courage they could muster.

Then she realized that no guards were stationed at the front door of the bank. The blinds were drawn at the windows, and as best she could tell, no one watched the street from inside.

"Something's wrong," Neil said. "Something's happened."

"And five kids are in there," she said.

The work was not yet completed.

59

IF THE CHILDREN WERE IN SOME WAY IMMUNIZED against ultimate violence, for whatever reason, they would be safe in the street, watched over by the dogs. Neil ought to be able to accompany Molly into the bank.

Their exemption from this holocaust, however, was no more than a theory, even though supported by some compelling evidence. With only theory to go by, Molly could not leave them without an adult defender.

If one of them had to go into the bank alone, Neil insisted on being the point man this time, but his intention was not met with enthusiasm by Virgil. The dog refused to accompany him. Indeed, the shepherd sat on the pavement in front of the door, blocking entrance.

Neil reached over the dog to open the door, but he discovered that it was locked.

When Molly approached, Virgil rose to his feet and wagged his tail. She reached for the door, which opened before she touched it.

As previously during this odyssey, this infernal tour, the inanimate seemed to harbor intention.

With an embrace and a kiss, Neil conceded the point position to Molly. He returned to the children and the dogs in the street.

During the walk to the bank, she had ejected the magazine from the

9-mm pistol and had replaced the expended cartridge. Ten rounds were loaded, ready. In the pockets of her jeans, she carried a few spares.

Flashlight in her left hand, pistol in her right, she shouldered open the door and followed Virgil inside.

The only bank in Black Lake and environs—constructed in 1936, when depositors needed to be reassured by a financial institution's grandeur—did not measure up in splendor to larger banks of that period in any major city, but it was impressive in its own modest scale. Marble floors. Six marble columns. Marble wainscoting. The surrounds at the tellers' windows were ornamental dark bronze with polished fluting and nickel inlays.

Throughout the lobby, in the tellers' enclosure, in the open area of service desks behind the marble railing, ample light was provided by Coleman gas lanterns, which hissed softly like dreaming snakes.

Molly switched off her flashlight and tucked it under the waistband of her jeans, in the small of her back, leaving both hands for the gun.

Although more than twenty adults, plus five children, had left the tavern with the intention of stocking and fortifying the bank, only four adults, three men and a woman, were in the lobby. They stood side by side, in a line, facing the row of teller windows, their backs to the door.

They didn't turn when Molly entered, which seemed odd, for the door had made some noise, and the dog's claws ticked on the floor, inspiring a sleet-storm of echoes from every marble surface.

From the back, she recognized only one of the four: Vince Hoyt, the history teacher and football coach.

"Vince?"

He didn't turn.

"Everything okay?" she asked.

None of the four acknowledged her.

Seeking guidance, she looked down at Virgil. He had abdicated leadership and, favoring Molly with a solemn gaze, waited for her to act.

She crossed the lobby to the line of four, noticing that they stood stiff, heads up, shoulders squared, essentially at parade rest, except that their arms hung slackly at their sides.

"What's going on?" she asked, and knew the answer when she came around the end of their formation.

They had no faces.

60

HERE WAS THE PHENOMENON THAT CASSIE HAD DE-
scribed: people without eyes, noses, mouths, each face smooth from ear
to ear and from hairline to the rounded bottom of the chin, the color of
pale clay, as glossy and featureless as fired ceramics.

They should have been dead, for they could not breathe.

Although their chests did not rise and fall with exhalation, inhalation,
they twitched perceptibly from time to time, and their throats moved as
they swallowed. In two of them, a racing pulse throbbed visibly in their
temples. And in every case, their hands, slack at their sides, trembled.

They radiated an anxiety that was almost palpable, almost keen
enough to smell. They were without faces, but they were still somehow
alive—and profoundly afraid.

Somewhere in the bank were five helpless children, and no doubt
with them was a thing with faces in its hands. Because its kind seemed to
be omniscient, it would know that she had arrived.

Virgil still would not lead, but he stayed bravely at her side, though
visible tremors passed through his flanks.

She opened the low bronze gate to the tellers' enclosure, and stepped
into the realm of money, realizing that money had no meaning anymore.

At the back of the tellers' enclosure, a low railing separated that space
from a hallway. She opened another gate and led Virgil into the corridor.

Three Coleman lanterns were evenly spaced along this passage. Nothing disturbed the silence except the hiss of gas burning in the mantles, behind the clear heat shields.

Here the floor was carpeted. The dog made no sound.

Five doors were set in the east side of the hall, three in the west side, all with frosted-glass panes in the top half. Some bore the names of bank officers. Another was labeled REST ROOMS. Two were not marked.

The entrance to the walk-in vault waited at the end. Set in a steel architrave, a massive round stainless-steel door, ringed with three-inch-diameter locking bolts, stood open.

Behind the doors with frosted glass, the rooms were dark. She considered them for a moment but then trusted intuition and passed them warily.

Cassie's fearful voice played in memory: *They can take your face and keep it in their hands, and show it to you, and other faces . . .*

In the vault at least one lantern glowed. She could see no one in the vestibule just beyond the deep jamb.

. . . faces in their hands . . . crush them in their fists, and make them scream . . .

Molly was fifteen feet from the vault door when she felt in mind and marrow, in blood and bone, the return of the airborne leviathan. It was cruising in from the north-northeast, seeming to compress the atmosphere below it, so that she felt like a diver deep in a marine abyss with a great weight of ocean on her shoulders.

A few steps from the vault, she heard a drizzle, turned, and saw Virgil urinating against the wall. Bladder emptied, he came to her, tail tucked, shivering, but still game.

"Good boy," she whispered, "brave boy."

At the threshold, fear gave her pause. Mouth dry and hot, hands cold and damp. The checked pistol grip slippery with sweat. She tried to bite back a shudder, but her teeth chattered for a moment like castanets.

She crossed the three-foot-deep, curved steel jamb. Immediately beyond, the day gate stood open.

Directly ahead, past the small vestibule, lay a rectangular chamber lined with safe-deposit boxes. A lantern glowed there, but the room proved to be unoccupied.

To the right of the vestibule, in a steel-framed doorway, a gate stood open. Light beckoned beyond.

Even here in the vault, she could feel the rhythmic throb of the great engines in the mountainous ship making way above the town.

She passed through the gate. To the left lay the money room—shelves laden with cash, coins, and ledgers.

Here, too, were the five children, sitting on the floor, backs against a wall, alive but terrified. And here, as she should have expected, was Michael Render, her father.

61

RENDER HAD KILLED FIVE CHILDREN IN HER SCHOOL-
room, twenty years ago, and here were five more at risk.

As if he knew what she was thinking, he said, "The magic number are
present, aren't they?"

She would have expected the vault walls to cast his voice back in
metallic echoes, but they muffled, softened. Although his words were
mocking, he sounded like a funeral director, murmuring in respect of the
dead.

Molly held the gun in both hands, pointed at his handsome face. "I'm
taking them out of here."

"Dead, maybe."

"Nobody dead but you," she said, "if it comes to that."

" 'If it comes to that,' " he repeated mockingly. "You're too morally
confused to do the right thing, Molly dear. You could have shot me at the
tavern, but you let me go. Let me go to commit what horrors?"

She shook her head. "You're underestimating me."

Quaking, tail tucked, head low, Virgil slipped past Render to join the
children.

Render produced one of his killer smiles, of the intensity and warmth
that had charmed her mother into marriage. "What do they call it when
you murder your own father? Patricide, I think."

"I have no father," she said.

"You tell yourself you don't, but you aren't convinced. You know that I came to your school that day because I loved you and didn't want to lose you."

"You've never loved anyone but yourself."

"I loved you so much that I killed to get you that day, killed whoever stood in my way, just to have a chance to raise you as a good father should."

He took a step toward her.

"Stay back," she warned. "Remember, I shot you twice that day."

"And in the back," he agreed. "But you were innocent then, and less aware of the *complexities* of right and wrong."

He took another step and reached one hand out to her, palm up, as if in a plea for an emotional connection.

She backed away from him.

Still approaching, he said, "Give Daddy a hug, and let's sit down and talk about all of this."

Molly backed into the open gate between the money room and the vestibule. She could retreat farther only if she left the room—and left him with the children.

He kept coming, hand out. "Your mother always believed in the power of love, the wisdom of *discussion.* She said anything can be accomplished with good will, with *compromise.* Didn't she teach you those values, Molly?"

She shot him in the chest. The vault did not muffle the clap of the gun, but rang with it, as if they stood inside a giant bell.

She heard the children scream and was peripherally aware that some of them covered their ears with their hands; some covered their eyes.

The slug jolted Render. And his eyes widened. And he smiled.

She shot him again, a third time, a fourth, but he did not go down. Four bullet holes marked his chest, but no blood spilled from him.

Lowering the gun, she said, "You were dead already. Dead when you came to the tavern."

"When everything began to fall apart, some of the guards at the sanitarium would have turned us loose," he said. "Out of pity, out of compassion, rather than leave us caged like animals, to starve or worse. But there were two who wouldn't have it—and shot us in our cells before they left for home."

What stood before her was not her father, but a simulacrum of exquisitely convincing detail. Now it changed, and became what it really was: a mottled black-and-gray *thing* with a face that seemed to have once imploded and been badly reconstructed. Eyes as large as lemons, protuberant, crimson with elliptical black pupils. From shoulders ridged with spiky plates of bone, leathery wings hung folded along its sides.

She knew that she stood now in the presence of a prince from another star, one of the species that had come to take the earth.

When it showed her its big, taloned, and powerful hands, she saw a face in each. Unlike the faces in the fungi, these had some dimension, and looked even more real, more disturbing than those she had seen earlier. In the left hand, the face of Michael Render. In the right hand, the face of Vince Hoyt, the football coach standing faceless now in the lobby of the bank.

The ET closed its enormous hands, and from within its clenched fingers, she heard her father screaming in agony, and Vince Hoyt.

When it opened its hands, the faces had changed, and now she saw a famous politician in the left, a famous actress in the right. These, too, cried out in misery when it crushed them in its fists.

Molly felt light, without any weight at all, as in a dream, as if she might float out of this place and into another chamber of the nightmare.

The thing's mouth was as ragged as a wound, and when it spoke, she saw teeth like broken glass. "I'll let you keep your face and walk out of here with four of the lambs. But only four. You choose the one to leave behind."

Heart knocking hard enough to shake her body and make the pistol jump in her uneasy grip, she looked at the five children, who had heard the creature's proposition. She would die before she left any of them.

She met the crimson eyes, and as strange as they were, she nevertheless could *read* them, and realized a truth. Like the walking corpse of Harry Corrigan, like Derek Sawtelle in his tweed jacket and hand-knotted bow tie, like Michael Render, like the talking doll and the walking colonies of fungi, like nearly everyone and everything that she had encountered since waking to the sound of rain, this was an agent of despair, intent upon reducing her to hopelessness.

They had used the bloody tragedy of her childhood, the abiding grief at the loss of her mother to cancer, her deepest fears, her greatest self-doubts, and even her love for the work of T. S. Eliot—which had always given her strength and inspiration—to confuse her, to exhaust her, to induce in her a black despondency that would leave her a hollow woman, a paralyzed force, of no help to the innocent.

There were many things about these events that she didn't understand yet, that she might never understand, but she knew one thing for certain, even if she didn't know why it should be true: *As long as she had hope, they could not touch her.*

"You have no power over me or them. I am their tutelary," Molly declared, surprised to hear the word escape her, for it was not one she had ever used, though she knew that it meant a special kind of guardian. "I'm taking them out of here. All of them. Now."

It reached for her face. Its spread talons extended from her scalp to below her chin, from ear to ear, and its touch was as cold as ice, and greasy.

She did not pull back. Or flinch. Or breathe.

After a hesitation, the thing drew its hand away from her.

The ET stared at her for a moment, and though its expressions were as alien as its face, she knew that it was filled with hate and fury and frustration.

As if it were suddenly weightless, the thing rose from the floor, floating upward as, moments ago, she had feared that she herself might have done. It passed through the ceiling, perhaps drawn up into the colossal ship passing over Black Lake.

62

IN THE MARBLE LOBBY, THE FOUR FACELESS PEOPLE were gone.

With five children in tow, led by a scampering Virgil, Molly joined Neil and his brood in the street as the low fog bank began to lift and dissipate.

Through the shrouds of purple mist, the passing mother ship was visible. So low, just above the treetops. The vessel revealed such a radically different surface from what movies had prepared her to see that Molly stood gazing up in a state beyond astonishment, so far beyond awe and terror that a curious calm befell her.

No metallic sheen as in a thousand films, no festival of lights as in *Close Encounters of the Third Kind,* no battleship architecture as in *Star Wars,* but instead something that appeared to be organic and infinitely strange. Here passed a silently gliding leviathan armored in places with chitinous plates similar to those of an insect, but in places scaled, in places smooth and pale and tender and pulsing as if a gargantuan slow heart boomed within, in other areas bristling with rows of spikes or horns, also cratered with what appeared to be wounds, lesions, sores, stippled with writhing knots of tissue resembling snarls of tentacles, deeply crusted with malignant-looking excrescences.

The most incredible features of this *corpus malignus* were the human faces embedded like blinking eyes throughout its surface, tens of thousands of faces, *millions* of faces, men and women of all races, revealed and then occluded only to be revealed again as membranes opened and closed over them.

On and on it came, vast in length and breadth, its entire shape too large to be extrapolated from this one aspect, in mass and volume greater than the combined mass and volume of all the ships of sea and air that humankind had constructed throughout its history, a thousand times greater, a thousand times a thousand. Although its propulsion system— and the process by which it defied gravity—continued to produce not one decibel of sound, the leviathan accelerated until the features on its surface began to blur, came faster and faster across Black Lake, mile after mile, and faster still, and then as it continued coming, it began also to rise through the gradually thinning fog, which soon shrouded it again, and rose out of sight.

Seconds after this massiveness vanished, the soundless throb of its engines ceased to wash waves of phantom pressure through Molly. Still in the leviathan's thrall, however, she stood gazing into the purple mist for half a minute, perhaps longer, as did Neil and the children, until a sudden downpour drenched them.

63

WHEN THE STORM BROKE, THEY RETREATED TO THE
bank, which was brightened by Coleman lanterns and which seemed to
be safe. A search of the rooms turned up no menace, human or otherwise.

Torrents pounded the earth, though perhaps only half as hard as in the
first deluge. This rain was not luminous, and it smelled like rain should
smell, fresh and clean.

The downpour gradually washed the murk out of the sky, and for a
while the day beyond the windows brightened from the unnatural plum-
purple gloom to the familiar gray light of an autumn storm.

Some supplies had been transported to the bank before the ETs had in-
terrupted the fortification plans. Molly discovered cases of lantern fuel
that for weeks would provide them with well-illuminated quarters. Neil
found blankets, cartons of canned meats and fruits, boxes of crackers,
cookies, candy, fresh bread and cakes.

They piled blankets three thick to make a series of comfortable beds
on the lobby floor. The wealth of dogs would provide additional padding
and warmth. A fourth blanket, tied in a loose roll with lengths of cord,
made an adequate pillow.

As the day waned, a watery twilight sluiced through the town. The
streets were quiet, and except for the rush of rain, so was the sky. Remarkably quiet, considering recent events. Molly did not trust such stillness.

By nightfall, after taking the dogs out for a last toilet, they had checked all the window locks, engaged the deadbolts, and dragged barricades of furniture in front of the doors. The ETs themselves could not be kept out if they chose to phase through ceilings, walls, or floors, but the strange beasts of their home-world ecology would be held at bay.

Molly continued to believe that the children were sacrosanct and that, as their tutelaries, she and Neil were also untouchable, but she wasn't taking any chances. Besides, there might be men like Render still loose in the world, and from monsters of the human kind, they had no protection except guns.

They could prepare only a cold dinner, but the variety and quality of treats qualified as a feast. They sat in a lamplit circle on the floor, thirteen children and two adults, surrounding an array of open cans and boxes, passing one another whatever was wanted.

At first they ate in a silence born half of weariness and half of shock. Soon, however, the comfort of food and the sugar content of warm soft drinks enlivened them.

Quietly, they spoke of their daunting experiences, swapped stories, groped toward an understanding and acceptance of what had happened. And tried to imagine what might happen next.

The five rescued from the vault told of watching parents and others abducted before their eyes, floated off the floor and through this very ceiling, during a period when the mother ship must have been passing over at too high an altitude to be felt. Some of the abductees had wept in the ascent; others had laughed; but none had resisted.

"Yeah, laughing," said Eric Crudup, recalling his grandmother's extraction through two ceilings and a roof. "Going up, they lose it. Nuttier than a can of Planters."

Their losses were so monumental that they could not yet grasp the dimension of them; therefore, they were not yet cast into grief. But Molly knew that grief would come when the shock subsided.

Curiously, no one raised the issue of the organic appearance of the mother ship, perhaps because it differed so dramatically from anything they had seen in movies that they didn't know what to think about it—or were afraid to consider possibilities.

By eight o'clock, they bedded down for the night.

Neil insisted on taking the first watch and promised to wake Molly for her shift at one o'clock in the morning.

She expected to lie awake, tormented by images of horrendous destruction and by nervous speculation about the future, but she fell asleep within seconds of putting her head on the makeshift pillow. She did not dream.

Five hours later, Neil woke her. In spite of his promise, he had intended to let her sleep, but the depth of his exhaustion convinced him that he would soon doze off, leaving them vulnerable.

With the pistol at her side, Molly sat in a chair in the soft lamplight, listening to the rhythmic breathing of the sleeping children, the occasional snores of the dogs. For the first time, she had the solitude and the peace to brood about what difference might exist between the wonders she had seen and her interpretation of them. Some elusive truth still teased at the limits of her reason, but she could not quite seize it.

Tutelary. A guardian, a protector, especially one with special powers. Although it wasn't an archaic word, it wasn't one that she remembered having used before in either her writing or conversation; yet it had come into her mind as precisely the right word to ward off the ET in the bank vault. *Tutelary.*

A few minutes before three o'clock in the morning, the rain stopped.

She went to a window to pull aside a blind, but returned to her chair without doing so. She was afraid that clinging to the window would be some fungoid form, human faces screaming silently in the rounded surfaces of its strange flesh.

64

WITH DAWN, THE TRAMMELED SUN WAS FREED FROM chains of rain and nets of mist. As if rising in celebration, it painted the eastern heavens with the glow of roses, blued the remainder of the sky, and gilded the windows of Black Lake.

Molly, Neil, the children, and the dogs left the cold marble lobby of the bank for the warm morning in the street. They stood at first in quiet rapture, faces to the sky, mouths open as if to drink the sun's golden wine.

Only thirty-six hours had elapsed since they had seen sunshine, but Molly felt as if half her life had passed since she had last enjoyed this delicious warmth on her face.

One of the children was the first to notice the restoration of all things. "Hey, all the crap and creepazoids are gone!"

The strangulation of blackish moss had rinsed out of the trees and off the buildings, dissolved, and washed along gutters into storm drains.

The phantasmagoria of fungi, both those that walked and those that rooted, had vanished. What remained was right: sodden grass, dripping shrubbery, washed-out flower beds of gluey mud.

No monkeylike forms capered on the roofs, and nothing red and ravenous crawled through the trees.

Molly felt almost as though she had dreamed it all—or were dreaming now.

The earth had been taken by an extraterrestrial species as ruthless as might have been a race of intelligent crocodiles. The future had promised an end, and soon, to the human experience and the eradication of every human achievement. Yet the future that had been inevitable was not. Here in the still point, the dance of life went on, moment by moment.

She could not comprehend what had happened, what those princes from another star had intended to accomplish, whether they had in fact accomplished it, or why they had gone.

A flicker of alarm trembled her heart when she glimpsed movement in the sky, but she saw that this, too, was good and right. Overhead a hawk turned in a widening gyre.

The bark of a dog, not one of theirs, drew her attention to the north end of Main Street. The Irish setter, first seen the previous day, led three adults and a group of children toward the bank. The number of kids in that procession had increased since she had waved at them on Marine Avenue.

Another bark, this time from a curly-coated mutt of many breeds, announced the approach of another group from the south end of Main Street. One adult, seven children, and a golden cat that guarded their western flank.

Molly felt Neil's gaze, met his eyes, moved to him, and took his hand.

A third group—four adults, more than twenty children, and a host of dogs—called out as they approached through the small park across the street.

Of all the shocks and astonishments of the past thirty-six hours, none had affected Molly more profoundly than this, and certainly none had lifted her heart as this lifted it.

In a quarter of an hour, the last of nine groups arrived, and Molly was able to tally the surviving population of Black River, where once more than two thousand people had lived. Twenty-two adults, most of them parents. One hundred seventy-six children, more than half of whom were orphans now. Forty dogs, seven cats.

65

THAT GATHERING ON MAIN STREET OCCURRED ON Thursday morning, and by the end of breakfast, all twenty-two adults agreed that they must move the children out of Black Lake, to a more comfortable location in the lowlands to the west.

This was September, and winter would soon come to the mountains. With no electricity, with no natural-gas supply, and with no long-term source of fuel oil, they needed to establish a settlement in a more accommodating climate.

They spent that day assembling a caravan of vehicles and packing for the journey. Food, drink, clothes, mementos. Weapons, too, though they hoped they would never need them.

Thursday night, they bedded down throughout the bank, in every room but the vault. Most slept, but some could not, waiting for the sound of torrential rain.

The night passed without a storm.

Friday morning, they set out from Black Lake in a caravan of three school buses, two eighteen-foot box trucks, and fourteen SUVs. All the fuel tanks were topped off, and if they needed gasoline en route, they expected to be able to siphon it from abandoned vehicles.

They had no idea what to expect, but what they found to the west was more of what they had left. Blue skies empty of everything but birds. Sodden landscapes slowly drying out. Deserted towns.

To Molly, as to everyone, the War of the Worlds appeared to have ended in greater mystery than it had begun. Where had the victorious armies gone, and why?

Some freeway bridges should have been washed away; but none were. Molly saw little evidence of flood damage, even in areas where rivers would have overflowed their banks, drowning whole communities.

Occasionally they encountered snarls of abandoned cars, which had to be moved, but for the most part, the highways were deserted and offered easy travel.

During the westward journey, they encountered three caravans much like theirs. Many children and their tutelaries, numerous dogs, some cats, and even one pet parrot that had been taught some scraps of Emily Dickinson but no T. S. Eliot.

In the lowlands, where many millions had lived—and died—Molly expected to encounter suburbs that had become charnel houses stacked with corpses, the air thick with the stench of decomposition. But they saw not one cadaver, and the air was sweet.

Each of the other caravans had its own destination, and in time the Black Lake group proceeded on its own again, all the way to the Pacific coast and Newport Beach, where two of the tutelaries had family about which they were concerned.

Like the children of the mountains, the children of the coast had survived. The only adults were those who had rescued and protected the young. Many were parents whose sense of responsibility extended beyond their own families.

The residents of the coast welcomed newcomers. There were empty cities to be filled, a vast loneliness of streets and parks and malls and suburbs.

That Friday evening, Molly walked hand in hand with Neil to the beach and stood near the surf line to watch the sunset. A few ships lay broken along the shoreline, but none were visible on the sea.

What of China? Europe? England? Empires gone. And yet Earth abides.

Knowing the comfort that she took from the poet, Neil quoted two lines of Eliot: " 'Between the conception and the creation.' "

She continued: " 'Between the emotion and the response.' "

" 'Falls the Shadow,' " he finished.

The sun painted a benediction on the western sky, first gold and orange, then fiery red, then purple, which ushered in, but only for a few hours, the night.

66

SHE AND NEIL, VIRGIL, TWO OTHER DOGS, AND EIGHT
children took for themselves an abandoned house on a bluff above
the sea.

In the early weeks of this new life, they had little time for contemplation, for puzzling out what had happened to them and to the world.

Supermarkets and warehouses stocked with canned food would last
the reduced population for years, though not forever. Strategies for long-
term survival had to be devised, and much hard work had to be done to
implement those plans.

Remarkably (or perhaps not), the only adult survivors, the tutelaries,
proved to be a diverse lot with a surprising breadth and depth of knowledge and experience for such a small number. They were doctors, den-
tists, nurses, engineers, architects, carpenters, skilled mechanics. . . .
When a complete directory was compiled of those living on this immediate section of the coast, it seemed as though every surviving adult had
been *chosen* not just to save the children but for the talents he or she
could bring to this larger purpose.

In mere days, selected public gathering places had electricity provided
by portable generators. The grand scheme promised electrical service to
some neighborhoods within a year.

Medical clinics were established. Drugs were scavenged from pharmacies, to be rationed until a simple pharmaceutical industry could be reestablished.

The millions of dead could not be found, nor any smallest example of the alien ecology that had flourished so briefly.

For a long time, the stars would be regarded with suspicion, and perhaps for even longer, dogs would be treated less like pets than like family.

Every day, in a thousand small ways, civilization was pulled back from the brink.

In October of that year, hardly a month after Armageddon, Molly became a teacher and discovered greater joy in this work than she had ever known on the *other* side of books.

Once a priest, Neil had left the Church when he reported his rector for child molestation and discovered that his bishop lacked the wisdom, the will, and the strength of faith to purge the offender from the priesthood. Here along the coast, he first served this new community as a first-rate cabinetmaker, but by Christmas he found himself with a congregation again.

Molly had met him on the last day of his priesthood. On an afternoon when her heart had been troubled, she'd gone into a church just to sit, to think. Eventually she'd gone forward in the deserted nave to light a votive candle in her mother's memory. Quietly saying good-bye to his church, Neil had been standing in the chancel, in the complicated geometry of colorful light from a stained-glass window. His face had been so perfect, his eyes so kind, that she had mistaken him for a statue of St. John the Divine, until he moved.

The New Year came and was marked by only quiet celebrations in respect of the dead, but there was pleasure in life, more by the day.

Through the winter and into the spring, Molly continued to be intrigued with the healthy psychology of the children. They had not forgotten their loved ones, and spoke of them often, but they seemed to be under a dispensation from grief. And from nightmares. They did remember the terrible things they had witnessed, but almost as if they had seen them in movies. More so than the adults, they were able to live in the moment, at the still point of the turning world, where the dance of life occurred.

In April, Molly learned that she was pregnant.

67

ON A WARM DAY IN JULY, IN HER FOURTH MONTH
with child, when school was in recess until September, Molly sat on her
patio overlooking the sea, in the shade of a whispering phoenix palm.

On the glass-top table before her was one of her mother's books,
which the world had forgotten even before the world had ended, but
which she treasured and reread from time to time.

She had set the book aside after discovering a reference to Noah and
the ark.

When Neil appeared with glasses of iced tea on a tray, she said, " 'The
flood, the ark, the animals loaded two by two, all that Old Testament
bullshit . . .' "

He raised an eyebrow.

"I'm quoting Render in the lavatory at the tavern. But Neil . . . besides
sin and selfishness and stone idols and that sort of thing, does the story
of Noah suggest any special reason that the world was wiped clean?"

Settling into a chair with his own glass of tea and a biography of W. B.
Yeats, he said, "In fact, yes. A tolerance of murder."

She wasn't sure she understood.

"Most people had become too tolerant of murder," he elaborated,
"punished it too lightly, even excused it when it was in the service of
utopian visions. Why?"

"There's a reference in Mother's book." She indicated the volume on the table. "I was just wondering."

He sipped his tea and lost himself in the life of Yeats.

For a time, Molly stared at the sea.

Hitler killed more than twenty million. Stalin fifty million. Mao Tse-tung as many as a hundred million. More recently, two million had been murdered in Sudan, another two million in Rwanda. The list of holocausts went on and on.

In the name of religion or political justice, in the pursuit of a better world through one ideology or another, mass graves had been filled, and who among the murderers had ever been punished, aside from a few Nazis convicted at the Nuremberg trials more than half a century ago?

No clouds were gathered over the sea. Blue met blue at a nearly invisible horizon.

Every day in the old world, so recently vanished, the news had been full of stories of suicide bombers, street-gang shootings, men who killed their pregnant wives, mothers who drowned their children, teenagers who shot their classmates. She remembered reading once that the average time served for murder in the Old United States had been seven years.

Render had never seen a prison, only sanitariums with counselors and rose gardens.

The more she thought about these things, the more she realized that the children's psychological recovery and their reluctance to dwell on their ordeal was matched by the adults' strange disinterest in discussing the ETs. Why had they traveled thousands of light-years, murdered millions, begun to reinvent the earth, but then departed?

Surely this should be the primary subject of discussion for the next century. But as the children were under a welcome dispensation from grief, the adults—including Molly herself—seemed to have granted themselves a dispensation from reason and from curiosity, at least in regard to the end of the world.

Rather than interrupt Neil, she went into the house, found a thick book of famous quotations, and returned with it to the patio.

She remembered something that she'd heard on the speakerphone when Neil had been talking to his brother, Paulie, in Hawaii: "—having great wrath because he knows that he hath but a short time." Those words had come through amidst static when telephone service had begun to break down.

As her key word, she looked under *wrath* in the index. She found the reference quickly. The quote was from *Revelation,* chapter twelve, verse twelve:

Woe to the inhabiters of the earth and of the sea, for the devil is come down unto you, having great wrath because he knoweth that he hath but a short time.

Come *down* unto you? Was not Hell thought of as a place below?

In the bedroom of their house on that night in September, when Molly had awakened Neil from a nightmare, he had stood gazing at the ceiling, feeling the passage of the leviathan for the first time, and had said, ". . . sift you as wheat." When she'd asked him what he meant, he hadn't remembered speaking those words.

Suspecting that this, too, was a quote, she spent a quarter of an hour with the fat volume on the table before her, and found the source. *Luke,* chapter twenty-two, verse thirty-one:

And the Lord said, Simon, Simon, behold, Satan hath desired to have you, that he may sift you as wheat.

Molly gazed at the sea.

When she picked up her glass of tea, she was surprised to find it empty. She didn't recall finishing it.

She went into the house, got the pitcher from the refrigerator, returned to the patio, and poured more tea for herself and for Neil.

"Thanks, honey," he said.

She remembered something the scar-faced psychopath had said in Bradley and Allison's house, regarding his intention to "sacrifice" those children: "Them that rule the world" wanted the children, the innocents, more than anyone, but "kids ain't for sifting."

Although the day was hot, a chill found her here in the shadow of the phoenix palm.

After a while, she said to Neil, "I'm going to take a walk on the beach."

"Want company?"

"Enjoy the biography. I'll be fine."

Switchback stairs led down from the bluff to the beach. At the bottom, she took off her shoes and carried them.

The astrophysicists say there are more stars in the universe than grains of sand on all the beaches of the earth.

They say that our universe is one of many, perhaps one of an infinite number.

She walked on warm galaxies of sand, strolled across universes, stooped to pick up a shell: a small nautilus with a chamber that seemed to curve away to infinity.

They say God made the universe. The astrophysicists don't say it, but perhaps wiser men do.

They say that Heaven is another realm apart from this one, which might mean that it is another universe.

She scrunched dry sand between her toes. It was hot. She moved to the edge of the surf, where the sand was hard-packed and cool.

They say that certain arrogant angels rebelled, and that God threw them out of Heaven into Hell, which is a realm apart from both Heaven and Earth. Another universe?

She walked south along the beach, and the lapping surf washed her feet.

Astrophysicists—them again—tell us that black holes, which are collapsed stars of incredible density, are most likely doorways between universes.

Is death perhaps its own black hole, through which we change universes?

A single cloud appeared in the south, drifting silently north-northeast.

The leviathan had cruised the sky in silence because it had no engines nor any need of them; it was not a mother ship but a father ship, and not a ship at all. It was a thing of godlike power, the master of a universe beyond this one, a spirit of dark design having grown vast and hideous with the consumption of that one delicacy that it favored.

Who is the ultimate agent of despair, the master of deception, the emperor of lies?

Molly returned to the soft warm sand and searched along the border between beach and wild grass until she found a small stick. She returned to the sand that had recently slipped out of reach of the ebbing tide but that was still wet. She dropped to her knees.

An extraterrestrial species, hundreds or thousands of years more advanced than we are, would possess technology that would appear to us to be not the result of applied science but entirely supernatural, pure magic.

With the stick, Molly began to print words in the sand, calling them from memory.

New thought: *A supernatural event of world-shaking proportions, occurring in a faithless time when only science is believed to have the power to work miracles, might appear to be the work of an extraterrestrial species hundreds or even thousands of years more advanced than we are.*

Her hands shook so that she had to pause from time to time in her printing. The words in an alien language, heard on the radio, transmitted from the space station after all the astronauts aboard had been killed, were engraved now in the sand before her. Her love of words, her passion for poetry, her ability to memorize verse with ease, had served her well.

Yimaman see noygel, see refacull, see nod a bah, see naytoss, retee fo sellos.

She had no way of knowing that these spellings were correct. She had rendered them phonetically, as they had sounded to her.

Expect deception. These are the words of a consciousness that sees right as wrong, wrong as right, that finds joy in pain, pain in truth, truth in lies, that looks at all things upside down and backwards.

The slowly drifting cloud shadowed the words on the sand.

In a while, the sun found them again.

The surf murmured, murmured, and ebbed away from her makeshift tablet.

She saw *soles* first. *Sellos,* minus one *l* and spelled backwards. And she knew the correct spelling must be *souls.*

The word *is,* when spelled backwards, may be pronounced *see.*

With the stick, she worked a translation under the first line that she had engraved: *My name is legion, is Lucifer, is Abbadon, is Satan, eater of souls.*

She tossed the stick into the surf.

With one hand, she smoothed away both lines of words. In the last sluice of a breaking wave, she washed her hand.

She considered the luminous craft that had hovered over them more than once in Black Lake. In its light, she'd felt so profoundly analyzed and so intimately *known* that she had been ashamed, as if she had been naked before strangers. Not a craft. A benign spirit. Her guardian.

Of the countless millions who had been taken, floated through ceilings, drawn through floors: Some screamed in the transit but some laughed. Different destinations.

She retraced her path along the beach, to the stairs in the bluff, and climbed to the patio.

Neil was still occupied with the life of Yeats. He looked up. "Nice walk?"

"Incredible," she said. "I've decided to write another book."

"Might not be book publishers for a few years."

"Doesn't matter," Molly said. "Ambition has nothing to do with this. I'm writing it for an audience of one."

"Me?"

She took the biography from his hands, put it aside, and sat on his lap. "Maybe I'll let you read it, too."

"If not for me, then who?"

She patted her belly, in which the baby grew. "I'm writing it for her—or him. I have a story I want to tell her, and if anything happens to me before she's old enough to hear it, I want the story written down for her to read."

"Sounds important," Neil said.

"Oh, it is."

"What's it about?"

She put her head upon his shoulder, and with her face against his throat, she whispered, "Hope."

	51		75	
	52		76	
	53		77	
	54		78	
30				

D